Love and Pursuit: Three Jazz Age Tales of Crime and Passion

by

C. K. Charlotte

A Wild Rose Press Bouquet

This is a work of fiction. Names, characters, places, and incidents are either the product of the author's imagination or are used fictitiously, and any resemblance to actual persons living or dead, business establishments, events, or locales, is entirely coincidental.

Love and Pursuit: Three Jazz Age Tales of Crime and Passion
COPYRIGHT © 2017 by C. K. Charlotte

Cover Art by *Diana Carlile*

The Wild Rose Press, Inc.
PO Box 708
Adams Basin, NY 14410-0708
Visit us at www.thewildrosepress.com

Publishing History
First Vintage Edition, 2017
Print ISBN 978-1-5092-1851-6
Digital ISBN 978-1-5092-1852-3

A Wild Rose Press Bouquet
Published in the United States of America

Table of Contents

Love and the Pursuit of Law

by

C. K. Charlotte

Prologue

Summerbrooke, Oxfordshire, May 1925

"Hurry, Tom!" Robert Farmer, running through the sun dappled woods of Summerbrooke—the Oxfordshire estate of Baron Fitzgerald Henderson, yelled to his best friend Tom Payne. "There'll be hell to pay if his lordship's gamekeeper catches us poaching."

"Wait, Robert!" Tom stopped before an ancient elm tree. "Let's search for birds' nests."

Without pausing for a response, Tom clambered up into the hollow tree, then gasped out loud. Glancing down inside the elm, he had spied the empty eye sockets of a skull, staring up at him.

"Whatever is it, Tom?"

"I—I—don't rightly know," stammered Tom, "a dead animal, maybe."

"Bloody Christ," muttered Robert as he climbed up to Tom and pulled the skull from the gnarled branches. With a second curse he dropped it, for the human skull still held the remains of some hair and, just barely attached to the rotting flesh beneath the jaw, a sliver of lilac silk.

Chapter One

Smythe and Company, Lincoln's Inn Fields,
London
September 1925

"I will not, I simply will not," said Ivy Smythe,
stomping her foot. "I did not become one of the first
women barristers in England to represent aristocratic
scum such as Bryan Henderson."

"The Honorable Bryan Henderson, my dear," her
father and law partner, Edward Smythe, calmly
responded. "Educated at Oxford, second son and—
since the untimely death of his older brother Frederick
in the Great War—only heir to Baron Fitzgerald
Henderson, landed gentry and member of the House of
Lords. Hardly scum, as you so delicately put it."

Turning to face her father, Ivy caught sight of
herself in a mirror above the mantel. She observed a
petite frame drawn up to its full height, tendrils of
chestnut hair escaping from a tight bun, and determined
blue eyes. She crossed her arms and shook her head.
"No."

"Ei incumbit probation qui dicit, non qui negat,"
her father intoned. "You cannot have forgotten the most
important precept of English law, my dear."

"The burden of proof is on he who declares, not on
he who denies," recited Ivy. "Or, in plain English,

innocent until proven guilty. But that does not mean I have to spend my time representing him. Have *you* forgotten the effort I expended to become a barrister? My application to become a student at Lincoln's Inn originally refused and my ultimate acceptance coming only as a result of my petition to the House of Lords and the passing of the Sex Disqualification Removal Act of 1919? I want to campaign for women's rights, defend the downtrodden, work for change, not represent what the newspapers incessantly refer to as one of the 'Bright Young People.' "

"All well and good to have ideals, my dear, but campaigning for women's rights and defending the poor will not necessarily pay for chambers," her father responded.

Ivy surveyed the legal chambers in which she stood. Her mother had died when she was very young, and she had basically grown up in these chambers beside her barrister father. Situated in Chancery Lane, Lincoln's Inn was surrounded by a brick wall separating it from the street. As all four of London's Inns of Court, it consisted of three squares. As Ivy and her father, many of the barristers trained at Lincoln's Inn maintained chambers in Lincoln's Inn Fields. The offices of Smythe and Company resided in the former Oldecastle House, originally constructed in 1641 as a private residence. Ivy loved the mahogany paneled walls, floor to ceiling bookshelves, brass sconces, marble fireplaces, and plush leather furniture.

She also loved her father, the challenge of learning and applying the law, and the thrill of being one of the first women in a prestigious profession. Britain and the world were changing since the Great War, and Ivy was proud to be a part of it. Large estates were breaking up, class distinctions were loosening, and women had more power and more choices. She did not want to waste her time on Bryan Henderson, dissolute, aristocratic playboy when there was so much important work…

Her thoughts were interrupted by her father, who she suddenly realized had been speaking to her for some time. "At any rate, there's no indication that young Mr. Henderson had anything to do with the poor unfortunate girl found dismembered on his estate. No one even knows her identity. I have simply agreed to consult with the Henderson family and their solicitor. Before the war this investigation into the Hendersons' private affairs, merely because they own the estate on which the body was found, would never have even taken place. Baron Henderson is an important client for this firm and…"

"Body? Dismembered?" Ivy interrupted. "Whatever are you talking about?"

"Do you not listen to a thing I say, my dear? Worse yet, do you not read the news in the *London Times*? *The Telegraph*? Even the *Mirror*? The papers have been full of nothing for weeks, but reports of the body found at Summerbrooke and the ongoing police investigation."

"A body on the Henderson estate?" Ivy repeated.

"Bloody hell," her father replied. "Yes, that is precisely why we are meeting with young Mr. Henderson. Two boys, poaching on Summerbrooke, found a human skull inside the hollow trunk of an old elm tree. Upon further investigation, the police found not only the human skull, but an almost complete skeleton, a crepe soled shoe, and fragments of rotted clothing. Closer examination revealed that the body was a woman approximately twenty-seven years old, five feet tall, with raven hair. The police estimate she had been dead for at least sixteen months before she was discovered. No sign of disease or violence were found on her body, but attached to her skull as well as her torso were fragments of silk."

"Silk," Ivy repeated easing into the soft, aged leather of the nearest chesterfield.

"Yes, lilac silk," her father continued. "The coroner declared it murder by strangulation and stated the poor girl was probably murdered first and then pushed into the trunk of the tree while still warm. The body would not have fit into the hollow trunk after rigor had set in, of course. Despite exhaustive searches, no trace of the girl's identity has been found."

"And the police think Bryan Henderson had something to do with it?" Ivy shivered.

"No, no," her father began, but then abruptly stopped. "Well, the absolute truth, my dear, is I just do not know. The police do want to meet with young Mr. Henderson, and the press are inflaming matters. The *Mirror* and others have been enjoying a field day carrying on about the young people of the upper classes and their disregard for decorum, lack of respect for their elders, wild driving, and outlandish parties. Young Mr. Henderson's escapades are featured frequently, and I have to think this is influencing…"

Ivy interrupted, "Bryan Henderson is in the press in an unfavorable manner? I simply cannot believe his mother's secretary would allow it." Bryan was sounding a little more interesting.

"Where have you been?" her father bellowed. "Studying law has positively ruined you. In the past, the

Times and the *Telegraph* may have limited coverage to what the upper classes themselves provided, but this new lot—including the *Mirror*—is much more likely to print the bad as well as the good. Since the Great War, the gentry have been victimized by national taxation, the breaking up of their estates, the loss of their staffs, and now the disrespect of the press. There is just no end to the humiliation. Over the last year, I have seen articles on a defrocked vicar, a nightclub raid involving lords and ladies, and a genteel murder. All of these indiscriminately served up by mass market fish wraps now focusing on the new youth cult and their society games."

"Society games?" Ivy was beginning to think the study of law may have really ruined her. "What society games?"

"Well, just look at today's press. The *Mirror* is reporting a midnight chase in London by the Society of Bright Young People. Fifty motor cars no less, on a treasure hunt through London searching for a prize of a few pounds. Even Tallulah Bankhead, the actress, was there. The article goes on to describe 'flapper dresses and shingled heads; a crawl in a none too clean section of Covent Garden in search of clues; concluding with a splendid breakfast and a string band entertaining the group after their strenuous adventures.' Glamour, money, famous names, and snob appeal—the *Mirror* has it all. Is this what the Great War was about? To save England for this?"

Her father had worked himself into a frenzy, but Ivy was fingering her hair restrained in its bun. Shingled hair?

"I am not at all in favor of these bright young

people and their antics," her father continued. "But when Baron Henderson, who has been so loyal to this firm, asks me to speak with his son, duty compels me to do so. I agreed to meet with him here today, and I need your help, Ivy."

Ivy had stopped listening. "I think I shall find that *Mirror* article," she said absently, "perhaps there is a photograph."

****

Ivy sat in her office staring into space. As one of the first women called to the bar in England, she had not had time for frivolity. Actually, she had not even had time to think of it. What had she missed? She wondered. Her perusal of the back issues of the *Mirror* revealed all sorts of changes. Hair was shingled. Dresses were above the knee, loose around the waist, beaded, feathered, and fringed. Hats had been replaced with glittering bands circling the head. Jazz had replaced classical music; the Charleston had replaced the waltz. Young people no longer favored formal dinners and debutante parties, but rather trips to clubs with names like the Gargoyle and the Night Lite.

Ivy sighed, then looked up as a quick knock preceded her father's entry into the office. Behind him was the most beautiful human being Ivy had ever seen. His golden hair flowed above green eyes flecked with gold, as well as intelligence. His face was angelic. He was tall, slender, but well formed. His expensively tailored clothes showcased his figure. She stared, forgetting to breathe.

"Ivy, I want you to meet…"

Ivy attempted to stand but knocked over her cup of tea, chipping a cup from the bone china set which had been in chambers for as long as she could remember. Liquid spread over her copies of the *Mirror*. As she bent to blot it, the image of the young man before her stared up from the page with his arm around an equally attractive young woman.

I hate her, Ivy thought, surprised by her reaction. Her father and the young god accompanying him moved forward simultaneously to help her mop up. She quickly turned the *Mirror's* page, sending tea flying. Mortified she looked up to find her father eyeing her curiously and the young man unsuccessfully hiding a smirk.

"May I be of some service, Father?" she asked crossly.

"Allow me to introduce myself, *mademoiselle*," the young man interrupted haughtily. "The Honorable Bryan Henderson, son and heir of Baron Fitzgerald Henderson." He flawlessly executed a court bow while adding, "At *your* service."

Of course. Ivy retreated to her chair. The devil, masquerading as the most beautiful man on earth. Rich, idle, degenerate. Creating a public nuisance by speeding around London in expensive motorcars taking part in scavenger hunts. What was he doing in chambers? In her office?

"You may remember," her father began sternly, "I mentioned that matter involving Summerbrooke? That young Mr. Henderson would be coming to chambers to discuss the unfortunate incident on his father's estate."

Ivy vaguely remembered something of this nature.

"Unfortunately, I have been called away to attend to another matter at Old Bailey. Highly unusual, I dare say. But what is one to do. I thought you might meet with Mr. Henderson and begin to understand the situation so our chambers may better be of service."

Ivy opened her mouth to object, but her father had already taken his leave.

Bryan, that is how Ivy insisted on thinking of him, leaned insolently against the credenza that once graced her mother's dining room and now held her law books. I will not grant this young fool the respect of a title no matter how beautiful, she thought petulantly.

"Please have a seat," she managed to offer aloud, gesturing to one of the two leather club chairs facing her desk.

"I prefer to stand. I cannot imagine that this will take any time at all. I have a number of matters to attend to, and I do not intend to discuss my legal concerns with a mere girl."

Frowning, with hands clenched, Ivy stood. "I will have you know sir," she began, "that I am a barrister admitted to Lincoln's Inn. Furthermore, the Sex Disqualification Removal Act of 1919 has made the matter of gender in the practice of law irrelevant."

Bryan laughed, unkindly. "The matter of gender irrelevant," he said moving his gaze over her body as though she wore no clothing at all. "Yes, I can see why you might consider that a positive development. For myself, however…"

While Ivy fought to find civil words, he stood to his full height. Approaching her desk, he bowed, then forcefully grasped her hand and kissed it, brushing his lips against her skin. Ivy gasped, as the kiss tingled up her arm, caressed her breasts, and wormed into the very interior of her being. She closed her eyes, not knowing if she wished him to stop or continue. But Bryan merely turned and left the room, closing the door ever so softly behind him.

Ivy sat and lowered her forehead to her desk, immersing her bangs in a cold puddle of tea.

****

"So?" Her father sank into the club chair Ivy had so recently offered to the annoying Bryan Henderson. "What did you learn from young Mr. Henderson?"

Ivy looked at him blankly.

"I say Ivy, are you well? You don't quite seem to be yourself. I inquired what you learned about the corpse found at Summerbrooke. Morbid, but interesting, don't you agree?"

Ivy shook her head, further loosening her hair. "Not a thing."

"Not a thing?"

"He refused to speak with me because I am a woman. Most haughty, annoying, worthless man I have ever had the displeasure to meet," she said, softly massaging her hand.

"That may all be so, my dear girl. But he is the son of one of our most esteemed clients. When will he meet with us again?"

"I have no idea. He left abruptly, and I hope never to see him again."

"Ivy," her father said impatiently, "campaigning for women's rights is all very good on your own time, but our job, indeed our duty as barristers trained in the law, is to serve our clients. I want you to send a note around to young Mr. Henderson's club apologizing for your behavior and setting up a second meeting as soon as possible. This is not a request, young lady," he added as he left the room.

Ivy sighed and put her head back down on the still damp spot of tea on her desk.

Chapter Two

Black's Club, London

John, a long-time clerk for Smythe and Company, cautiously approached Black's Club on St. James Street the following day. The reputation of Black's Club—one of the oldest and most exclusive gentlemen's clubs in London—was well-known to John. Why just last week the *Mirror* reported gambling aristocrats left a member lying on the pavement outside the club during a thunderstorm, rather than abandon the bets they placed on whether he could rise of his own accord.

John approached the front door, bypassing a bow window jutting out from the ground floor. "Incessant London drizzle," he muttered, lowering his umbrella and ringing the bell.

A young maid, in a black and white uniform, immediately answered the door. "May I help you, sir?" She tossed her head and smiled.

John was immune to her charms. "A note for young Mr. Henderson, if you please, miss."

"Oh, Mr. Henderson." She giggled unceremoniously, while John rolled his eyes. "He's not here. Still at the Cavendish with Lady Sitwell I imagine." Another short giggle followed. "But you can leave it with me, if you like."

"Thank you, miss, but I've been instructed to wait

for a reply."

"Oh, well if you must," she began, but then looking up added, "If that don't beat all, here he comes now. Quite early in the day for him to be returning, actually."

****

Bryan Henderson moved jauntily along St. James swinging his umbrella at his side, despite the weather, and brushing his blond locks from his eyes. He was thinking not of the evening he had spent with Lady Zita Sitwell and the other bright young people at the Cavendish, but rather of the newest barrister in the chambers of Smythe and Company.

Bryan had never had the opportunity to meet a less attractive or charming young woman. That hair style, let alone the long herringbone skirted suit, should be enough to discourage any healthy male's thoughts. Nevertheless, there was something about her that had kept her in the back of his mind all evening and upon waking this morning. That small act of kissing Ivy's hand had positively electrified him. He could not help but wonder, what would it be like to hold her tightly and really kiss her? To move beyond kissing to caressing? His body stirred.

Bryan, educated at Eton and Cambridge, the heir of a baron, attractive, and wealthy, had never had any difficulties attracting women. The Great War had left London terribly short of handsome young men of all social classes. Bryan, too young to serve, had spent the difficult war years away at school. He had done well at Cambridge and, while his older brother Frederick was alive, little else was expected of him. He considered himself fortunate, because as the second son of Baron Fitzgerald Henderson, he had the advantages of wealth with few of the responsibilities. He spent most of his time as one of the bright young people, attending parties and clubs. As a member of an aristocratic family, he found many of the changes wrought by the war—worker conflicts and the lack of dependable staff, increased crippling taxation, loss of prestige and privilege accorded the aristocracy, women in the workforce—distressing. But not so distressing that he was moved to act.

The death of Frederick in the Great War had begun to change things. As the eldest and only living son of Baron Fitzgerald Henderson, he was now expected to learn to run the family estate, marry well, and produce heirs. As heir to a large estate and son of a baron and peer in the House of Lords, he also would eventually have a great deal of influence, socially and politically. It was a large responsibility, but one which he wished to fulfill well if only to please his father and honor the memory of his brother.

The question was how to begin. Particularly how to begin without giving up the social gatherings and bright young companions he so enjoyed. The police investigation into the macabre findings at Summerbrooke further complicated matters.

As Bryan's thoughts turned to the corpse at Summerbrooke, he looked up and saw the maid and an unknown man beckoning to him from the steps of his club. Could this have to do with the police investigation?

****

"Sir," the maid interrupted his thoughts, "this is John, a clerk with Smythe and Company. He has a message for you."

"Mr. Henderson," said John, handing Bryan the note, "the pleasure of a reply is requested."

"Insulting," Bryan muttered as he opened the note to find it was written by Ivy, rather than her father.

Delivering correspondence on an important legal matter from not only a junior barrister, but a female one, indicated a distinct lack of respect for his position. Nevertheless, he smiled. How convenient to have a request for a second meeting, he thought. How easy it would be to show the young female barrister just who was in control.

He turned to the clerk. "Tell Miss Smythe I will meet her for dinner at Claridge's, Saturday evening at seven. My usual table."

"But, sir, it is a business meeting intended for chambers."

Bryan smiled. "And please, ask her to dress appropriately."

Leaving the maid gaping, he moved into the club and the billiard room for the afternoon's entertainment. But once out of sight, Bryan breathed deeply attempting to dispel the panic that had gripped him upon first glimpsing John and believing the police had come to question him. It was only a matter of time until the police determined the identity of the woman in the elm. Once her identity was known, how long could he conceal his connection to her?

Chapter Three

Claridge's and Cavendish Hotels, London

Ivy stepped from the taxi precisely at seven, wearing exactly the same suit she had worn when first meeting Bryan several days earlier. John's admonition to wear something "appropriate" had prompted another tirade about the seriousness of women barristers, and she had almost refused to come. In the end, however, she decided to come exactly as herself: tweed suit, hair neatly coiffed in its bun, and sensible shoes.

Claridge's façade of roman stone rose impressively before her. A grand old hotel, founded in 1812, it was purchased by the Savoy Group in 1894 and had been demolished and replaced. Claridge's had flourished after the Great War due to demand from aristocrats who no longer maintained a London house and as a result of parties thrown by London's bright young people. It was their influence, according to the press, which had encouraged Claridge's to recently modernize. Ivy admired the jazz modern mirrored foyer designed by art deco pioneer Basil Lonides as she passed through to the restaurant. She particularly loved the magnificent engraved glass screens.

Her heart nearly stopped as she eyed Bryan standing across the dining room at his table. Covered in white linen, set with Waterford crystal and bone china, and crowned with a centerpiece of white roses, the table was beautiful—but Bryan outshone it. Featuring a rakish grin, blond hair falling across his forehead, and a beautiful Saville Row suit paired with a bow tie, he was irresistible. A hat and cane rested on the table, as though he might later be going dancing.

The other diners were equally well dressed. Many of the women sported the new flapper style of flashy evening wear. Ivy looked down in some dismay at her unfashionable suit which had seemed like such a good idea just hours before.

If Bryan noticed her dismay, he hid it well. "Our champagne now, please, James," he said to the waiter as he seated Ivy. To Ivy he added, "I ordered the roast with Yorkshire pudding; that seems to be very much your, um, style." Ivy watched him turn away, to conceal a smirk. Ivy having worked all day—unlike him she thought unkindly—was starving, and however old fashioned, she did love a good English roast. Bryan sipped the champagne James had poured, and in an attempt to prove her sophistication, she joined him. The best champagne she had ever tasted, even if it was only her second; it bubbled in her brain making her smile.

"How lovely you look," Bryan said.

She grimaced. "We should discuss your legal matter."

"Legal matter? I certainly will not discuss it before dinner."

With a sigh, Ivy settled back and decided to enjoy herself if only to spite Bryan. He oozed charm. "Tell me about your father? Tell me about studying for the bar? Why a barrister? Have you always been interested in the law?"

Ivy found herself talking endlessly all the while staring into his unique green eyes with the golden specks that matched the brilliance of his hair and honeyed skin. He was indeed the most beautiful man she had ever met, and he never seemed to take his eyes off her. She felt like the most important person in the world. I could become accustomed to this, she thought to herself, momentarily closing her eyes to enjoy the moment.

"Well, well, what have we here?" a cultured female voice inquired.

Ivy opened her eyes to see a woman who might have been Bryan's sister, she was so beautiful. But the placement of his arm around her waist and the kiss she gave him on the lips made it clear she was not.

"Meeting with my barrister, my darling Zita." Bryan stood. "Miss Smythe, allow me to introduce Lady Zita Sitwell. Zita, my barrister, Ivy Smythe."

"Right." Zita raised her perfectly arched eyebrows at Ivy. "I dare say you need one."

Ivy, remembering her reason for meeting Bryan, crashed quickly back to earth.

Zita, however, continued. "We'll see you later at the Cavendish, of course, Bryan? We are all going." Turning to Ivy, she added, "You must come as well. You are dressed so well for it!" She smiled and, giving Bryan a second public kiss, sashayed from the room.

Ivy closed her mouth, which she suddenly realized had been hanging open. "Where do such creatures come from?" she murmured.

****

"So, dessert, a little more champagne, then off to the Cavendish, my lady." Bryan smiled.

"I have work to do tomorrow. It will be a busy day," Ivy responded.

"I will not accept 'no' for an answer. I am the client. But first, more champagne."

An hour later, despite her best efforts, Ivy found herself in a taxi headed to the Cavendish. It was only at this point that she looked down and realized she was dressed entirely inappropriately. Even for a barrister.

"Oh no," she moaned quietly.

But Bryan was oblivious, carrying on about the Cavendish. "It's a wonderful hotel. King Edward VII maintained a personal wine cellar; there are remnants remaining today. It's rather faded since the war. Do you know the hotel has a portrait presented by the Kaiser? It used to hang over the mantel in the main dining room. Relegated to the men's room now, I'm afraid. Perhaps I can smuggle you in to see it."

"Dear God," whispered Ivy feeling queasy, although whether from the thought or the champagne she could not say.

"It is very comfortable," Bryan continued, "Edwardian. It is one of the favorite haunts for my crowd; we descend after midnight when drinks are available in the large drawing room on the first floor. But take careful note of who is there. The tradition is communal drink bills: the most affluent person in the room is expected to pay. We may want to leave a little earlier if it turns out to be us."

Ivy smiled at the use of "us" in spite of herself.

The taxi stopped on Jeremy Street, and Ivy found herself in front of a hotel with a brick front and large plain doorway. The music inside was loud. "The best jazz," Bryan confided, "although some at the Gargoyle

Club might disagree."

The air was warm and perfumed by rose, jasmine, and lily of the valley. It was the essence of Arpège. The Lanvin fragrance which for Ivy defined the moment in the decade when women really started to find themselves. Its black bottle was an icon.

The large drawing room was crowded with partygoers, as well as too much furniture. "The owner is quite fond of estate sales," Bryan whispered.

Ivy spied red plush settees and morocco leather chairs, estate maps, archery targets, croquet mallets, and polo sticks, all mixed in with photographs of men on horseback and yachts in full sail.

"Bryan, darling!" yelled Zita, crossing the room, throwing her arms around him while simultaneously exposing a fair amount of pale cleavage and kissing him soundly on the lips. "Oh, and you've brought your little friend—your barrister." She smiled coldly at Ivy. A line from an old poem came unbidden to Ivy's memory: *her breasts were white as snow, and just as cold.* As is her heart, thought Ivy.

Zita dragged Bryan off to dance the Charleston, without a backward glance. Ivy stood abandoned in the center of the faded and dusty, but opulent, drawing room.

"Bryan abandon you, old girl?" a male public school voice intoned. "Come have a drink with me."

Before she could object, a tall, attractive stranger had moved her to a sofa in the corner of the room and handed her yet another glass of champagne. "Down the hatch, old girl. There you go; you'll feel much better in no time."

"Let me introduce myself. I'm Stephen Bernard,

the oldest son of the Earl of Glenconnor, but everyone calls me Cedric. You are?"

Ivy eyed him cautiously. Also perfectly, if extravagantly, dressed and lovely to look at. Does Bryan know any plain people, she wondered. "Ivy Smythe, Bryan's barrister," she answered firmly.

"Quite, quite." Cedric nodded his head and dispelled sprinkles of gold dust from his hair while simultaneously unknotting the lovely spring green scarf wound about his neck and placing it in his lap. "Couldn't be anything else now dressed like that could you, old girl? But tell me are they really allowing girls to be barristers now? What has the war wrought? Father would be appalled."

Ivy responded quickly, describing her legal studies and practice. Cedric was an admirable conversationalist and better listener. She found herself relaxing and eventually, after several more glasses of champagne, nestling into the crook of his arm.

She had just started to fully enjoy herself, when Bryan returned. "Having a good time I see," he said with a smile.

"Relax, old boy, just keeping the embers burning so to speak. Have a glass of bubbly?"

"I think it's time I got my *barrister*," he emphasized the word, "home. She's had quite a night."

"Right, right, well here take my card, old girl." Cedric handed Ivy an engraved calling card. "Do stay in touch." He softly kissed her hand. "Oh," Cedric remembered, "I forgot to ask, my dear, why does our Bryan need a barrister?"

Bryan turned quickly to Cedric, and Ivy was certain Cedric winked at him. "I'll have more to say to you later, much more," Bryan said crossly.

Ivy felt a little flutter as Bryan put his arm around her and urged her through the door.

****

Cedric's question jogged Ivy's champagne drenched mind. Dear God, thought Ivy seated comfortably in the taxi, as rain poured down throughout the streets of London. We never talked about the case, the body in the tree. She had to at least broach the subject of the corpse found at Summerbrooke, if for no other reason than to appease her father at breakfast in the morning.

"Um," she started turning toward Bryan, "about that woman?"

"Zita? Oh, she's all for show, all for fun."

"No, not Lady Sitwell, the one found in the tree."

"In the tree?" Bryan asked visibly amused, as he turned toward her. "Whatever are you talking about?"

Somewhat exasperated, Ivy turned and opened her mouth to respond. Bryan's fingers traced her open lips, while his other hand grasped her waist. She thought to object; she did not behave this way in general, let alone with a client. But before she could do so, his tongue slipped gently between her teeth, and his hand fondled her breast before moving up and caressing her neck. Goose bumps flowed over Ivy, and she sighed softly.

Just as suddenly as he had begun, however, Bryan withdrew. Ivy opened her eyes and stared directly into his. She was not stupid; she knew he had just diverted the discussion from the woman found at Summerbrooke. But she also was not dead, and she knew her body had responded to Bryan in a way it had never responded before. As shocking as the interaction had been, she longed for more. She closed her eyes and tilted her head up, hoping for another kiss. But she was disappointed.

Bryan cleared his throat. "Now, about your new friend, Cedric."

"Oh!" Ivy exclaimed, misunderstanding. "That was nothing, just an avid conversation, and you were dancing—if that's what you call it—with Lady Sitwell. You can hardly be jealous of that."

"Dear, dear Ivy," Bryan said, laughing so hard he was crying. "Dear, dear Ivy."

His response was totally unexpected. "Whatever do you mean?" She brought herself up ramrod straight

"You don't know who Lord Stephen Bernard, also known as Cedric, is? You've never heard of him before? Of his, um, inclinations?"

Ivy frowned. "Whatever do you mean? Inclinations? He is a delightful man, well dressed, polite, wonderful manners, and a great conversationalist."

Bryan laughed again "Yes, dear Ivy, he is all of those things."

"Then why are you laughing? He is the perfect companion—much better than some, present company included, I might add."

Bran continued laughing. "Not in all ways, my dear Ivy, not in all ways. In fact, some might say not in the most important way."

"The most important way? What might that be?"

"You have no idea? Let me put it this way, he lives in Mayfair Mews, with a count."

"Mayfair Mews is obviously one of the most sought after addresses in London, and a count as a flat mate sounds delightful."

"Not as a flat mate, old girl," Bryan responded falling into Cedric speak. "They share a bed and what happens between consenting adults in bed."

"Why, what…" Ivy trailed off, the image having finally conveyed the impact of Bryan's meaning.

"My dear Ivy, I have so much to teach you." Bryan reached his hand up to caress her cheek. She closed her eyes and tilted her head up, expecting a kiss. Instead, his fingers traced her lips.

The driver suddenly broke into her thoughts. "We have arrived, sir."

****

Riding home alone, after walking Ivy to her door, Bryan wondered what was happening. He had kissed her solely to deflect the discussion of the woman in the tree. He was not yet ready to discuss it.

But something else had happened. Despite her prickly personality and unattractive appearance, something about that kiss had affected him. Enough that he wanted more. And what Bryan wanted, he generally got.

Alighting from the taxi at his own Mayfair Mews address, he muttered aloud a saying he had often heard his father use, "Damn barristers."

Chapter Four

Harrods Department Store, London

Ivy was still on Bryan's mind the following morning when a curious invitation descended on his doorstep. As always his mantelpiece, as those of his friends, was crammed with requests to attend balls and evening parties. Yet this piece of cream vellum was different from the others. It was printed, rather than engraved, and advertised what it touted as a "unique entertainment."

Bryan could not help but read it aloud. "Mr. Thomas Hardy and Mr. Stephen 'Cedric' Bernard, together with Miss Peacock and Mrs. Grant, request the pleasure of your company at St. George's Swimming Baths, Buckingham Palace Road, at eleven o'clock p.m. next Saturday evening. Appropriate attire is a Bathing Costume. Please bring a towel and a bottle. Each guest must show his invitation upon arrival."

At the bottom of the invitation was a handwritten note from Cedric. *Bryan, your invitation is conditioned upon your bringing your new barrister friend. It will do her such good. And I hereby wager one hundred pounds that you will not be able to entice her to attend. Cheers, Cedric.*

Bryan frowned. What was that infernal Cedric up to now? He could not imagine Ivy owned a bathing costume, let alone one which she could wear to such an event. Nevertheless, one hundred pounds was a worthy wager, and he had yet to pass up an opportunity to gamble. Further, it would divert Ivy's attention from the body found at Summerbrooke. The thought crossed his mind that it was also another opportunity to spend an evening with Ivy, but he quickly dismissed it.

Bryan telephoned a delighted Cedric to accept the challenge. He then immediately began to plot his offensive to obtain Ivy's presence. Her first objection would certainly be to the very thought of wearing a bathing costume to an evening party. Hence, his first task must be to gift her with the perfect bathing costume.

Entering Harrods from Bropton Road, Bryan found displayed the perfect costume. Something even Zita might wear. Made of silk, the lower part of the bathing costume was red, and the bodice consisted of rainbow stripes of blue, red, and yellow. Just the thing, but how could he convince Ivy to accept it. Further incentives were obviously required.

Turning the corner, he saw just the inspiration she would need. Despite her appearance and demeanor, Ivy was of the feminine persuasion. Displayed in front of Bryan was a dress no woman could fail to love and no man could resist touching. Of tightly fitted silver silk, the dress was low cut, sleeveless, and snug through the bodice. It was covered in pearls and silver sequins, so the light glanced off it in patterns fascinating the observer, and ended just above the knee with a row of glittering fringe.

Bryan had a plan that was sure to succeed. He would have the dress delivered to Ivy with an invitation to dinner at Claridge's—which she clearly loved—the night of the party. He would publicly present the bathing costume at dinner, where she could not possibly refuse, and spirit her away to the party. Thereby, earning his one hundred pounds, maintaining his winning reputation, and hopefully diverting Ivy further from pursuing the question of wrongdoing at Summerbrooke. Bryan smiled deviously as the clerk wrapped his packages.

****

It was a rainy evening, and Ivy was curled up on the divan in front of a crackling fire speaking with her father about legal matters, when the bell rang. "A package for you, miss, delivered by the Hendersons' boy," exclaimed the Smythes' housekeeper Hannah Greene, entering the parlor.

"A package from the baron?" asked her father.

Ivy opened the package and removed the sparkling silver dress. "Well, I dare say," sputtered her father. "Not quite what one would expect in terms of legal fees."

"From Bryan Henderson, not his father," Ivy corrected after reading the enclosed calling card. "Although I still cannot understand what on earth…"

"Oh, there's a note, miss." Hannah removed an envelope from her apron pocket and handed it to Ivy.

Ivy read aloud, frowning. "Dear Miss Smythe, It occurred to me this morning that we still have not discussed the legal matter which introduced us. Please accept this token of my apology for last evening and agree to accompany me to dinner at Claridge's next Saturday evening, when we might continue our discussion. Respectfully, The Honorable Bryan

Henderson."

"Splendid," said her father. "Now we can maintain the Henderson client relationship in good standing, and perhaps make some progress on this unfortunate matter of the damsel in the tree." Rising to leave the room, he added, "Bloody attractive frock if I may say so. You should spruce up nicely."

"Well, I never!" began Ivy.

"Begging your pardon, miss. The Hendersons' boy is waiting for your response," Hannah interrupted.

Passing through the entry hall, Ivy's father greeted the waiting messenger in a cheery voice. "Please tell young Mr. Henderson Miss Smythe is delighted to meet him on next Saturday evening for dinner," he said before proceeding up the stairs to his study.

Ivy shook her head in disbelief.

"Try it on, miss!" exclaimed Hannah who had raised Ivy since her mother's death so many years ago.

As if in a daze, Ivy slowly stood and held the sparkling dress over the suit she had worn to chambers earlier that day. Glancing in the mirror above the mantel, she gasped. It was beautiful! She could do anything wearing this dress!

But trying it on a short time later in front of her dressing mirror, Ivy groaned in frustration. The dress fit perfectly, but the rest of her was all wrong. Practically wailing, she called for Hannah.

"It's the hair, miss," Hannah opined. "It should be bobbed for that dress. I'd run off to Harrods tomorrow if I were you, before you have time to think too much about it."

****

Ivy entered Harrods' hairdressing court, with its

large reception lounge, pink and beige décor enhanced by mirrors, and pale pink Formica, with trepidation. No wonder it was advertised in the *London Times* as one of the most "sumptuous the world over" and a "revelation in modern design." Falling into the chair of the hairdressing cubicle, she gazed in amazement at the carefully placed telephone, clock, and rapid drying machine. Shaking the pins out of her bun, she addressed the chic attendant in her best accent, "a bob, please." Then closed her eyes.

An hour later the hairdresser announced, "*Voilà,* madam!"

Opening her eyes, Ivy stared at her reflection. Cropped to just below her ears, her chestnut hair danced in the lights of Harrods' salon. Her neck was revealed as slender and white as a swan, her deep blue eyes enormous.

"Lovely, madam, but perhaps a little color." The hairdresser smiled.

Another hour later, Ivy left Harrods in a daze with cake mascara and application brush, a push up tube of red lipstick, and a small pot of rouge. Although her recollection of doing so was spotty, she had also purchased a pair of silver satin t-strap pumps.

Chapter Five

Claridge's and St. George's Swimming Baths, London

Ivy walked into Claridge's for the second time in a fortnight, but no one recognized her. Not the doorman, nor the *maître d'*, nor Bryan, nor for that matter Ivy herself. Following Bryan's usual waiter James, Ivy glided across the room in her silver t-straps, swinging her hips and feeling the glittering fringe of her new dress brush against her knees. The silk swished against her body, and the sequins sparkled. Passing a mirror, she tossed her head, sending her bob swinging in time with her hips and creating ripples of light throughout the room.

The heads of male and female diners rotated to take her in, Bryan's among them. His expression was one of pure desire, which became quite puzzled when James stopped at his table, pulled out the chair, and seated Ivy.

"Surprised?" she said. "You can close your mouth now."

It was not until she spoke that Bryan's face registered recognition. "Ivy? Ivy! What have you done?"

"Like it, darling?" She smiled, enjoying this.

"I am speechless," he replied.

"Good, just how I like you." My visual

33

transformation seems to have changed my personality as well, Ivy thought. How curious.

"Ahem, well, I have ordered…"

"Oh, darling. I intend to order for myself this evening. I am the barrister at this table, after all. I'll start with champagne, James." She turned to the waiter.

Dinner passed quickly. Remembering Bryan's feelings about not discussing legal matters during meals, Ivy avoided broaching the subject of the body discovered at Summerbrooke. She focused instead on actively listening to Bryan speak about his feelings surrounding Frederick's death and his new responsibilities. In turn, she found Bryan genuinely interested in her challenges as one of the few women barristers. She found she thoroughly enjoyed this give and take among equals.

Over coffee, Ivy noticed the Harrods' box sitting on the empty chair next to Bryan. "Another dress?"

Bryan grinned mischievously. "Actually something a little different, for you of course."

"Really, Bryan, I cannot possibly accept anything else. The dress is more than enough. In fact, as your barrister I really should not have…"

"You will need this at our next event."

Ivy raised her eyebrows.

"Open it, at least," Bryan implored.

Slowly Ivy lifted the lid off the box. She stared with utter horror at the bathing costume. Where could one possibly wear this?

"For the Bath and Bottle Party!" Bryan exclaimed, apparently reading her thoughts.

"The what?" Ivy yelped, although she had read about the upcoming event in the *Mirror* and wondered whether Bryan would attend. Although she hated to admit it, she had also speculated on his appearance in bathing apparel. "I am afraid it is out of the question. Quite not my thing. Furthermore, may I remind you we agreed to discuss your legal matter this evening?" Ivy crossed her arms and frowned.

"Right. I promise, we can discuss the matter on the way. I must go, honestly. We can talk in the taxi, it's the only chance we'll have tonight." Taking her arm, then encircling her waist, Bryan whisked Ivy out to a waiting taxi before she could object further. "You can change at the party."

****

Once seated in the taxi, Ivy found her voice. "Well of all the…No more delays, tell me about the body found at Summerbrooke once and for all, so I may put an end to being kidnapped to these childish events!"

Bryan leaned close, so close Ivy could feel his breath on her neck as he whispered, "What do you want to know?"

"Did you know this poor unfortunate woman?"

His finger traced her jaw. "You look delicious, you know. Has the body been identified, then?"

Ivy shivered. Her nipples hardened; she could feel them against the silk of her chemise.

Bryan's fingers moved down her collarbone and traced the neckline of her dress. His open hand brushed against her bodice and paused to fondle her breasts. Ivy gasped.

"What was that? I didn't quite hear you. Come closer," Bryan entreated.

As if in a trance, Ivy leaned in to Bryan's warmth. Slowly he began to nibble her neck. His lips moved lower to the crevice between her breasts. Ivy felt the soft lapping motion of his tongue. "I, um…" Ivy began to object.

Bryan slipped his tongue into her open mouth and teased his tongue with hers. Gently he nibbled at her lips. Ivy began to squirm. Without breaking the kiss, Bryan lifted her onto his lap. Ivy began to feel her resistance melt. Through the thin material of her dress, she could feel him harden. Her body clung to his without any conscious thought. Bryan moved his hand upward on her thigh.

"We've arrived, sir. St. Bartholomew's Baths," said the driver.

Ivy thought she heard Bryan swear under his breath. She quickly slid off his lap, pulled down her dress, and opened her eyes.

****

Under the darkness of a sensual summer night, guests streamed into the public baths wearing dazzling bathing costumes. Ivy recognized Cedric at the door, perusing each guest's invitation. As Bryan handed over his invitation, Cedric looked up. Ivy smiled at him, but he failed to recognize her.

"I see my barrister friend failed to make it. So sad. Not often that you lose, old boy." Cedric held out his hands. "One hundred pounds, if you please."

Bryan glowered.

"I'm right here, Cedric!" Ivy declared, having no knowledge of the wager.

"Why, Ivy, is that really you? How ravishing you look! Is it really you, indeed? Or merely an impostor posing to assist Bryan in taking ever more of my money?"

Bryan elbowed him sharply.

"Ow! Oh I see," said Cedric. "I'll catch up with you later, old man," he stage whispered to Bryan. To Ivy he added, "Please go in, old girl, and save a dance for me."

Confused, Ivy entered the baths. Her eyes widened in surprise. Huge rubber horses and brightly colored flowers floated in water illuminated by spotlights. Cocktails were served in the gallery by servers wearing bathing apparel. They immediately offered Ivy a cocktail, invented for the occasion and christened the "Bathwater." Dancing took place to the strains of a negro orchestra. Guests leaped into the baths, where the water had been slightly warmed. A woman, unknown to Ivy, was giving wonderful exhibitions of diving. A group of Mayfair debutantes, whom Ivy recognized from the *London Times*, took sport in ducking those who came their way. Amid the carousing, a small amount of actual swimming took place.

Coming out of the changing cubicle, Ivy received many compliments on her bathing dress. She spotted Bryan looking marvelous, if surprising, in a pink vest and long blue trousers. Sipping her second, or was it her third, Bathwater, Ivy forgot her original apprehension. She danced until dawn, when the police arrived to encourage the partygoers to leave. Ivy, Bryan, and a large number of guests danced from the baths in their bathing outfits to the music of the negro band, shocking passersby on their way to work.

Reclining in the taxi next to Bryan, Ivy closed her eyes and dreamt of bobbing champagne corks and petal strewn tiles reflected in the skylights of St. George's Swimming Baths. Not until she felt Bryan's lips caressing hers did she open her eyes and realize she was home.

Chapter Six

Gargoyle Club, London

Ivy appeared at the breakfast table somewhat later than usual the next day. She had slept fitfully. She alternated between dreams of lovemaking with her newest client and nightmares of women stuffed in elm trees.

"Good morning, my dear," said her father, "or should I say good afternoon. I do believe I heard you come in about dawn. Peeking out to make sure we weren't being burgled, I almost thought I saw you wearing a bathing outfit. Quite an attractive bathing outfit. Nevertheless, I cannot imagine what the neighbors would say. I must have been dreaming, what?"

Ivy collapsed into her chair.

"Cat have your tongue?" her father queried. "Well, I do hope you learned something about the case because the *Mirror* certainly has." He handed the newspaper to Ivy.

"Please, Father, just tell me," she plead, her head on the table.

"A bit early for reading, is it, my dear?"

"Please, Father."

"Very well. The *Mirror* has an article on the unfortunate young woman found in the tree on the

Henderson estate. According to the *Mirror*, the identity of the victim was reported to the police several weeks ago by an Oxfordshire bar maid and suspected prostitute named Daisy. In the report Daisy stated that a known prostitute, called Elsie, who worked Highgate Road in Oxfordshire, had disappeared about a year and a half ago. Her description matched that of the body found at Summerbrooke."

"How sad," Ivy said.

"Wait, there's more, my dear. Several days ago, graffiti began showing up in Oxfordshire and in London related to the crime."

"In London? Where? What does it say?"

"On Dean Street on the front of some establishment called the Gargoyle Club, of all things. Apparently, it is another establishment frequented by the bright young people. In any event, painted in white on the building is the question: 'Who put Elsie down the elm tree on Henderson's estate?' In Oxfordshire, the same question was painted on the side of a two hundred-year-old obelisk on the Henderson estate. I am afraid things may be looking a little dodgy for young Mr. Henderson."

"Based on some graffiti and an unreliable police report? Really, Father. Where is your faith in our clients?"

Her father raised an eyebrow skeptically. "That's not quite all, my dear. There is a separate article of some interest."

"More graffiti?"

"No, another unfortunate young woman."

Ivy lifted her head to find her father watching her seriously.

"Really, Father, you cannot believe…"

"Just listen, please. The *Mirror* further reports that the police in London now also have the death of a young woman on their hands. At the Cavendish Hotel—very unsavory."

"The Cavendish?" Ivy paled, remembering her visit there. "Another death? Is it a murder?"

"Entirely unclear. There was a disaster with a chandelier. The woman was found hanging from it by her headband. Those present, including a judge, said the young woman—a member of the bright young people—was attempting to swing on it after a bit too much champagne, and something went horribly wrong. When the police arrived at the scene, her companions were bathing her forehead with champagne, except for the two who had fallen asleep! Can you imagine! Unfortunately, the poor girl was already dead. The police are still investigating."

"Is the identity of this one unknown?"

"Oh no. The identity of this one is anything but, my dear. Quite well known in fact, Lady Zita Sitwell. One of the bright young people and daughter of an earl."

A chill crept over Ivy. It was as though a ghost had walked over her grave, as Hannah would say. It was hard to believe the beautiful young woman who had danced with Bryan at the Cavendish just a few nights ago was now in the morgue. Danced with Bryan, the words repeated themselves in her head. Was it possible he was involved? "When did this happen?" Ivy hoped it was the previous night, when the Bath and Bottle party would at least provide Bryan with an alibi.

"Several nights ago. And this is what I have been

trying to tell you, according to the *Mirror*, young Mr. Henderson was at the Cavendish when Lady Sitwell's body was found."

Ivy laid her head back down on the table. How could Bryan not have mentioned this?

"I think it's time I sat down with young Mr. Henderson," her father continued. "We need to qualify his knowledge with respect to both of these episodes."

"We are meeting for lunch today," Ivy said, her head still on the table. "I'll try to find out more and establish a meeting time."

"Seeing quite a lot of that young man aren't you, my dear? Do be careful."

Careful? Ivy shuddered. If her father only knew. She had not the nerve to tell him that lunch was to be at the Gargoyle.

****

On his way to the Gargoyle Club to meet Ivy for lunch, Bryan could not help but smile. Although his original plan had been to teach Ivy a lesson about the proper hierarchy of men and women, he had been bewitched. Her newly bobbed chestnut hair, her slender figure, and deep blue eyes, combined with her intelligence and independence were refreshingly intoxicating. He wanted—no, he needed—to know her in every sense of the word. He had never felt so alive!

Bryan's euphoria was quickly quashed as he rounded the corner onto Dean Street and viewed the Gargoyle. He stared in horror at the graffiti splashed across its exterior. His family name was plastered across the club in the same sentence with the name of a prostitute well known to all of the beautiful young people, at least the male members. So shocked was he at seeing the juxtaposition of names, that it took him a moment to realize the import of the sentence: the identity of the corpse found on the grounds of Summerbrooke was now known to the police. He shuddered; how long would it take the police to realize he had known Elsie? Bryan's thoughts were interrupted by Cedric waiting for him outside the entrance.

"Hello, old boy. Quite a work of art, what?"

"You knew Elsie very well," Bryan said accusingly.

"We all knew her very well, old boy. In every sense of the word. We need to close ranks. The police are bound to question us. And, let us not forget, she was found on your land."

"My father's land. I was miles away in London."

"Exactly my point. We will need to agree to alibis. No firm date has been established for the death, but when it is, we must all have been attending a wonderfully decadent party."

Bryan's stomach turned. "I can't discuss this now. I am about to meet with Ivy."

"Ah, the charming barrister. Perhaps, we should have a group luncheon and discuss our options."

"No!" Bryan was adamant. "She's approaching us now. Promise me to say nothing, or I swear Elsie will not be the only body found crushed into a tree!"

"Bryan!" Ivy called, hurrying toward them. "I have so much to talk to you..." She stopped suddenly, seeing Cedric and the graffiti simultaneously.

"Good afternoon, old girl." Cedric bowed. "Shall we go in?"

****

Ivy preceded Bryan and Cedric into the club and

entered a small rickety lift. Cedric whispered into her ear, "It is said that those who enter this lift as strangers become very intimate friends at the end. I have not managed intimacy within this gilded cage as of yet, but I have my hopes." He smiled lecherously, leading Ivy to wonder if he was referring to her or the count.

Ivy exited the lift to find a large ballroom, a bar, a coffee room, and a drawing room. The Gargoyle served as a chic nightclub, home to the bright young people. In the evening, fashionable young men in dinner jackets and flappers in cloche hats danced the Charleston, champagne glasses in hand. But during the daytime, it was a refuge for writers, painters, poets, and musicians who were sold good food and wine at affordable prices.

Bryan had told her that the artist Henri Matisse, a member of the Gargoyle Club, had designed the Moorish interior mirrored with pieces of eighteenth century glass.

"Eroticism imbued with mystery." Cedric winked at her. "Look for the ghost of Charles II's mistress, Nell Gwyn. I have glimpsed her several times."

Ivy, though fascinated with her surroundings, was quietly watching Bryan. Elegant as ever in his tailored suit, his blond hair falling over his eyes, she wanted nothing so much as to touch him. If only Cedric could be distracted toward other pleasures.

As if on cue, Cedric turned into the bar. "You'll have to excuse me, Bryan. I have business to attend to here." Kissing Ivy's hand, he joined a group of young men at the bar.

"Thank God," breathed Bryan. "I have arranged a private dining room for the two of us. We have some things to discuss."

"Eroticism imbued with mystery?" Ivy asked, tossing her head. "Or elm trees and chandeliers?"

****

Bryan led Ivy into a small alcove closed off from the larger dining room by velvet curtains. Inside, a small, oval mahogany table sat on a Turkish carpet between two brocade sofas crowded with velvet pillows. A decanter of ruby red wine with two Waterford glasses sat on the table.

Bryan closed the curtains, took her hand, and led her to the closest sofa. Looking into Ivy's eyes, he took a deep breath. "We need to talk…about everything."

Ivy sighed. Her nipples were erect; her thighs tingled. But she needed to know: was her strong desire for a murderer? "Start with the chandelier."

Bryan removed his hand. Ivy resisted the temptation to snatch it back. "What happened to Zita was horrible. I came to the Cavendish just as they were throwing champagne on her face. I have no idea what happened. But the judge, who was one of her many lovers, says it was a tragic accident."

"And you? Were you also one of her lovers?" Ivy pressed.

Bryan put his face in his hands. "Yes. We have known each other a very long time." Bryan's shoulders shook. "I am sorry."

Ivy reached over and poured them both a glass of wine. "Drink this, you'll feel better."

Bryan looked up. "Do you believe me?"

"I don't know," said Ivy, suddenly the barrister. "I still do not have all the facts."

Bryan reached out to touch her face, and Ivy slid back. As much as she wanted to feel his touch, she needed to know his heart. "You have had intimate relationships with many women? Prostitutes perhaps?"

Bryan looked up guardedly. "Why would you want to know of this?"

Ivy snorted. "Did you not read the graffiti on this very building? Do you not think it odd that graffiti concerning an Oxfordshire prostitute is turning up on a London building connected to the bright young people?"

Bryan remained silent.

"Certainly," Ivy continued angrily, "you are aware the police believe this 'Elsie' is the very woman found at Summerbrooke? At your family estate!"

Bryan placed his head in his hands and mumbled.

"Answer me." Ivy was almost yelling. "Now!"

****

His head still lowered in his hands, Bryan winced. He should be concerned about his situation, but his only thoughts were of Ivy. How beautiful she looked! And how exciting she was when she was passionate, even if it was in the pursuit of law rather than love! His body stirred. He must have her!

Slowly he raised his head, trying his best to look sheepish. "I am sorry."

"Sorry? Sorry?" Ivy was still angry. "For what exactly? For Lady Sitwell? For Elsie?"

"For disappointing you." He looked directly into her eyes brushing a forelock of hair from his forehead. "I'm better than this. I want to be better than this. For you. For us."

"I…I…" Ivy stammered, clearly taken aback.

Realizing the thaw in her attitude, Bryan reached across to touch Ivy's hand. He was pleased when she failed to withdraw it, and brought his other hand to her cheek forcing her to face him. "I need you."

"Need me?"

Seeing something new in her eyes, Bryan leaned over and kissed her. Very, very gently. Testing the waters.

Slowly Ivy responded, returning the kiss hesitantly at first. Touching his face, his hair, his neck. Then more passionately. Easing her tongue between his teeth and tickling the inside of his mouth. Gently sucking at his ear and then his neck.

Bryan groaned. How could such simple actions have such effect? How he wanted her to touch him—everywhere! To feel himself inside her. He felt his passion growing, stretching against the fabric of his trousers. I must have her, here, now, he thought. Slowly, he moved her to a prone position on the seat of the brocade sofa.

"Wait!" Nearly throwing Bryan off the sofa, Ivy suddenly sat up. "Wait," she repeated.

Bryan looked at her in disbelief. "For what, exactly?"

Sitting up straight and moving away, Ivy tidied her clothing. "I will not be diverted again. I am your barrister; we must discuss recent events."

"Recent events?" Bryan eyed her incredulously.

"At Summerbrooke!" Ivy was clearly riled again.

Bryan just stared at her.

"I must know what happened. You must tell me!"

"I cannot. Not here, it's too...too sordid. But, I swear..."

The curtains were pulled back. "Swear to what old boy?" Cedric entered the alcove. "Your undying love?

47

Eternal fidelity?"

Cedric turned to Ivy. "Come, come, old girl. Not that gullible are we? What with all that's been going on…"

Bryan interrupted, "Cedric, we would appreciate some privacy, please."

"Won't hear of it, old boy," Cedric quickly responded. "Entirely too serious. Let's order some bubbly, what?"

Ivy had had enough. "I am sorry, I must go. Father expects me. But Bryan, we must talk. In private. Come to chambers tomorrow." Ivy's voice sounded cold even to herself. Cold as my heart, she thought.

"I can't. I promised Father I would come to Summerbrooke."

Ivy cocked an eyebrow skeptically.

"Summerbrooke, old boy?" Cedric questioned. "Indeed, what can be happening at Summerbrooke?" His tone was almost as cold as Ivy's.

"Business. Personal business," Bryan retorted.

"Indeed," said Cedric.

Ivy crossed her arms, raised her eyebrow even further, and tapped her foot. "Yes, indeed."

Bryan shrugged helplessly. "Ivy, I am sorry." Then suddenly, "Why don't you come with me?"

"To Summerbrooke? Whatever for?"

"We can talk. You can speak to Father; your firm does represent him. See the estate."

Ivy cocked her head skeptically.

"To say nothing of the offending elm tree," Cedric added.

Chapter Seven

Summerbrooke, Oxfordshire

Ivy found the journey to Summerbrooke magical. The air was fresh and bright; Bryan's roadster roared along the curves of the country roads. Passing through the wrought iron gates, Ivy gasped. Henderson House sat at the end of a long and winding drive under a canopy of trees shading formally landscaped park lands. It boasted a grand façade with an imposing flight of stairs leading to the first floor. Arrayed on the staircase, the family, and what appeared to be an army of servants, awaited Bryan's arrival. Ivy turned to Bryan questioningly.

"They are arranged according to their station," Bryan informed her, without irony.

Lord and Lady Henderson stepped forward to meet the small red coupe. "So wonderful to see you, dear." Lady Henderson kissed Bryan on both cheeks. Ivy braced herself, but Lady Henderson only turned to her to say, "We are delighted to have you in our home."

"Yes, thank you; but of course this is not actually a social visit…" Ivy began, anxious to dispel the impression she was at Summerbrooke in any capacity other than her professional role of barrister.

"Here, here. Plenty of time for that business later," Lord Henderson interrupted. "Come inside; come

49

inside."

Ivy ascended the staircase and entered a high ceilinged hall. Eyes wide, Ivy took in the polished marble floors, limestone arches, and massive oak table displaying a group of bronzes with flanking candelabra modeled with figures of Roman goddesses. "How beautiful!"

"Please, make yourself at home," said his lordship.

"Gertrude," her Ladyship said, turning to her maid, "take Miss Smythe up to the Damask Room to change before dinner." She turned to Ivy. "You brought your maid?"

"Um…no," Ivy replied, while behind his mother's back Bryan offered her a mischievous wink.

"Right. I'll send up one of the housemaids to assist with your dress and hair. Dinner is at seven o'clock; cocktails in the drawing room at six thirty. Gertrude can help you find your way."

Ivy followed Gertrude up to her room. Passing over the threshold, she turned full circle to admire the stunning views east, west, and south. "The south terrace, the deer park, and the cutting garden, miss," Gertrude explained.

Ivy merely nodded, turning to view the room itself. There was no doubt in her mind why it was called the Damask Room. Every window was hung with silk damask draperies in the most beautiful shade of blue. Even the walls themselves appeared to be covered in the luxuriant fabric. The fireplace boasted an antique marble and gilt fireplace surround and mantel. A small settee, writing desk, and huge mahogany four-poster bed with blue damask canopy completed the room.

Promptly at six thirty, Ivy entered the drawing

room. Opening off the entrance hall, it was huge. At least ninety feet long, it was divided into three sitting areas. Ivy chose a spot on the green baize sofa in front of the fireplace which boasted a large limestone hood painted with hunting scenes. The walls displayed three silk and wool tapestries with detailed pictorial designs personifying prudence, faith, and charity. Ivy was surprised to see several other guests in the large room. She had hoped to have an opportunity to speak to Baron Henderson about the discovery of the young woman's body on his estate.

****

Bryan loved Summerbrooke, Henderson House, and most particularly, the drawing room. But this evening, he only had eyes for Ivy. Her chestnut bob gleamed in the firelight. Her peacock blue frock highlighted her eyes and enhanced her slender frame. But what captured his attention most was her animated discussion with his elderly neighbor, Lord Fortnoy, and his dissolute son, James. Usually gatherings at Henderson House divided up along gender lines, the gentlemen talking about horses, hunting, or automobiles. But James was clearly enthralled with Ivy's discussion of her life as one of England's few female barristers. An unexpected twinge of jealousy passed through Bryan's consciousness. She is mine, he almost said aloud.

As Bryan made his way across the room to the green baize sofa, he caught his father's eye. Baron Henderson inclined his head toward Ivy, raised his glass, and smiled. Sidling up to Bryan, he whispered, "Fascinating and beautiful." Bryan nodded but continued toward the sofa to claim Ivy's attention. In passing, he wondered if his father had conspired with his old friend and barrister Edward Smythe to introduce him to Ivy for reasons beyond the law.

****

Ivy enjoyed talking with James and was pleased to be seated next to him at dinner. But her eyes strayed continuously to Bryan who sat at the other end of the long oak dining table resplendent in his tailcoat. The dining room was also impressive, with two built-in gilt trimmed throne chairs and a triple fireplace flanked by armor. The fireplaces sat beneath one high relief panel depicting a fox hunt. Pennants hanging in the room commemorated staff and family members who fought in the Great War.

The dinner was delicious. Never had Ivy so much enjoyed food or drink. Dinner began with a soup course with sherry, followed by a fish course with white wine, mutton cutlets served with champagne, a meat pie accompanied by potatoes, vegetables and Burgundy, venison served with traditional game chips and claret. Just as the table was cleared and Ivy breathed a sigh of contentment believing she was finally finished, new glasses and cutlery were set out and dessert was served: ices, followed by fruit and nuts, complemented by port and Madeira.

****

Following dinner, the ladies moved to the drawing room, the gentlemen relaxed at the dining room table, drinking port and smoking cheroots. Bryan usually loved this time with his father and the other men, but found himself unable to concentrate on anything but Ivy.

"Quite a girl you've found there," said the elder

Lord Fortnoy. "Wish James here could find someone like her."

"Actually, sir," Bryan responded, hoping to deflect any interest James might have, "she's my family's barrister."

"Yes, yes, I understood that. Quite an interesting conversation we had about the body found in the old elm. She was interested to learn the extent of your acquaintance with the poor unfortunate girl."

"What did you tell her?"

"Nothing, old chap, nothing at all. We few remaining gentry must stick together, what?"

James smiled, knowingly.

****

Ivy awoke the next morning to brilliant sunshine. As was common in the social interactions of the landed gentry while at their country houses, the ladies and gentlemen were to spend the day apart. Bryan had warned Ivy of his father's refusal to move out of the Edwardian age on their drive from London.

As a lady, it was only appropriate for Ivy to sew, gossip, read, or walk after breakfast. Normally she would chafe at such restrictions, but today she was anxious to walk the estate and find the much discussed elm tree.

Setting out across the parklands, her mind drifted to Bryan. How different he was here than in London. In London he was all play, gambling, drinking, and carousing, if truth be told. It was easy to be drawn to his bad boy side and his good looks, but not really so difficult to believe that he could be involved in a heinous murder.

At Summerbrooke he was interested in the estate

and his family, cognizant of the responsibilities he had inherited upon the untimely death of his brother, and anxious to please his father and make him proud. Here, it seemed impossible that he could be involved with anything as vile as the intentional death of a prostitute, let alone stuffing her body in a tree.

Ivy left the formal gardens and cut across a field. Surely if anyone was watching her from the house, they would wonder. Upon that thought, she turned back to look at Henderson House. Again facing forward, she saw a figure riding toward her. Sitting erect upon a magnificent stallion, the figure was a handsome one. Tall and fit, blond hair flying. She smiled as Bryan rode up to her. "I thought this morning was golf with the gentlemen," she said sarcastically, "or some other activities not fit for young ladies who must remain passive."

Ignoring her jibe, Bryan dismounted. "I thought you might want to see more of the estate than your ladylike chains allow. I have come to rescue you."

"Indeed. To where?"

"The river, it has always been my favorite spot. Rowing, fishing, dreaming; it was my summer haunt when I was a boy."

Despite herself, Ivy was interested. Born and raised in London, and familiar primarily with the Thames, Ivy found it hard to envision the idyllic life Bryan described. But her duties called. "And might we visit the notorious elm tree?"

Bryan sighed with resignation. "Of course." Reaching for her hand, he pulled her up to the front of the stallion.

Seated before him and riding across the fields, Ivy

felt Bryan's arms around her and relaxed her body into his. The stallion's powerful muscles massaged her thighs through the wool of her trousers, and Bryan's legs fitted around her as the rough terrain bounced his body against hers. Entirely new sensations enveloped her, not an unpleasant experience.

Reaching the elm tree, they dismounted. The scene was desolate; nothing remained to assist Ivy in understanding the senseless act of violence that had occurred there.

"This is it. Have you seen enough?" Bryan asked.

"We must talk about this. I am your barrister. My knowledge can only help you."

"Very well. What do you wish to know?" The better self, which Bryan evidenced when at Summerbrooke, emerged.

"Did you know her?"

"Know her?"

"Bryan…"

"Yes. I knew her. We all knew her. She would sometimes accompany Cedric and others to the Cavendish. She would sometimes accompany James to Paris. She sometimes accompanied my brother to the local pub. We—the young gentry—all knew her."

"Cedric? I thought…"

"Yes, he much prefers the company of men in his bed, but he is not above enjoying the company of women out of it or in it if the need arises."

"Did you…did the need arise with you?"

"With Elsie? God forbid, no. Give me some credit."

"Was she ever here?"

"At Summerbrooke? Not that I know of, but of

course I spend most of my time in London."

"Have you asked your father? Others on the estate? In Oxfordshire? Have you learned anything at all?"

He shrugged. "The prevailing rumor is that it was a local tradesman known as Jack Morris. Jack's sister claims Jack confessed to family members that he met a prostitute named Elsie in the Rusty Nail, a local pub. Jack said Elsie became drunk and passed out while he was drinking and playing darts in the bar. Insulted, he drove her to Summerbrooke. Once on the estate grounds, he put her in a hollow tree with the hope that in the morning she would wake up and be frightened into seeing the error of her ways."

"Why Summerbrooke? How did he know about the tree?"

"Oh, he has done odd jobs at Summerbrooke and neighboring estates since he was a boy. He knows the grounds as well as any of us."

"Have the police confronted Jack? What does he say?"

"Nothing. He died in a mental hospital before the body was found."

"A mental hospital? How odd. Why was he there?" Ivy involuntarily shivered.

Bryan frowned. "That's the oddest part. Jack Morris was confined to a mental hospital several months before the body was found because he had recurring dreams of a woman staring out at him from a tree."

Ivy shook her head. "A horrible story. Have the police questioned the sister?"

"I don't know. I have told you everything. I swear. Yes, I did know Elsie as did most of my set. I heard from Cedric that she was the corpse in the tree…"

"From Cedric? How did he know it was Elsie in the elm?"

"Local gossip, I imagine. In any event, I have no idea how she ended up in such a bloody resting place. It may have been Jack Morris; it may have been someone else. But it was not me."

Ivy eyed him cautiously. She did believe him, but she was not done. "And what of Lady Sitwell?" she asked.

Bryan hung his head and muttered.

"I beg your pardon?"

Bryan looked up and grasped Ivy's hands. "I have already explained all that. It was a difficult time in my life. It was a mistake to bed her. But she was so alive, so charming…"

"And so you hanged her from a chandelier." Ivy, in her hurt, reverted to the skills she had learned as a barrister in cross-examination.

"No!" Bryan pulled back his hands so quickly Ivy almost lost her balance. "I told you. I wasn't at the Cavendish when it happened. The judge said it was an accident. They were playing at acrobatics and…" A sob escaped Bryan's lips.

Ivy stood by helplessly. She had met Lady Sitwell, as well as her friends, and experienced the Cavendish. Unlikely as playing at acrobatics was in her circle, she was not surprised to hear it happened in Zita's.

Bryan looked into her eyes. "Tell me what you're thinking. Do you hate me? Should we return to Henderson House before I do some unspeakable harm to you as you believe I have done to every other woman I have known?"

Ivy met his gaze and shook her head. "I want to believe you. Convince me." She opened her arms invitingly.

****

Rather than the romantic convincing Ivy was expecting, Bryan grabbed her around the waist and put her back up on his stallion. Mounting the steed behind her, he whisked her through the woods to a small boat beached on a winding river deep within Summerbrooke.

Grabbing the oars, Bryan rowed effortlessly though the water. Ivy found it a welcome relief to talk of things other than death. She smiled at Bryan and stretched her arms, dangling one hand in the river.

"You are so relaxed, here," he said.

"And you are so different."

"I love Summerbrooke. My brother Frederick and I spent many happy hours here. It was paradise."

"You were close to your brother?"

"Five years older, and the heir, he was my hero. I wish you could have known him. He was kind, generous, and intelligent. His death in the war was a huge loss to me, my family, and the estate. It took several years for normalcy to return here at all, and it will never be the same."

"And now you're the heir."

"Not something I ever wanted or was prepared for. It is a huge responsibility. The land, my parents, the house, the servants, the estate, everything depends on me. Plus the changes since the war, labor unrest, taxes. I want to do well by Summerbrooke and my family. It's my duty. It's important for me to fulfill it."

All of this had been said while looking out over the landscape, but suddenly he turned his golden gaze directly on her. "I care."

"I know." She reached out to touch his hand but immediately pulled back from the electrically charged contact.

"I know you don't understand," she continued, "but that's how I feel about the law. The law is structured, but it has the ability to adapt to changing times and has kept England free for centuries. To be one of the first women barristers is such an honor. I want to prove myself and make my father proud. Changes are coming for England, probably for the world; the law will help us make our way."

Bryan continued to gaze at her but turned the boat toward shore and let it nestle in the reeds. He reached for her hands. Cautiously she stepped forward to grasp his.

"I want to tell you," Ivy began. "I feel so much closer to you at Summerbrooke. You are so different here."

"And I am so awful in London?"

"No, not awful. But capricious, superficial. Here..."

****

Bryan had been watching her carefully while she spoke. The riding had disheveled her. It still surprised him to see women in trousers—a fairly new development since the war. But on Ivy they looked splendid. They showed off her figure, in a way her suits or even her flapper dresses did not. She wore a plain white blouse which buttoned down the front, and the top button had strained as she moved across the boat to grasp his hands.

Slowly, without thinking, he leaned forward and

kissed her. Her lips were warm, whether from the day's exertions or his nearness he could not be sure. She reached up to touch his cheek, and he felt his groin stir.

Being careful to balance the boat, he pulled her to him. Her lips parted when he inserted his tongue. Then he moved down her neck licking softly. Undoing the offending top button of her shirt, he reached in and gently stroked her nipples first one then the other. They responded immediately, as did Ivy.

She whispered, "More."

He moved his tongue to her breasts. Favoring each nipple as he had done before, but now gently sucking as she arched with pleasure. She groaned loudly, "More, please."

He cupped her bottom and brought her on to his lap. In pants, her legs separated easily to hug his waist. Although the boat rocked perilously, he drew her body close to his. She wrapped her legs more tightly around him, felt his manliness throbbing against her as she began a slow dance.

He let out a long breath. "We need to find somewhere we can…"

"Hello, old boy," came a hearty voice followed by the sounds of thrashing through the bushes. "Gertrude thought I might find you here."

Ivy and Bryan turned suddenly toward Cedric's voice. The boat rocked violently, dumping them unceremoniously into the river.

Chapter Eight

Metropolitan Police Station, Central Criminal Court, Old Bailey, London

Bryan sat at the table directly in front of the bow window that jutted out from the first floor of Black's Club. All he could think of was Ivy. Her hair and the way it blended into the curve of her jaw. Her swanlike neck. Her small perfect breasts. He must find a way to win her confidence. If only...

Shaking his head to clear his thoughts, he unfolded the morning's edition of the *Mirror* laid out next to his tea service. The lead story involved the disappearance of yet another young woman. Violette Saunders, aged twenty-two, was a dancer and prostitute in London. Last seen a fortnight ago, she was feared dead. The police were investigating, but had no leads. At least I haven't made her acquaintance, Bryan thought wryly.

His thoughts were interrupted by the sudden entrance of the young maid accompanied by two uniformed police officers. One short and portly. The other tall and thin. "Sir, these gentlemen wish to speak with you."

Bryan was on his feet. "Has something happened? Is someone injured?"

The taller officer stepped forward. "Sir, I am Inspector Ravendale." Indicating his partner. "This is

Officer Glen. We have come to ask you a few questions."

Bryan quickly sat again. "I do not care to answer questions at the present time. It is not convenient. Please leave."

Ravendale ignored his request. "Sir, I must insist. What is your name?"

"The Honorable Bryan Henderson, son and heir of Baron Fitzgerald Henderson, of course. You must know that."

Glen took hold of his right arm. "Please come along, sir."

"I will not. Whatever is the matter with you? I have just told you who I am." Bryan's lowered voice quivered with anger.

Ravendale calmly responded, "I am an inspector of police. You must consider yourself in custody in connection with the willful murder of Elsie Gordon at the estate of Summerbrooke, Oxfordshire."

"Is that all?" Bryan growled.

"For the moment, sir," Glen declared politely.

"Thank you."

"Your welcome, I'm sure, sir," said Glen with a smile. "Come along now, sir."

"And where might we be going?"

"To the police station of course. To meet with Chief Inspector Fox," said Ravendale.

"But first we much search you, sir," interrupted Glen, still smiling.

"Of all the bloody impertinence!"

"Please stand and empty your pockets, sir."

"I will not!"

Ravendale stepped closer. "Yes, sir, you will and

immediately if you please."

Bryan stood and with an exasperated sigh, emptied his pockets of their only contents: pound notes. "Are you satisfied?"

"Very, sir. Now please come with us."

****

At the Metropolitan Police Station, Bryan met with Chief Inspector Fox. "Good morning to you, sir," Fox politely began.

"There is nothing good about it, Chief Inspector. I demand to be released. What possible evidence can you have against me?"

"Do you truly wish to know?"

"I do wish to know."

"I may tell you. But this is a very serious charge, and first I must introduce you to someone."

"Whom?" Bryan pulled himself up to his full height to convey his importance.

His gesture was lost on Fox. "Detective Inspector Collins, New Scotland Yard. Would you like to know his specialty?"

Bryan only glared in response.

"Fine. I shall enlighten you. Detective Inspector Collins has been the supervisor of the Yard's fingerprint department since its formation in 1901. Since 1902 the Yard has collected over one hundred fifty thousand sets of fingerprints."

"Fingerprints? Fingerprints?"

"Yes, indeed. And here is Detective Inspector Collins to collect your fingerprints now."

Collins entered the small, windowless room and nodded to Bryan. "Good morning, sir." He carried a copper plate with a roller, a bottle of ink, and what appeared to be a police form. He spread a layer of ink over the plate. "Now, sir, if I may have your right thumb, I will place it upon the plate so its ridges take up the ink. I will then place your thumb on this paper"—here he indicated the form—"and it will leave an imprint. It will not hurt at all, sir."

"I most certainly will not provide my thumb. I am leaving immediately." Bryan moved toward the door.

Fox stepped in front of him. "I'm afraid that's not possible, sir. I must advise you that you are under arrest for the murder of Elsie Gordon, that you may not leave, and that you are to provide your thumb to Detective Inspector Collins immediately."

With an exaggerated sigh, Bryan complied.

"And now, Chief Inspector," Bryan demanded as Collins left the room, "I would like to know the evidence you have against me."

"All in good time, my boy. All in good time." Fox nodded solemnly and left the room. The heavy door clanged shut.

Bryan stared in horror. He knew he was innocent. And he had told Ivy the truth, he had known Elsie but never intimately, and he certainly had not murdered her. Would Ivy believe him? If not, his life was truly over.

****

Ivy entered Old Bailey several steps ahead of her father. News that Bryan had been taken into custody on charges of murder had quickly spread through Lincoln's Inn. Ivy was furious with Bryan, the police, her father, everyone. She and Bryan had become so close at Summerbrooke. She believed he was innocent of murder. Was that not true? Could she defend a murderer? Should she, given how close she and Bryan had become? Oh, why did life never proceed as planned?

"Where is he, Officer?" she demanded of Glen, a man she had known since childhood.

Glen regarded her coldly. "Whom?"

"Mr. Henderson, of course!"

"And whom shall I say is calling?" Glen responded with a mischievous grin.

"His barristers!" Ivy's father, having finally arrived, announced. He was winded but equally as angry as Ivy.

"Why, hello, Mr. Smythe. How nice to see you. I will be glad to escort you to the prisoner."

"And my daughter?"

"Well…I don't rightly think…"

"Who is also a barrister!" Ivy interjected.

"A barrister, imagine! Blokes, did you hear that?" he yelled to the group of officers huddled nearby. "They're letting girls be barristers, now!"

Ivy reached out as if to slap him, but her father quickly caught her hand. Turning to Glen he added, "You will regret that, I guarantee. Take us to Mr. Henderson now, please."

Glen shrugged and turned to lead them down a narrow passage.

The door opened, and Ivy's eyes and heart went immediately to Bryan, hunched over the table. He lifted his head, despair evident in his eyes. "Ivy! Mr. Smythe! Thank God!"

"Not another word, Bryan," said Ivy's father.

"Who is in charge here, Officer?" he asked Glen.

"Chief Inspector Fox."

"Bring him to me at once."

Several minutes passed before Fox entered the room. "How may I help you, sir?" he asked Ivy's father. "And of course you, my lady." He smirked.

Fearing physical violence, Ivy's father moved between them and spoke quickly. "Why are you holding this man? What is he charged with? What possible evidence can you have against a young sir of such an esteemed background?"

Fox paused for emphasis. "The prisoner is under arrest for the murder of Elsie Gordon at Summerbrooke. As to evidence, to begin with the body was found on the Henderson estate. Further, we have several witnesses who will testify the prisoner knew the victim. Quite intimately, according to one"—Fox checked his notes—"Stephen Bernard, also known as Cedric. Third, said Cedric reports the prisoner had recently had a falling out with Miss Gordon over the cost of her services. And fourth, we expect the thumbprint we have just taken from the prisoner will match the bloody print found on the fragments of lilac silk wrapped around Miss Gordon's neck at the scene of the crime."

Ivy locked eyes with Bryan and shook her head. Even in the hands of the metropolitan police, he was as attractive as ever. Part of her wanted to run to him and hold him passionately. The other part of her wanted to run to him and crush his larynx with her bare hands. He had ruined her career. Ruined her! She could never forgive him. She turned to leave.

"Ivy, wait!" Bryan implored. "Ask them about Morris! Ask them about Cedric! The police must have his report wrong; it was he—not I—who was intimate with Elsie."

Ivy walked out, slamming the door. Her eyes filled with tears, and a strangled sob escaped her throat.

Chapter Nine

Smythe and Company, Lincoln's Inn Fields, London

The following days were unbearable for Ivy. Bryan remained in police custody, but try as Ivy might, she could not put him out of her mind. His smile, his hands, every facet of his being haunted her.

Her father worked around the clock researching the law, reviewing documents, talking to witnesses, preparing his case. He forbade Ivy from having anything further to do with Bryan or, as he expressed it, "any of his bloody cases." Bryan had only been charged with Elsie Gordon's murder. Nevertheless, the police believed the murder of Elsie Gordon and the disappearance of Violette Saunders, reported in the press, were connected. Her father privately expressed to Ivy his concern that the police also suspected Bryan in Violette's disappearance.

Despite her negative feelings regarding Bryan, Ivy believed her duties as a barrister required her to continue his representation. Her father, however, vehemently disagreed. Alone with him in chambers early on the morning of the third day after Bryan's arrest, Ivy dared to broach the subject again.

"Father, there must be something I can do to assist the defense. You know I am the better researcher." Ivy smiled wanly.

"Absolutely not! Your relationship with young Mr. Henderson has compromised the case far too much already. Attend to our other clients. And please try not to fall in love with them!"

Ivy was aghast. "Whatever do you mean? I never said anything about Bryan to lead you to believe… I…I…I only met with him at your request. You forced me to take him on as a client."

"Yes, my dear. And how I rue that day. As to what you did or did not say," her father continued, "do you think I am blind? That I have not watched you change your hair, your wardrobe, your manner of speaking and walking because of him? That I have not watched you mope about one moment and become giddy with glee the next because of some meaningless action by young Mr. Henderson?"

"Father! I never…"

"Oh yes, my dear, you did. And I admit that at first, God forgive me, I was pleased to see you finally take an interest in a young man. But did you have to choose a murderer!"

"Father, please." Ivy hung her head.

"Do not 'Father' me, young lady. You have compromised the legal ethics of this office and potentially destroyed your career by cavorting with a client. Our only hope is that this not come to light publicly. I insist that you have nothing else whatsoever to do with Mr. Bryan Henderson."

Ivy was silent. Her father was right, of course. Personal involvement with a client by a barrister would be viewed as unprofessional by almost everyone. What had she been thinking?

John, the office clerk, bounded into chambers. Excitement reverberated from every pore.

Her father turned irritably. "What is it, John? We are trying to work here."

"I've just come from outside the *Mirror*, sir. There's news about the other pro—skirt. You know, sir, Violette, the other pro—skirt we thought might be linked to young Henderson."

Ivy looked up in horror. She thought her father had only voiced that concern to her.

"John, enough of that," her father commanded.

"Very well, sir." John turned to go. "Just thought you might want to know the police have found the body."

Ivy could not contain herself. Risking her father's wrath, she blurted out, "Where? Where did they find it?"

"Don't want to interfere with the master's work now," John replied sullenly.

"For bloody's sake, John," her father exploded. "Tell us."

"Might there be some tea left, sir? Another wet morning it is, sir."

"Tea, Hannah!" her father yelled to the Smythe housekeeper. Hannah had been relocated to chambers for most days, as her father was spending all of his time there.

"Thank you, sir." John settled in front of the fireplace, enjoying his cup of tea.

"Yes, yes. This better be worthwhile," said her father.

"Oh, it is, sir," said John, warming to his tale.

"Then tell it, man!"

"Well, you know William Blaine at the left luggage office of Kings Cross railway station," John began.

"No," Ivy said, "actually we…"

Her father gave her a sharp look. "Please, continue John."

"He had several complaints about an ungodly smell and hellish fluid leaking from an unclaimed trunk. He alerted the Metropolitan Police, and Chief Inspector Fox opened the trunk to find the body of a young woman.

"Naked she was, according to the blokes at the *Mirror*. Naked as a jaybird!" John tittered.

"All right, John," her father said. "Let's move on."

"Well, almost naked," John corrected. "She was wearing a torn scarf around her neck. Strangled according to the blokes at the *Mirror*."

Ivy looked meaningfully at her father. "What kind of scarf, John?' he asked.

"The blokes wouldn't say, sir."

"What did the woman look like? How do the police know the corpse in the trunk is Violette Saunders? Did someone identify her?" her father continued.

"Don't know that either, sir. Guess we'll just have to wait for the evening edition of the *Mirror*."

"I'll go to the police station and see what I can find out." Ivy moved toward the door.

"You'll do no such thing, young lady," her father quickly responded. "I'll go myself. I want to check on young Mr. Henderson at any rate."

He added, "John, in the meantime, return to the *Mirror*. See what else you can discover."

As John and her father left chambers, Ivy slid into John's vacated chair in front of the fire. Hannah silently entered the room with a tray of tea things and sat beside her.

"Oh Hannah," Ivy sighed. "What does this mean? I'm so confused. I thought the law would be clear, black and white. It's not, it's all gray. I don't know what to think."

"There, there, dear." Hannah gently hugged her. "I know you have feelings for the young gentleman. Things will all work out. They always do."

Ivy pulled back in surprise. "Feelings for Bryan? I don't know what you can be talking about? Have you been speaking to my father?"

Hannah shook her head and smiled. "No need to talk to Mr. Smythe. I know."

"You don't know anything, Hannah!" Ivy cried as she flounced from the room.,

****

Ivy actually managed to complete some work for other clients by the time John and her father returned to chambers. Just minutes apart, they both told the same story although John had been at the *Mirror* and her father at the police station.

Her father summarized. "The body in the trunk was that of Violette Saunders, aged twenty-two, a dancer and prostitute in London, known to consort with the bright young people. Violette was identified by the police from a photograph provided by her flat mate, Evelyn Warner. In her missing person's report, Miss Warner stated that when last seen Violette was wearing a red cloche hat, a string of pearls, and a black dress. However, Violette was naked when found in the trunk. No clothes were found in the trunk or its vicinity."

Ivy looked up at her father. "What of the scarf

around her neck John alluded to earlier? Was that in error, then?"

"Let me finish, please, Ivy," her father responded. "When found in the trunk, Violette was naked but for a light green silk scarf, of fine quality according to the police, wound around her neck. The police believe the scarf was used to strangle the victim. They are also examining fingerprints found on the trunk."

"A green silk scarf," Ivy mused. "What does Bryan say?"

"Nothing," her father replied glumly. "Nothing to me, at least. Other than to say he never met the girl and knows nothing about her untimely demise."

Ivy brightened. "That's good news then."

John and her father looked at her dubiously. It was her father who responded. "I'm afraid the police have other ideas, my dear."

John interrupted, "The *Mirror* too, miss."

With a warning look at John, her father continued. "Two young prostitutes, known to frequent the haunts of the bright young people, both strangled with pieces of silk, and shoved into unlikely hiding places: a tree and a trunk. Even I must admit, the similarities are troubling."

Chapter Ten

Smythe and Company, Lincoln's Inn Fields, London

The following days passed slowly. "Father, isn't there anything we can do?" Ivy asked.

"Only wait," her father replied. "The police have the bloody fingerprint from the lilac scarf found at Summerbrooke, as well as the prints found on the trunk from the murder of Violette Saunders. They, and we, must now wait for the comparison of the fingerprints by Scotland Yard with those of young Mr. Henderson."

"I cannot wait any longer." Ivy shivered with distaste at the thought of the murder scenes as well as fear for Bryan.

"You will and you must."

Ivy began to protest, but her father held up his hand. "And, young lady, no matter what the outcome of this unfortunate matter, you must have no further dealings with young Mr. Henderson. His father has told me that, even if he is ultimately released, he will be sent abroad. It will be impossible for the young man to function effectively in Britain—running the estate or assuming any responsible position—his reputation is ruined. A lesson in choosing one's friends wisely, if ever I heard one. What he was thinking while making friends with the bright young people is beyond my comprehension."

"Why, the last time I was at the station," her father continued, to Ivy's dismay, "that Cedric chap appeared—at Old Bailey you understand—with his elaborately coiffed hair, flapping his hands and sauntering around the room. Nowadays so many boys are girlish," her father complained. "It's the way too many of the gentry have grown up since the war. At any rate, for all practical purposes young Mr. Henderson's life is over."

As is mine, now, thought Ivy, retiring to her office to attempt to accomplish some client work as her father labored over Bryan's case. How boring her life was after the magic of Bryan. How could I ever have wanted to become a barrister? she asked herself morosely.

Several hours later, Hannah came in with a cup of tea and found Ivy staring vacantly into space. As much as Ivy tried to focus on her next case coming to trial, her mind kept returning to Bryan. Not just his smile or the way he touched her, but the way his entire case had unfolded. Something had been tugging at the edge of her consciousness since reports of the finding of Violette Saunders' body had first surfaced. Hannah's entrance interrupted her concentration just long enough for the sought-after thought to surface. The green silk scarf! She had seen one before, but where?

"Hannah," Ivy began, "do you know where I might have seen…"

Her question was interrupted by the sound of a new, but nevertheless familiar, voice in chambers. "Excuse me, miss," Hannah said as she hurried out the door. "I must fetch tea for your father and his guest, now that Chief Inspector Fox has arrived."

Her father was expecting the Chief Inspector? "Highly irregular," Ivy muttered under her breath as she left her desk and moved toward her father's office.

"There is something you should know." Ivy overheard Fox explaining to her father. "The papers will be printing it soon. I thought I owed it to you to tell you in person."

"Please, Chief Inspector, come in and sit. Ivy, you as well, quit lurking. Hannah, some tea, please," her father called out.

Seated with tea, pleasantries dispensed with, Fox cleared his throat. "Well, sir, the reason I am here is this. We may have another suspect in the murders of Elsie Gordon and Violette Saunders."

"Indeed," her father said, while discreetly motioning to Ivy to remain still.

"Yes, sir. Evelyn Warner, Miss Saunders' flat mate, disappeared shortly after she made the missing person's report, and well, sir, we feared the worst. But Miss Warner returned to her flat yesterday, and it turns out she had only been visiting her sister in Brighton."

"Right," her father said, exhibiting a remarkable amount of patience in Ivy's view.

"Yes, sir," Fox responded in his plodding manner.

"Pray go on."

"Well, sir, we asked her what else she could remember about the last time she had seen Miss Saunders. And sir, it was quite illuminating."

Her father merely nodded. Ivy tried hard not to roll her eyes.

"Miss Warner reported that on the day Miss Saunders disappeared, she had had a row with one of her..." Fox paused and looked at Ivy for a moment. "Um, a row with one of her 'regulars,' if you know what I mean, sir."

"Quite," said her father.

"This young gentleman—and a gentleman he was, sir, according to Miss Warner—had arranged to meet Miss Saunders at the flat but was exceedingly late. While waiting, Miss Saunders had quite a bit to drink. By the time the young gentleman arrived, Miss Saunders was obviously drunk, according to Miss Warner, and very angry. Miss Saunders accused the young gentleman of being overly familiar with"—he paused and shot a furtive look at Ivy—"a waiter at the Cavendish known as Tony. The young gentleman became incensed and yelled insults at Miss Saunders. Apparently this went on for some time. Indeed so long that Miss Warner ultimately had to leave to meet one of her own 'regulars.' "

"I see," her father said calmly, "and you believe there is some connection between this young gentleman, his argument with the unfortunate Miss Saunders, and her disappearance, do you?"

"Yes, sir. You see, sir, it is the last time Miss Warner saw Miss Saunders. When she returned from her rendezvous, Miss Saunders was gone."

"I understand, but..."

"And sir," Fox concluded in a rush, "the young gentleman was wearing a green silk scarf. In fact, Miss Warner has identified it as the scarf found on Miss Saunders' body."

Ivy gasped, suddenly remembering where she had seen the green silk scarf before. Her father gave her a stern warning look, before continuing in his calm lawyerly voice. "Chief Inspector, do we know the identity of the young gentleman?"

"Not exactly, sir. But Miss Warner recalls his nickname as Cecil."

Ivy could be still no longer. "Not Cecil, Cedric," she blurted. "You've seen him, Father. His legal name is Stephen Bernard. His father is the Earl of Glenconnor." Turning to Fox she added, "Cedric was the witness who claimed Bryan fought with Elsie over the costs of his services!"

"Ivy!" Her father shouted, recognizing the earl's name. "You cannot be recklessly accusing members of the aristocracy without some proof."

Ivy, not to be deterred, blundered on. "Cedric has a lovely spring green silk scarf. I saw it myself. At the Cavendish, no less. And he knew Elsie Gordon. Knew her, um, in the biblical sense." Ivy snuck a sideways glance at her father, who suppressed a smile at the euphemism, then rushed on. "He was a 'regular' as the Chief Inspector would say. Cedric also had access to Summerbrooke, and"—Ivy stopped a moment to catch her breath—"and that must be the reason he fabricated that story against Bryan!" Ivy concluded, having just realized it for herself. "Cedric hoped to deflect suspicion from himself!

"Bryan is innocent!" Ivy practically shouted. "I must speak to him. Now!"

"Sit down, young lady," her father ordered. "You will do nothing of the kind until the police have finished their business." Turning to Fox, he added, "Chief Inspector, it appears you have quite a lot of business to attend to this afternoon."

"Indeed, sir. I best be going."

"We will momentarily allow you to take your leave. But as young Mr. Henderson's barrister, I must ask. Has the young sir been exonerated on the fingerprint evidence?"

Fox shook his head. "Too soon, sir."

Ivy groaned. How could she have forgotten the fingerprints? Could they possibly be Bryan's? If so, would he be hanged?

Chapter Eleven

St. Marks Place, London

Bryan walked slowly through the dismal London drizzle mulling his options. Much to his relief, he had been released from police custody earlier in the day. His father, however, was now waiting for him to return to Summerbrooke and prepare for his future. The prodigal son, he thought wryly to himself. But he could not go without seeing Ivy. All he could think of was Ivy's blue eyes teasing him, testing him, setting him on a better course. Her slender body, which he so longed to touch. He had gained his freedom, but he feared he had permanently lost Ivy. She had worked so hard and took such pride in becoming a barrister. How could he hope that she would want to continue a friendship, let alone something more, with someone once accused of not one murder, but two! Now that he was released, he would not even have the excuse of calling on her as his barrister.

He felt numb. The rain intensified and lashed his face. He walked on, unaware of where he was heading. Earlier in the day, being unable to find the Smythes in chambers, he had checked their address planning to come to their home to thank them for all they had done for him. Now, looking around, he found himself on St. Marks Place, the small quiet square on which the

Smythes resided. The townhouse was dark, except for a single light on the second floor.

****

Ivy sat in her dressing gown at a writing desk near the fireplace in the minuscule sitting room adjoining her bedroom on the second floor of One St. Marks Place. The fire was lit against the chill, and Hannah had just brought in a pot of tea. Outside the French doors was a small balcony overlooking the garden. With the doors slightly ajar, she could hear the rain dancing against the slate. French doors also opened off the sitting room to her bedroom, which included a canopy bed with white linens and a white chaise smothered in blue pillows. These two small rooms and tiny terrace had been her mother's refuge during her prolonged illness. Ivy sat at the desk tonight thinking of her mother and wishing she could have an old-fashioned heart to heart discussion.

She could not imagine her life without Bryan. She loved the law and enjoyed being a barrister, but she wanted more. She wanted a family, children. She wanted someone to share her bed and her heart. Truth be told, she wanted Bryan. She shook her head, if only he wasn't accused of murder. Ruefully she thought, I need to find some way to meet men other than my profession!

Suddenly the French doors leading to the terrace flew open, startling Ivy. She moved to close them, wondering when the peaceful rain had morphed into a violent storm. Pushing aside the draperies, she brushed a human form and would have screamed had a hand not covered her mouth.

She looked up to find herself staring into Bryan's eyes. "I just want to talk to you. May I release you?

Will you promise not to scream?"

Ivy nodded.

Bryan uncovered her mouth but kept his other hand around her waist.

Ivy blurted out the first thought that came into her head. "You escaped! How?"

Despite himself, Bryan chuckled. "No. The police released me. The fingerprint evidence finally came in; the prints didn't match. The police are fingerprinting Cedric now."

"You're innocent." She leaned into him.

"Yes, of everything. Will you ever believe me?"

Ivy chose not to answer the question. "You said you wanted to talk to me. Why?"

"To thank you and your father for everything you've done. And"—he looked down into her eyes— "to sincerely ask for your forgiveness."

"Forgiveness? For what?"

"For everything. For my arrogance, for failing to respect you as a barrister, for my friendship with Cedric, and all of the bright young people, actually. For being shallow and superficial, when you are serious and accomplished. For being heedless of my own head and heart." Bryan paused. "I have had a lot of time to think over the last fortnight. Mostly I've thought about you. Fearing I'd lost you forever as a result of my foolishness." Bryan bent his head and kissed Ivy's brow. His arm, encircling her waist, clutched her tighter.

Ivy reached behind him and latched the doors, then led him to a small settee in front of the fire. "I should ask forgiveness as well."

"Never." He pulled her closer, kissing her throat.

"Yes, Bryan, I was judgmental and high-handed. I..."

Bryan interrupted her with a soft, seductive kiss. His tongue teased the corner of her mouth. There's no need to resist any longer, thought Ivy. I want this. I need this. She pressed herself against him, nibbling his ear, grazing his lips with her tongue, then his neck.

Bryan sighed and leaned her back against the settee. Slowly he began to undo the ribbons on her dressing gown. His hands were hot, and his breath ragged. Ivy shivered with anticipation. His fingers played with her nipples, through the silk of her gown. Slowly undoing the ribbons, he moved his mouth to her breasts.

Ivy surrendered. He infuriated her, but she wanted nothing more than to feel him inside her, tonight and every night. "Please," she murmured. "Please don't leave. Please don't stop."

Bryan raised his head to look directly into her eyes. "Ever?" he asked. "Do you trust me? Will you stay with me?" Ivy answered by sliding her arms around his neck, wrapping her legs around his waist, and nipping his ear.

Bryan cupped his hands around her buttocks and stood, holding her against him. Ivy felt his large, prodding erection and pressed against him. Bryan gasped and flexed. Ivy laughed and squirmed, enjoying the sensation.

Bryan growled in pleasure, carried her through the doors to her bedroom and gently laid her on her back on the chaise. Ivy had been wearing only her dressing gown, and now untied, it opened, exposing her. Bryan knelt on the floor before her and ran his hands over her breasts, down her sides, and between her thighs. Ivy mewed and thrust her pelvis toward him in longing.

"Not yet." He grinned as he brought his tongue between her thighs.

Ivy writhed in pleasure. Eyes closed, breathing heavily, she could wait no longer. "Please. I want to feel you inside me. Now!"

Bryan raised his head, smiling. "I thought you'd never ask." He stood and thrust into her. Ivy gave a yelp of pleasure, felt Bryan's shudder and release, and also climaxed.

A few minutes later, she reached out to stroke him. "More," she said.

Bryan grinned. "I've created a monster. A few minutes of leisure, please, my lady."

Ivy gently ran her fingers over his erection, then rubbed her thumb on its tip in small circular motions.

Bryan's breath quickened, and he bent down, picked her up in his arms, and moved her to the bed. Quickly undressing, he climbed in beside her.

Admiring his body sprawled before her, Ivy circled his nipples, then resumed her long firm strokes.

Bryan groaned.

Ivy pushed him on his back and straddled him. She bent over him, suckled his nipples, and rocked her hips against him.

"Ready?" She lifted up and placed his long, hard erection between her legs. She gently lowered herself, until she felt him throbbing inside her. Slowly she moved up and down. He arched and bucked. She leaned back and continued riding.

Bryan cried out and in one motion, rolled over so Ivy was beneath him. He looked her in the eyes and, when she smiled and nodded, plunged inside her. This time they climaxed together.

Ivy awoke early the next morning to find Bryan gazing at her. She grinned and stretched. Then reached out to stroke him.

"Ivy! You are shameless," he said with a laugh. "Will you marry me?"

"If I agree, may I have my way with you?"

"Every day," Bryan responded, "but not now. Now we must talk. Your household will be awake soon."

"My father!" Ivy wailed. "Whatever shall we tell him?"

Chapter Twelve

Smythe and Company, Lincoln Inn's Fields, London

The first time Ivy had cried out in true pleasure, Bryan knew he must marry her. That conviction was only strengthened by the sensation of his own climax, which was unlike anything he had experienced before. Not only was she beautiful, she was accomplished. And of all wonders, she professed to love him as much as he loved her.

He would love only Ivy for the rest of his life. He must convince the world of his honorable intentions despite the anticipated disapproval of Edward Smythe, the plans of his own father to send him to Europe, his arrest, and the open questions surrounding the murders of Elsie and Violette, and the mysterious death of Zita.

Leaving Ivy early that morning, he had driven to Summerbrooke. Although difficult, he had convinced his father of his love for Ivy, his desire to marry her and have a family, and to learn to manage Summerbrooke and the family's other holdings. Surprisingly, his father had long suspected his feelings for Ivy and was more than willing to forego his exile in Europe provided he lived up to his responsibilities. He knew his father loved him without reservation and believed in his innocence, but convincing Edward Smythe would be more difficult.

The first step would be to clear his name of criminal suspicions. To that end he had asked his father and Chief Inspector Fox to accompany him to the Smythe chambers. He prayed his efforts were successful. They must be successful; he could not live without Ivy.

****

Ivy sat at the desk in her office, sipping tea, waiting for Bryan, and reliving each and every delicious detail of the previous evening: the kisses, the touches, the pledges of love. Bryan must convince my father to bless this marriage, she thought. Suddenly she realized she was the barrister, trained in persuasion. She had the skills to accomplish this. Quickly, before she lost her nerve, she went in to speak to her father.

At four o'clock that afternoon, Bryan, Baron Fitzgerald Henderson, and Chief Inspector Fox entered chambers. Ivy was in the anteroom, speaking to her father.

"Well, well, to what do we owe this pleasure?" her father inquired of Baron Henderson with a sly smile. To Bryan he added, "So glad to see you out and about, away from police supervision, my young sir. Let's try to keep it that way, shall we."

Ivy winced.

Her father was undeterred. "Baron Henderson, I see you have collected your prodigal son to send off to Europe. Quite right that."

"Actually," Baron Henderson began before being rudely interrupted.

"And good afternoon to you, Chief Inspector. What news have you? Not here to re-arrest Mr. Henderson, I hope."

Ivy's jaw dropped as she stared in horror at her father. Whatever has gotten into him, she wondered.

Fox looked quizzically at the elder barrister but answered cordially. "No sir, not at all. Just wanted to bring you up to date on the case—young Mr. Henderson being your client and all."

"Yes, yes. Quite appreciate it. Let's all retire to my office. Hannah, tea!" yelled her father.

****

Ivy preceded her father, Bryan, the baron, and Fox into chambers. Hannah brought tea, and they were all seated.

"Now then," said her father, "please proceed, Chief Inspector."

"Well, sir, you know of course that we believe Elsie Gordon and Violette Saunders were strangled with silk scarves, one lilac and one green."

"Yes, yes, go on."

"And you may know, Scotland Yard ultimately determined the fingerprints of young Henderson did not match those found at the murder scenes of either Miss Gordon or Miss Saunders."

"Yes, yes. But the young sir could have worn gloves, could he not?" her father jovially responded.

Bryan gazed at the elder barrister in horror.

"Now, Edward," Baron Henderson implored, "that's hardly appropriate."

"Ha, old boy, merely jesting. Need a sense of humor, what?"

Baron Henderson merely harrumphed. Ivy and Bryan exchanged glances.

"But then again," her father continued, "one never

knows. Have you determined the origin of the fingerprints?"

"Actually…" Fox began.

"Just a moment, Mr. Smythe," Bryan interrupted. "Do you actually believe I am capable of committing not one, but two, such heinous murders? You impugn my honor! You are my barrister, let alone…"

"Let alone what, dear boy?" the elder barrister asked, not the least offended.

Ivy intervened, "Father…"

Fox interrupted. "Actually, we believe we do know the origin of the fingerprints. We cannot confirm it until we hear definitively from Scotland Yard, but…"

"Well, you cannot be positive than, can you, Chief Inspector?" her father inquired.

"Father…" Ivy objected in exasperation.

"Actually, sir, I am." Fox again interrupted.

"Positive, Chief Inspector?"

"Yes sir. We have a confession."

"Confession, you don't say?" They all leaned forward in anticipation.

"Yes. A confession."

"Why in bloody hell didn't you say so?"

"Because," Fox said impatiently, "it's impossible to get a word in edgewise. And, sir," he added in a more conciliatory tone, "we just obtained it."

"I would have thought…" began her father.

Ivy had entirely lost her patience. "Who?"

"Who, my dear?" asked her father.

"Yes, who confessed?"

"Lord Stephen Bernard, also known as Cedric. We took him into custody based on information we received from several sources. Not the least of which is yours, my dear," he said to Ivy. "We asked him about the green silk scarf, and bloody hell if he didn't confess."

"To Elsie and to Violette?" asked Baron Henderson.

"Yes, and actually to several others."

"Others!" they all exclaimed. "Who?"

"I have yet to confirm those, so I cannot disclose identities. They were other unfortunate young women forced to support themselves by..." Fox paused and looked at Ivy. "...unnatural acts, one might say."

"You mean prostitution," Ivy pressed.

"Um, yes. Although I am hesitant to use those types of words in front of a young lady."

"Ivy is a barrister!" Bryan all but yelled, earning an affectionate smile from Ivy.

"But why?" Ivy asked. "How?"

"I am not sure we will ever know why," Fox said. "He says the women cheated him, took advantage. Blokes at the Yard think most of his heterosexual encounters were with, um, prostitutes. How is easier. In both cases we have investigated, he had an ongoing relationship with the women"—he paused and looked at Ivy—"the prostitutes, who trusted him and were not afraid to be alone with him, never expecting to be strangled in a fit of anger."

Ivy shivered. Bryan massaged her hand.

"And what of that bright young thing hanged from the chandelier, Lady Sitwell?" her father asked. "Did Cedric do her in as well?"

"Scotland Yard has long believed that to be an accident, sir," Responded Fox. "Cedric only confirmed it. Unfortunate hijinks gone wrong."

"And what of that Morris chap? The one who died in the insane asylum?" asked Bryan, anxious to resolve all of the open issues in one sitting.

"Also an unfortunate case, but we never believed Mr. Morris murdered Miss Gordon. He was just a poor, unstable man who undoubtedly heard rumors about the murder and was severely influenced by it."

"Well, then," said her father. "It appears young Mr. Henderson…"

"That's right, Mr. Smythe," Fox rushed to conclude, "is no longer under suspicion."

"And," her father continued with a wink toward Ivy, "is free to marry."

"Mr. Smythe!" exclaimed Bryan, while hugging Ivy.

"What my dear boy? Do you think I do not know what goes on under my roof? I told Ivy days ago she was in love. When I saw you sneaking out of my house early this morning, my belief that the feeling was mutual was confirmed. I expect the wedding will be sooner, rather than later," he added mischievously, slapping Baron Henderson on the back. "Hannah! That champagne!"

****

The end of the evening found Ivy and Bryan on the first floor terrace at One St. Marks Place, following a celebratory dinner prepared by Hannah and attended by her father and Baron and Lady Henderson.

"I am so happy," breathed Ivy ensconced in Bryan's arms.

"And so beautiful, and so smart, and so…"

"Oh, do continue."

"I am serious. However did you convince your

father to accept me?"

"Convince him? I was as surprised as you were!"

"Indeed." Bryan pulled her close and kissed her playfully. "Indeed."

"Indeed," said Ivy, the barrister, smiling to herself while simultaneously planning her wedding and her next trial.

Love and the Pursuit of Justice

by

C. K. Charlotte

Prologue

Brighton, England, March 1926

Henrietta Copperway walked slowly beside her best friend Cordelia Simons, prayer book and Bible in hand, on her way to St. Mary's Church. Reverend Price was presiding over the funeral of her long time neighbor, Mrs. Mabel Greenville, this morning, and Henrietta found it necessary to stop and sob loudly every few feet.

"I cannot believe Mabel's gone." She sniffed and dabbed at her eyes with the monogramed handkerchief given to her by her late husband on her thirtieth wedding anniversary. "Her hair may have been gray and her face lined, but she was only forty-five years of age!"

"I remember when Mabel and George Greenville first moved to Brighton," Cordelia said. "They were so happy. George was a successful solicitor; he purchased Ramsey House. The neighbors talked, it was such a large residence for just the two of them. But then they were blessed with two beautiful children, Suzanne and Henry. And even after Henry went off to Oxford, Suzanne stayed to care for her parents. Such a lovely family."

"Things have not been so lovely lately." Henrietta glanced behind her and lowered her voice. "I hear

George's legal practice shows little growth. Mabel confided he was frequently preoccupied and spent more and more time in London."

"*Tsk, tsk.*" Cordelia made a disapproving sound with her tongue. "No good ever came of spending extra time in London; no wonder Mabel's been having those fainting spells."

Henrietta interrupted, "Mabel has been complaining of pains around her heart and in her abdomen for years. Dr. Morris blamed them on a weak heart and the change of life."

"*Tsk. Tsk.*" Cordelia weighed in.

Henrietta continued unabated. "Eileen, the Greenville's maid, says she served the usual luncheon to George, Mabel, and Suzanne on Sunday: a glass of Burgundy and a beef joint with vegetables, followed by a gooseberry tart with custard. Almost immediately, Mabel complained of stomach pains. George gave her more Burgundy, which made her violently ill. George and Suzanne carried her upstairs to bed. Then George ran across the street for Dr. Morris, who dispensed medications and promptly left."

"Well, I heard from his nurse, Nancy Nemeth," Cordelia chimed in, "that the medications contained bismuth and morphine. And when she went back to check on Mabel, she found her vomiting. Nancy gave Mabel a dose of medicine, but there was no noticeable improvement. So when Nancy returned a second time at midnight and Mabel was even worse, she asked George to fetch Dr. Morris. But old George dallied most curiously on his short mission across the road; an hour later, Nancy sent Suzanne to fetch her father."

Cordelia paused to make sure she had Henrietta's

full attention. "And when Suzanne finally retrieved him, he was alone and smiling! Nancy was incensed. 'You must fetch the doctor without delay,' she told George. But old George, although he went out again, returned almost at once to say he could not roust the doctor. Nancy was forced to fetch the doctor herself. He administered some pills, but it was too late. Within the hour, poor Mabel had passed on."

"However," Cordelia paused for emphasis, "not before saying, 'this is all George's fault!' "

Henrietta's eyes widened as her wits worked overtime. "I have heard talk George has been seen around London...with a young thing with curly, cropped hair wearing trousers, no less."

Cordelia gasped. "You don't think George—?" she began, but her question was temporarily quashed by a stern glance from Reverend Price as they entered St. Mary's.

Chapter One

The Cavendish Hotel, London, April 1926

Graham Wetherington rushed through the streets of London, trying to keep pace with his law partner, Ivy Smythe Henderson, and her husband, the Honorable Bryan Henderson, on their way to the Cavendish Hotel. As the newest barrister at Smythe and Company—a firm consisting of Ivy and her father, Edward Smythe— Graham often found himself hurrying after Ivy. One of the country's first female barristers, Ivy was a force to be reckoned with.

Graham found Bryan, a member of the landed gentry, no less impressive. Nevertheless, Bryan— formerly a member of London's Society of Bright Young People—was a great deal more fun. Graham was familiar with the story of the Henderson courtship, conducted while Ivy and her father worked to clear Bryan on charges of murdering several young prostitutes. He considered them an odd, albeit now happily married, couple.

Stop! Graham silently reprimanded himself. It is not your responsibility to analyze your partner's marriage. It is your responsibility to win cases! The son of a physician and a veteran of the Great War, Graham could still not believe his luck in landing a position with Smythe and Company. Ivy and Edward had both trained at Lincoln's Inn, one of London's four Inns of Court, and maintained chambers in Lincoln's Inn Fields. The offices of Smythe and Company resided in the former Oldecastle House. Constructed in 1641 as a private residence, it still retained the mahogany-paneled walls, floor to ceiling bookshelves, brass sconces, and marble fireplaces original to the structure. More importantly, the cases handled within its hallowed halls were some of the most important in the country. Why, just yesterday…

Bryan interrupted Graham's thoughts. "At last, we have arrived!"

Graham gazed at the unassuming brick front and large plain doorway of the Cavendish Hotel. Even outside, the music was exceedingly loud. "The Cavendish has the best jazz in the city," Bryan confided.

Graham nodded his agreement and entered a drawing room crowded with bright young people, as well as too much furniture. "The owner is quite fond of estate sales," Bryan whispered as they maneuvered around red plush settees and morocco leather chairs, estate maps, archery targets, croquet mallets, and polo sticks, all mixed in with photographs of men on horseback and yachts in full sail.

"Let's dance, Bryan!" Ivy dodged a settee and angled her husband toward the dance floor.

Bryan smiled at Graham. "Excuse me, duty calls."

Graham stood alone, observing the room. Since returning from the Great War, he found it difficult to reconcile the London before him with the one he had left behind. He feared the stench of the French trenches would haunt him forever. He shook his head to clear his thoughts. "Must move on, old man, must move on," he murmured.

A commotion at the door caught his attention. A large, rambunctious group entered the hotel. Laughing and joking, they took over the room. From the sound of their accents, at least a portion of them were Americans. Graham had no sooner formed this thought, when he heard it echoed by a matron nearby. "Americans! Detestable people, loud and vulgar; they have the most appalling accents." Graham heard her confide to her companion.

At that exact moment, a surprising apparition entered the room. Tall and slender, with ivory skin, shining eyes, and curly cropped ebony hair, the figure's mannerisms suggested a female. But the clothing was mannish, topped with a fedora, and accessorized with an instrument case and a short riding crop. Graham stared in fascination.

Seemingly feeling his gaze, the figure waved the crop in his direction, removed the hat, and provided him with an impish grin. Simultaneously, she—it must be a she, thought Graham—grabbed a flute of champagne from a passing waiter and released a deep, but decidedly feminine, laugh. Graham laughed as well. Who was this woman?

Again the matron behind him voiced his thoughts. "Who is that young woman? The one wearing the men's clothing?"

"Oh Elizabeth," her companion responded. "Haven't you heard? The new darling of the bright young people: Diana Vanderwell, southern belle from Nashville. Very nouveau riche. Her father owns a publishing dynasty, I believe. The *Mirror* calls her the

'Tennessee Princess.' "

"Nashville?"

"Tennessee, dearest. The 'northernmost southern state,' as they say in America."

"Right," Elizabeth replied, in a tone which suggested the circumstances were anything but. "One would think such a father could at least purchase his princess an appropriate frock."

Graham's eavesdropping was interrupted by the tap of a riding crop. "Have we met before?" asked an evocative southern voice.

Graham gazed down into dark violet eyes, surrounded by heavy black lashes and framed by a crop of ebony curls. The vixen in men's clothing smiled up at him, while continuing to lightly strike him with the crop.

"*Harrumph*," uttered the matron Elizabeth, as she moved her companion away.

"Young woman, please..." Graham attempted to express his outrage at being summoned for attention by the use of a riding crop. But the violet eyes held him mesmerized. He had never seen such eyes: nearly purple with coquettish lashes. The eyes of a little girl locking herself into his memory. He tried again. "I am quite sure I would have remembered a prior meeting, madam."

"Madam? Madam!" The faintly outraged, southern voice accosted him. Its owner manipulated the riding crop to caress his face.

Graham felt outrage, as well as desire. He took a step back.

"Desire, then fulfillment?" She chuckled.

Graham, struck utterly speechless, simply stared.

"Ah, well. Later, if you are very good, I will play my sax for you," she whispered breathlessly. Tapping him once more with her riding crop, the violet-eyed apparition vanished into the crowd.

****

"Graham! Graham! Are you in there?" Ivy waved her hand in front of his face.

"Looks as though you have been bewitched, old boy," added Bryan. "Made the acquaintance of Diana Vanderwell, I see."

"You know her!" Ivy and Graham responded simultaneously.

"Only by reputation." Bryan slipped his arm around Ivy's waist. "Only by reputation."

"I should sincerely hope so," Ivy said under her breath.

"She is known rather fondly among the bright young people as the Tennessee Princess. Her father is quite wealthy, as I understand it. Although, as an American, she has no title of course. Such a pity." Bryan shook his head, then brightened. "But she plays the saxophone!"

"Yes, so I have heard," Graham responded drily.

As if on cue, the band suddenly broke into "You're in Tennessee as Sure as You're Born." Graham was dismayed; Diana's entourage delighted. "Sing, Diana! Play, Diana!" Her companions waved their champagne bottles and stomped their feet.

Diana nodded solemnly in Graham's direction and bowed to the crowd. Still grasping the riding crop, she climbed atop the piano and broke into what Graham thought could only be described as a Southern rendition of "The Lady Is Good," written for the popular musical of the same name. Her sensuous voice mesmerized him.

Completing the first verse, she widened her eyes, slowly licked her lips, and pointed the crop in Graham's direction. The crowd at the Cavendish roared their approval. Graham felt Bryan punch him on the shoulder in a sign of male comradery.

Ivy was oblivious. "Time to take our leave, boys. Busy day tomorrow."

"Wait!" Graham insisted. "I must make her acquaintance."

"I thought…" Ivy began.

Graham ignored her as he purposefully moved toward the piano. Diana gracefully stepped down and met him halfway. "Did you like it? Did you like it very much?" The vixen purred and rubbed the crop against his arm. "I'm not done yet."

As Graham stood with his mouth agape, Diana returned to the piano. Unlatching the instrument case, she removed and assembled the saxophone. Then, climbing back on top of the piano, she played "The Lady Is Good" as an instrumental. Her body and the instrument were one, writhing and bobbing until both glistened with perspiration. How I wish to be that instrument, thought Graham as he writhed slightly himself.

All too soon the performance ended. Graham looked down to find Diana once again beside him, tapping his arm with the riding crop. It was a sensation he no longer found offensive. "Now that you have witnessed all of my talents, dear boy, allow me to properly introduce myself: Miss Diana Vanderwell, the Tennessee Princess." She bowed.

Tongue tied, Graham reached into his pocket and

brought out a sterling silver case. He removed a vellum card and, with a slight flourish, handed it to her.

"A gift," she said mischievously. Turning the card over, she read aloud: "Graham Wetherington, Barrister, Smythe and Company, Oldecastle House, Lincoln's Inn Fields."

Diana lifted her eyes to meet his, smiled widely, stood on tiptoe and—still holding the saxophone— threw her arms around him. Pressing her body close to his, in what Graham found a most encouraging manner, she kissed him firmly on the lips. His whole body responded, to his embarrassment. But the vixen merely laughed and prepared to kiss him again, this time with parted lips. His whole body ached to receive her attentions.

"Come, darling, work tomorrow. No more distractions." Ivy interrupted, slipping her arm through Graham's and pointing him toward the exit.

"Tough break, old man," Bryan added bemusedly.

Graham followed obediently but could not help looking back when he reached the door. Diana stood watching him, stroking the saxophone.

Chapter Two

Rose Cottage, Chelsea

Diana awoke the next morning with sun streaming through the windows of her overgrown Chelsea cottage. When first arriving in London, she had checked into the Ritz. But several months into her stay, a dear friend had suggested he might be able obtain a lease on Rose Cottage for her use.

Diana had accepted his offer and now found herself in a meandering home she had come to love. The rooms were large with low beamed ceilings, the windows were leaded with diamond panes, the oak floorboards were uneven, and there was a great deal of knotted wood everywhere. Furnished in an overabundance of chintz, every available space was covered with books; books lined the walls, lay stacked on tables and chairs, and formed towers on the floor. The garden surrounding the cottage was a watercolorist's dream: herbaceous borders, rockeries, cutting beds, and water gardens in delicious profusion. Diana hoped to convince her father to purchase Rose Cottage for her on his next trip to England.

As her mind drifted to her father and her home in Nashville, she frowned. It was entirely more likely that her father—rather than purchasing real estate for her in England—would cajole her into returning to Tennessee.

Diana had been raised in a Georgian mansion overlooking the Cumberland River on the outskirts of Nashville. Her father, Howard Vanderwell, had acquired the home from his second wife, one of America's richest women. She had died leaving Diana's father a substantial legacy, which he parlayed into a thriving publishing empire. As an only child, Diana had been denied nothing. In exchange, she had served as Howard Vanderwell's emotional center. As Diana matured, the father-daughter relationship formed a merry-go-round of affection and disappointment. Diana ultimately fled to London to escape the relationship.

Although she had been successful in putting distance between herself and her father, she repeated the pattern of their relationship with every man she met. Diana would draw close, then suddenly break away. Something about the serious young barrister she had met last night intrigued her. Perhaps he would be different?

Diana's thoughts drifted back to Graham. Tallish, wavy dark hair, with blue-green eyes, he was muscular with a military bearing. But a barrister, how much fun could he be? Particularly after the men she had come to know in London—members of the bright young people, landed gentry, artists, authors, musicians. With a few exceptions, wealthy men who were not above offering to assist in defraying her expenses. Her father provided her with a generous allowance, but her expenses were substantial. To date, no barristers could be found among the group and only one solicitor: George Greenville.

George was a Brighton solicitor she had met at the Cavendish more than a year ago. A friend of a friend with whom she had long since lost contact, George had pursued Diana with a vengeance. He insisted on enjoying her company whenever he was in London and in exchange was generous with small favors: dinner, theater performances, gifts of clothing and jewelry. George was gentlemanly and attentive, if somewhat tedious.

****

A knock at the door interrupted Diana's thoughts. "Come in, Mary."

Mary—her cook, maid, and confidant—peered around the corner. She carried a tray with tea, scones, and the London daily newspapers. "Good day, miss. I left you sleep a little longer this morning, given the late evening you had." She raised an eyebrow. "You had a good time then, miss?"

Diana stretched and sat up. "Very interesting. I met a young man who somewhat intrigued me."

"Oh, pray do tell, miss," sighed Mary, sitting on a rose chintz settee. "What does he look like? Is he a member of the Society of Bright Young People?"

Diana paused, considering her answer. "No, he is, serious…manly. Not so girlish as the men who associate with the bright young people. Thoughtful, as though he knows things."

"A lord?"

"Maybe…no…I do not think so. Wait, I have his card here somewhere. Hand me my instrument case, Mary." Rummaging through her saxophone case, she found the card. "Graham Wetherington, Barrister," she read.

"Oh no." Mary moaned. "Not a man of the law. That Mr. Greenville who visits is so terribly boring."

"Not all…" Diana began.

She was interrupted by Mary's screech. "Dear God in heaven, I almost forgot!"

"Forgot what, Mary? And please learn not to scream. My poor head, darling."

But Mary continued screaming as she pulled the newspapers off the tray and began madly turning pages, nearly upsetting the tea service.

"Mary, what in heaven's name is the matter with you?"

"Mr. Greenville, miss. His photograph is on the front page of the *Mirror* this morning."

"Well, that's hardly reason to…it is probably a legal notice related to his practice. He is a solicitor, after all."

"Would his business have to do with murder, miss?" Mary asked skeptically.

"No, no, of course not. George is a solicitor. He would not try murder cases. He drafts wills and contracts and…" Diana stopped in mid-sentence. "Murder? Whose murder? Are you sure, Mary?"

"Yes, miss. Here in the *Mirror*. It says Mr. George Grenville is being investigated by the Brighton police for murder."

"It must be a mistake. Whom would George, of all people, murder? How?" Diana stifled a smile. "Unless he bored them to death."

"The *Mirror* says he is being investigated for murdering his wife, miss."

Diana leaped from bed, upsetting the tea tray herself. "Wife? Wife!"

"Yes, miss. He may have poisoned her according to the *Mirror*. Look, if you don't believe me!" Mary, clearly disgruntled, held up the *Mirror*. Diana observed the newspaper did indeed include a very unflattering picture of George Greenville under the headline: *Brighton Solicitor Investigated for Poisoning Beloved Wife.*

Grabbing her spectacles, which only Mary ever saw her use, Diana snatched the newspaper and carried it to her writing desk. She read aloud from the *Mirror*:

"George Greenville has been described by his neighbor Henrietta Copperway as a 'wag, a man keen on sporting bets and a favorite with the ladies.' Greenville set up his solicitor's practice in Brighton shortly after his wedding to Mabel Greenville nee Rockford, and life looked good. But the business never prospered, and his family life was thrown into turmoil with the rapid deterioration in his wife's health.

"A condition that had at one stage been diagnosed by her doctor as 'the change of life' was giving cause for concern on a recent Sunday. There was severe sickness. Poor Mrs. Greenville was convinced that the culprit was 'the gooseberry tart' because 'it always disagrees with me.' But this was far more than a 'disagreement' for Mrs. Greenville fell into a coma and died."

Diana paused to shake her head, then continued reading:

"Before long, tongues began to wag. All sorts of tales were spread about the deceased's last few days and Greenville's frequent trips to London. According to Mrs. Copperway, Greenville made the excursions to visit 'a brazen American hussy with cropped curls, wearing men's trousers.' Rumors intensified when, despite his recent visits to London, Greenville proposed last week to a local woman: his wife's nurse, Nancy

Nemeth. Only two months having passed since poor Mabel's demise, mention of 'murder' became rampant.

"The gossip reached such a level that the police proposed to exhume the body for forensic examination. When Greenville was informed of this, he replied, 'Just the very thing—I am quite agreeable.' Last week, Mabel Greenville's remains were exhumed and found to contain 0.25 to 0.5 grains of arsenic. The Brighton police are now investigating Greenville for murder. Will the staging of an inquest be the second Mrs. Greenville's wedding present?"

"A brazen American hussy! Indeed!" Diana was incensed. She removed her eyeglasses and threw them on the desk.

Mary giggled. "Who would have thought old Mr. Greenville had it in him! Always so plodding he was. Now he's murdered his wife to marry a nurse. Quite exciting! Did you know of her, miss?"

"No! I never even knew of his first wife! And now to think I've been referenced in an article in the *Mirror*, of all newspapers, about adultery, poisoning, and inquests! What if Father hears of this? I will be forced to return to Tennessee," Diana wailed. "Oh, I am ruined, circumstances could not possibly be any bleaker. I…"

The chiming of the bell startled Diana and sent Mary scurrying to answer the door. "What next?" Diana muttered sullenly.

****

A few moments later found Diana and Mary standing in the front hall of Rose Cottage with a poorly dressed messenger. "A letter for Miss Diana Vanderwell, if you please, from solicitor George

Greenville."

Mary gasped. Diana reached for the letter. "I am Miss Vanderwell."

"A signature is required, miss." The messenger held fast to the letter.

Diana sighed, signed for the letter, and sent Mary to find a farthing for the messenger's cooperation. "Shall I wait for a reply, miss?" he inquired.

"Certainly not." Diana could hear the trepidation in her voice, as she brusquely dismissed the messenger and moved into the parlor. Removing a pile of books, she sat on a chintz sofa and turned the letter over in her hands.

"Open it, miss," Mary implored. "Aren't you curious? Do you think Mr. Greenville may have sent his confession? Oooh, it is exciting!"

Diana looked up horrified at Mary's enthusiasm. Before she could change her mind, she grabbed the ivory letter opener and sliced through the heavy cream vellum envelope. Shaking out the folded legal stationery, she read aloud, voice shaking:

"My dearest Diana,

I have been trying hard to reach you this last fortnight, but no luck, always you were out. Now I want you to think very carefully and to send me a reply as soon as possible. There are many rumors about, but between you and me, this letter reveals the true position. My children have turned bitterly against you, and are of the belief that you and I together poisoned their mother. It is only right that you should know this, as you are the one I love most in this world, and I would be the last one to make you unhappy. Under the circumstances, are you prepared to face the music and be married? I want to do something quickly. Let me have something from you, my love.

Yours as ever,
George"

Chapter Three

Smythe and Company, Lincoln's Inn Fields, London

"Quite bedazzled by that creature last night, weren't you?" Graham winced under Ivy's teasing as they walked into chambers together.

"Ivy…" Graham began.

"Do not 'Ivy' me. I know when someone has been beguiled, Graham. You practically melted when she petted you with her saxophone. And why does she carry that riding crop?" Ivy laughed.

Graham groaned.

"Admit it, the vixen is under your skin. Perhaps a little fling will do you good. Bryan and I…" she began.

Graham could stand it no longer. "Have you seen this, Ivy?' He pulled a copy of the *Mirror* from his valise. "The Tennessee Princess has already enjoyed a fling, a quite public one."

Ivy frowned. Sitting down on the nearest chesterfield, she scanned the *Mirror*.

Brighton Solicitor Investigated for Poisoning Beloved Wife. Ivy scanned the headline. She looked at Graham questioningly. "It is shocking, a British solicitor accused of murder. But I don't see what this can possibly have to do with an American heiress."

"Read further," Graham said glumly.

Ivy returned to the *Mirror*. She read aloud: *"George Greenville's frequent trips to London…"* She stopped, then began again: *"Greenville made the excursions to visit 'a brazen American hussy with cropped curls, wearing men's trousers.'* Indeed Graham, there are any number of young women wearing trousers in London these days. Whatever makes you think this refers to Diana Vanderwell?"

The door to chambers suddenly burst open, and Edward Smythe rushed in, disrupting the conversation. "You will never imagine what I have just learned from that raconteur Marshall Phillips, while waiting for my case to be called at Old Bailey!" he yelled, shaking his fist.

"Father, sit down, please, before you have a heart attack," Ivy implored.

"That rascal Marshall has managed to secure the defense of the biggest murder investigation since that matter involving Bryan and Cedric."

"Please stop bringing up that unpleasant affair involving Bryan. You know he was innocent. I don't understand…"

Edward Smythe waved his hand dismissively and continued. "Greenville, that Brighton solicitor being investigated for murder, has become Marshall's client! The Greenville case would be a wonderful one for Smythe and Company. Although the poor man will most certainly be found guilty and hanged." He paused, rubbing his hands together. "But, no matter, the publicity would be priceless. Oh, Marshall is a rascal!"

Graham exchanged a look with Ivy. Together they asked, "George Greenville?"

"George Greenville is a Brighton solicitor being

114

investigated for poisoning his wife, Mabel! Have neither of you seen the papers?" Edward bellowed. "Young people these days. Out carousing last night and just now arriving at chambers, I imagine!"

"Actually, Father..." Ivy began, holding up Graham's copy of the *Mirror.*

The door to chambers burst open for the second time in an hour. "Fresh news from the blokes at the *Mirror*, just as you asked for, sir." John, Smythe and Company's clerk, bustled in.

"Splendid! What do they say, John? Ivy, Graham, listen to this."

"There may be an inquest, sir. The autopsy of Mrs. Greenville performed last week revealed 0.25 to 0.5 grains of arsenic."

"Yes, yes. That was in this morning's *Mirror.*"

"Yes sir, but let me finish," John said peevishly. "Not only did the autopsy show the presence of arsenic, but there were absolutely no signs of heart disease according to the coroner."

"Of course," Edward interposed impatiently.

"Despite the fact that was the cause of death given by the doctor on the certificate." John continued slightly louder. "And the blokes at the *Mirror* have learned that Greenville purchased weed killer containing arsenic several weeks before his wife died."

"You don't say."

"And," John continued, louder still, "Greenville opened and served the Burgundy drunk by his wife immediately before she became ill."

"Well..."

"And—" John was nearly yelling now. "—Mrs. Greenville had a healthy inheritance, but Greenville's law practice was floundering." Out of breath, John sat down.

"Good work, John. Bloody good work. Now if only Greenville had come to Smythe and Company," Edward mused. "Graham, you clerked for that rascal Marshall before joining us, perhaps you could..."

The request lingered uncompleted, as the door to chambers burst open for a third time.

****

Upon receiving the poorly dressed messenger with the unpleasant and unexpected marriage proposal earlier that morning, Diana had been in shock. She vacillated between obsessing over the impact the content of George Greenville's letter would have on her father's willingness to support her English lifestyle and the impact the letter would have on the Brighton police.

Overwhelmed, she had retreated to her bedchamber. Her eyes alighted on the calling card of Graham Wetherington at Smythe and Company. Gingerly holding the card, she had been overcome with a desire to see the mature, but utterly delicious, barrister. In all likelihood, the nonsense with George would come to naught. But from her father, she had learned it could never hurt to seek legal advice when confronted with an unpleasant problem potentially involving the police. And at the very least, it gave her an excuse to meet again with the young man who had so intrigued her at the Cavendish.

Cognizant of the dual purpose of her visit to Smythe and Company, Diana dressed carefully. She wore her Chanel dress of black crepe de chine. The bodice bloused slightly at the front and sides and had a tight bolero at the back. Especially chic, she thought, was the arrangement of tiny tucks which crossed the front. Over the dress she wore a white wrap coat with a black fur collar. Black satin t-strap shoes and gray silk stockings added to the look. A white cloche topped her ebony curls and completed the outfit.

Against the impressive entrance she had hoped to make, she found the silence of the four individuals staring at her in varying degrees of curiosity disconcerting. Her eyes paused with pleasure on Graham's countenance. He was even more handsome than she remembered. A shiver ran up her spine. She quickly shook it off and sought the advantage. "Is there so little work for barristers then? That you all stand about reading that fish wrap—the *Mirror*—all day?" The American twang was unmistakable.

Diana watched amused as Graham exchanged glances with the young woman he had accompanied last night. Diana recognized her from the newspapers as Ivy Smythe Henderson, barrister and wife of the Honorable Bryan Henderson. Why an attractive young woman would want to practice law was beyond her, but...

The elderly gentleman sniffed, interrupting her thoughts. "I am Edward Smythe, senior partner of this firm, madam. May we be of some assistance?" His disdain was palatable.

The score needs evening, Diana thought. "I, sir, am Miss Diana Vanderwell—daughter and heiress of Howard Vanderwell, the American publishing magnate. I wish to consult with Mr. Wetherington," she paused for emphasis, "on a private matter."

"Indeed. I am afraid Miss...Vanderwell, is it? That within legal chambers there are no 'private' matters as you so quaintly express it. Perhaps..." Edward paused, as Diana turned toward the door.

"Wait," Graham interrupted. "What Edward means to say is that perhaps this once an exception may be made, at least until I have an opportunity to determine if the legal matter is of an appropriate nature for Smythe and Company. Please, Miss Vanderwell"—he held out his hand—"accompany me to my office."

Smiling at Graham, Diana preceded him into a small room lined with bookshelves. She caught Edward's eye as she passed and winked.

****

"Now, Miss Vanderwell," Graham began as he closed the door to his office behind her, "to what does Smythe and Company owe this pleasure?"

Diana turned and—similarly to the previous night in the Cavendish, except that she no longer carried the saxophone—wrapped her arms around his neck and held him close. As the evening before, he found it a singularly enjoyable experience. Without thinking, he bent down and kissed her firmly on the lips. She sighed and snuggled closer, bringing him back to reality and the unseemly position in which he now found himself. Damn the informality of Americans! They were a bothersome lot! He loosened her arms and took a step back.

Seemingly unperturbed, she licked her lips and smiled. "Shall I sing for you then?"

"No! And if you brought the bloody riding crop, please keep it under wraps!" Graham felt completely out of his depth. "Why in God's name are you here?"

"Well then, if we are to be all business. I may, just may, have a slight legal issue."

Graham frowned in confusion. "A slight legal

issue? Of what nature? As an American you may not be aware, but barristers handle court proceedings. Smythe and Company specializes in criminal proceedings. I hardly expect…"

"You have perhaps been reading in the *Mirror* of George Greenville?" Diana interrupted.

Graham reflected on the *Mirror's* reference to the "brazen American hussy" he had read earlier that morning. Certainly it suggested an unsavory relationship, but not necessarily one involving criminal activity. "Yes, but…"

A quick knock preceded Ivy's voice. "Graham? We are due at Old Bailey, I'm afraid."

Diana gathered her things. "I should never have come."

"Wait. I must see you again. I will help you if I can."

Diana threw her arms around Graham once again. He hugged her briefly, then reluctantly stepped back. "Tomorrow. Dinner at the Savoy. Seven o'clock."

Diana nodded. She kissed him, hard, leaving him without a single thought in his head as he prepared to depart for court.

Chapter Four

The Savoy Hotel, London

Straightening the peaked lapels and satin cuffs on his tuxedo jacket, Graham exited the taxi outside of the Savoy's front entrance on the Strand at seven o'clock the following evening. The iconic stainless steel sign of the hotel name curved above the Savoy Court and was topped by the famous sculpture of Count Peter of Savoy.

Although he did not often frequent the hotel, Graham was well aware of its history. Opened in the late 1800s, the Savoy was famous as the first luxury hotel in London. It set new standards for technology, comfort, and luxury. The Savoy was the first hotel in London to be lit by electricity, as well as the first to feature electric lifts—known as ascending rooms. Guestrooms were connected by speaking tubes to various parts of the hotel, including the valet, maid, and floor waiter. Most of the rooms included private baths *en suite*, famous for their marble floors, cascading showers, and quick filling bathtubs.

The Savoy's parties were also legendary. As Graham proceeded to the River Restaurant, located on the south side of the hotel overlooking the River Thames, he saw tonight was no exception. The central courtyard of the hotel had been flooded and scenery erected around the walls to recreate Venice. Several dozen costumed guests sat in an enormous black and gold gondola floating in the center of the courtyard, being served by similarly attired staff. Just outside the courtyard, Graham passed a baby elephant encumbered with a five-foot birthday cake.

Graham stared in disbelief. It was often difficult for him to reconcile the hardships he had experienced in the war with the frivolity he encountered in such places as the Cavendish and the Savoy.

The thought brought him around to the reason he was at the Savoy. Which, in truth, quite evaded him. He had plenty of work awaiting him in chambers, and if he hoped to become known as an accomplished barrister in the criminal arena, he should be attending to it. His brief meeting with Diana the previous day had intrigued him, as did the woman herself, but he found it highly unlikely she had a legal matter worthy of the attention of Smythe and Company. It was mainly Edward's urging, hoping to somehow become involved in the Greenville matter, that encouraged him to come this evening.

Graham's ruminations were cut short as he entered the River Restaurant and caught sight of Diana. Her black curls, encircled with a seed pearl band, were as unruly as ever. Her dress rendered him speechless. As fit the formality of the Savoy, the dress was floor length. The neckline formed a low V, plunging to the waist, with a contrasting panel inset. The dress itself was made of a gold clingy fabric, but the inset was nude. It was quite a naughty look. The back of the dress was equally dramatic. Cut with a similar low V, it fell below the waist and lacked any inset whatsoever.

Several long strands of luminous pearls encircled her neck. Contrasting embroidery graced the hem. A large decorative brooch, with an Egyptian theme, anchored the waist. Graham knew the recent discovery of King Tut's tomb made all things Egyptian extremely fashionable.

Graham observed Diana as she spoke to an exotic-looking young man in full evening dress. The young man held a gold leash attached to a diamond choker encircling the neck of a white leopard. The leopard was petite, but quite alive. Diana gestured wildly with one hand as she spoke; with her other hand, she held her saxophone case.

****

Diana knew Graham had entered the room and was watching her. In fact, she had approached infamous Egyptian playboy Said Fusani as soon as she had glimpsed Graham. Known in London as Prince Fusani, although technically he was not a prince, he cut a striking figure. He had recently married Parisian Margarite Hagen. Ten years older than Said, Margarite was frequently portrayed by the *Mirror* and newspapers of a similar ilk as a "gold digger."

Feeling Graham's eyes upon her, Diana turned so he could admire both the front and back of the dress which she had chosen precisely for him. She needed to discuss the Greenville proposal and her legal difficulties, but she wanted him for more than his legal prowess. She had yet to meet a man she could not entice with the promise of sex and her inheritance. She was determined Graham not be the first.

After an appropriate time, to give Graham ample opportunity to admire her in her entirety, Diana kissed

Prince Fusani on the cheek and prepared to welcome Graham. Fusani pulled her back, grabbed her around the waist, and kissed her on both cheeks—in the European fashion. His expression, as his eyes traveled down and then back up the front of her dress, was not that of a recently married man nor even of a member of polite society. Diana was surprised to find herself embarrassed, delighted to find Graham hurrying to her side.

"My darling, I thought you must have been lost." Diana was unable to keep the relief from her voice.

"Indeed. It appears I arrived in the nick of time." Graham graciously kissed Diana's hand, then turned to the gentleman beside her. "I don't believe I have had the pleasure," he began, but the young man had disappeared.

"Never mind," said Diana, who had at last regained her equilibrium. "Shall we sit down for dinner? I don't know about you, but I am famished." Waving, she caught the attention of the waiter who promptly led them to their table.

"That, uh, gentleman was Prince Fusani?" Graham asked. "And the woman I see him ravishing now is Margarite, his wife?"

"Yes, of course."

"I have read of them in the *Mirror* and heard of her, shall we say, exploits in Paris. Before this evening, however, I have never actually seen either of them."

"Exploits? In Paris?" Diana asked. "I am American, please recall. I have enough trouble keeping up with British gossip, let alone European. Pray tell, what exploits?"

"Well," Graham hesitated, "the most public is that

she is a well-trained courtesan."

Diana snorted. "Well-trained? How much training can it possibly take?" Suddenly inspired, she slipped her foot out of her pump, wiggled her toes, and began to walk them slowly up the inside of Graham's trouser leg. "Perhaps she learned to do this?"

Graham remained expressionless, although Diana felt him tense. "Or this?" She placed her dainty silk-stockinged foot in his lap and pressed against his groin. "Or this?" She moved her foot slowly back and forth, then up and down. She had the satisfaction of feeling Graham's erection, beginning as a small bud then gradually growing and standing to full height as she stroked him with her toes. He softly groaned.

The waiter returned with the menus, and Diana withdrew her foot. Point made, she thought.

"You are…" Graham began.

"Amazing? Desirable? Unforgettable?" Diana smiled, superbly proud of herself.

Graham took a deep breath and turned to the waiter. "And what is featured this evening?"

Diana looked at the waiter, who clearly had some idea of what had taken place, and clarified. "He means, what is featured on the menu?"

"Oh," said the waiter, smirking, "roast sea bream. Although, the gentleman at the next table has just asked to order what you are having."

Diana laughed aloud.

Graham looked over at the next table to find Prince Fusani leering at him.

Diana put her hand on Graham's arm, gently restraining him. "The Savoy's specialties are aged Scottish beef on the bone or whole roast sea bream for two. Let's order oysters, then the beef with sides, and lastly peach Melba—the specialty dessert. Shall we?"

The meal was divine, the conversation fascinating. Once relaxed by several glasses of Merlot, Graham spoke freely about his time in France during the Great War and his experience with American servicemen. Diana was delighted to hear not all of the interactions had been negative, although Graham did admit he found Americans' optimism and childlike enthusiasm "immensely tiring." He also spoke of his respect for Edward Smythe and his hopes for his own legal career. Diana listened intently, comparing his interests and commitments to those of the other men she had known.

The meal ended all too fast; Diana was not willing to let Graham go. Taking the initiative, she grabbed Graham with one hand and her saxophone case with the other. "Off to the foyer and dancing."

"But of course." Diana noticed a look of surprise cross Graham's face, but he smiled compliantly.

Encouraged, Diana launched into a description of what he could expect. "You must know that the Savoy is known for its jazz, even in America. The hotel imports the best musicians from the United States to play in its famous bands: the Savoy Orpheans and the Savoy Havana Band."

Reaching the Thames Foyer, she enthusiastically discussed the stage and dance-floor. "These are permanently installed. Underneath the dance floor is a hydraulic system, allowing it to be raised by three feet to provide a larger stage for cabaret acts. "Oh," she exclaimed, "listen, they are playing Irving Berlin's 'Always.' Let's dance."

Diana urged Graham to the dance floor, folded

herself within his arms and swayed against him, softly singing the lyrics. She felt his body respond. She sighed and laid her head against his shoulder, wishing the moment would last forever.

Suddenly the band switched to a southern classic, "Wild Cat Blues." "My favorite!" Diana squealed, retrieving the saxophone case. Abandoning Graham, she joined the Savoy Opheans and began to play. The band moved seamlessly into "Kansas City Blues." Diana continued her playing and shimmying to the acknowledged delight of the crowd and, she hoped, Graham.

****

Several numbers later, Graham found himself seated in the American Bar, sipping a gin concoction from a martini cocktail glass. He gazed in amazement at the plush Art Deco design, with cream and ochre walls and electric blue and gold chairs.

"This bar at the Savoy Hotel was one of the earliest establishments to introduce American-style cocktails to Europe." Diana continued her travel monologue. "The head barman, Harry Craddock, is my fellow countryman." She waved to him as he worked the far end of the bar. "It's said he fled Prohibition in New York. He's famous for inventing the White Lady. It's what you're drinking," she added with a grin, "gin, *cointreau*, and fresh lemon juice. Heavenly, isn't it?"

Graham grimaced but held his peace.

"Finish it," Diana continued, "and I'll take you to see one of the most wonderful views in London."

Graham sighed. It was late, and he was exhausted, but he would gladly travel to the gates of Hell to spend more time with this fascinating creature. Despite all of her adventures this evening, she looked as beautiful as ever; her eyes shone with mischief. Who could resist her?

"Come on, drink up! One more adventure and I'll let you go." She stroked his cheek with one hand and picked up the saxophone case with the other. "Don't make me retrieve the riding crop."

"You have it?" Graham choked on his cocktail. How could he have forgotten the riding crop?

Diana patted the saxophone case with affection. Graham rolled his eyes and followed her to the lobby and, he assumed, the exterior door.

"Oh no. This way. The view is up here."

Graham raised his eyebrows but followed her to the brass plaque indicating "ascending room." The doors slid open at the push of a button to reveal a small mirrored room.

"Normally there is an attendant," Diana explained, "but at the latest hours, one has the adventure all to oneself."

The doors closed, seemingly of their own volition. Diana pulled on a brass lever, placing its arrow on "roof." Slowly, the room began to ascend. The bottom fell out of Graham's stomach.

Diana moved closer to him and placed her arms around his neck. She kissed him gently on the mouth, as she ground her hips against him. Unlike the dance floor, there was nothing subtle to this movement. It was the grind Graham knew from the follies in Paris during the war. But now it was being performed by a truly beautiful woman, one who fascinated him. He felt her tongue against his and the heat in his groin. His member rose. He reached out and stroked her nipples.

The speed of her hips increased, and she placed her leg around his waist. The movement of the lift increased the pleasure of their coupling. Graham began a pumping action with his hips. He must have her, now…

Suddenly, the ascending room came to a shuddering stop, and the door opened to reveal a middle-aged couple in evening wear waiting to descend. The woman coughed and turned her head, but the man smiled and clapped Graham on the back as he and Diana exited the lift.

Graham gasped at the view. Behind him shone the lights of London; before him the Thames River reflected the hotel.

"Fred Astaire and his sister Adele danced up here the last time they were in London," Diana confided to him. Grabbing his hand, she dropped the saxophone case and pressed her body close to his. Softly singing the lyrics to "Always," Diana began to dance. Graham could never remember being so happy.

Only upon returning home early the next morning did Graham realize he and Diana had never discussed the reason for their meeting at the Savoy: the death of Mabel Greenville.

Chapter Five

Smythe and Company, Lincoln's Inn Fields
London

Graham walked to chambers the next morning, thinking of Diana. How beautiful she was, how fascinating, how much he wanted her. Approaching the red front door with the brass lion's head knocker, he tried to focus his thoughts on the day's work.

"Cheers, Graham!" Ivy greeted him. "What have we learned about the legal needs of our newest client?"

"Newest client?" Did Graham imagine it, or did she leer at him.

"The ever popular Tennessee Princess? The woman you dined with at the Savoy last night in order to determine if her legal concerns were appropriate for our firm? The *Mirror* certainly has some juicy details to report."

"What..." Graham began, but was interrupted as Edward Smythe entered chambers.

"Well, well, my fine chap," Edward began. "It appears that due to your efforts, we may have a piece of the Greenville matter after all. Good show, I dare say. Good show."

"Father must have seen this," Ivy said to Graham, holding up the front page of the *Mirror*.

Inquest Tomorrow May Lead to Multiple Arrests

the headline screamed. Ivy read aloud from the *Mirror*:

"The Mirror *previously reported that solicitor George Greenville—under investigation for the poisoning of his wife, Mabel—recently proposed to Nancy Nemeth, Mabel's nurse. Only two months having passed since poor Mabel's demise, the gossip in Brighton ran rampant. Eventually, it reached such a level that the police exhumed Mabel's body for forensic examination. Her remains were found to contain 0.25 to 0.5 grains of arsenic."*

"Yes, yes," Graham replied impatiently. "All of this is well known."

"Wait, Graham. I suspect only you know this." She continued reading:

"The Mirror *has subsequently learned that Solicitor Greenville has proposed to not one, but two women over the last several weeks. The 'brazen American hussy with cropped curls, wearing men's trousers,' described in our original article, has been identified as Miss Diana Vanderwell. Miss Vanderwell is an American heiress and member of the Society of Bright Young People. A reliable source reports that Miss Vanderwell herself received an offer of marriage from George Greenville via messenger several days ago. Will anyone be surprised if tomorrow's inquest leads to several arrests?"*

Graham sat down heavily on the nearest chesterfield.

Ivy and her father exchanged glances.

"Graham, are you feeling unwell?" Ivy gently inquired.

"So, my young partner. What did you learn last night?" Edward interrupted, before Graham could answer. "Will Smythe and Company be representing the Tennessee Princess? Did she accept the marriage proposal?" He rubbed his hands together. "Does she have knowledge of the murder? Did she accommodate it?"

"Father! There is no indication in the *Mirror* that Miss Vanderwell was an accomplice," Ivy protested.

"There undoubtedly will be. Graham, as I told Miss Vanderwell yesterday, there are no private matters between barristers in chambers. The inquest is tomorrow, by God! You must cease this dithering and describe what transpired last evening."

"It was the most wonderful evening…" Graham began in a faraway voice.

"Yes, yes. But what of Mabel Greenville's murder?"

Graham forlornly shook his head. "Nothing."

"Nothing?" Edward was incredulous.

"We never had time to discuss the case."

"Nonsense. You were in her company the entire evening. What of this offer of marriage referred to in the *Mirror*?"

"I know nothing about it."

Exhaling deeply, Edward joined Graham on the chesterfield, just as the door to chambers opened.

****

Diana traveled to the chambers of Smythe and Company thinking of Graham and the utter magic of the prior evening at the Savoy. Graham was unlike any other man she had ever known. He made her feel important, valued. She had longed for such validation since she was a child.

Opening the morning edition of the *Mirror* and

learning that both her identity and her marriage offer from George Greenville had been disclosed filled her with dread. Not only for the ultimatum to return to Tennessee it would bring from her father, but also for the negative impression it would leave upon Graham. He had spoken at dinner of his fears for the integrity of British society after the war; the scandalous behavior he saw everywhere. Although he had not specifically identified Diana or her friends, she felt the sting of his allegations. What would he think upon reading the *Mirror*? Lastly, she had considered the legal ramifications of the article. She had originally assumed any arrests would be limited to George, and perhaps Nancy Nemeth. Could there be another arrest? Her? The thought was too terrifying to contemplate.

Diana realized she must speak to Graham. So pressing was her need to see him, she dressed without thought to her appearance. It was not until she burst through the red door and encountered the surprised looks of Ivy, Edward, and Graham that she realized she was wearing the exact ensemble she had worn yesterday: her Chanel dress of black crepe de chine with her white wrap coat and cloche. The only difference was she now clutched in her hands the letter she had received from George Greenville proposing marriage.

Graham leaped up from the chesterfield as if, Diana thought, to hold her. But to Diana's dismay, Edward stepped into his path. Edward gently seized her arm and guided her toward a large office; Diana realized it must be his.

"Hannah, tea," he yelled. "Now!" As a matronly woman wearing a black dress and starched white apron appeared with the tea service, Edward made a perfunctory introduction. "Miss Vanderwell, this is Miss Hannah Greene. I could not survive without her."

Edward waved Graham and Ivy into his office. "Graham, Ivy, inside. We have little time and many matters to resolve."

He then approached Diana, holding out his right hand. "All right, young miss, let us see what we are holding here."

With a sniffle and an embarrassed look at Graham, Diana surrendered the letter she had received from George Greenville.

Edward read the letter aloud in its entirety. Then he began to reread certain sections:

"There are many rumors about, but between you and me, this letter reveals the true position. My children have turned bitterly against you and are of the belief that you and I together poisoned their mother."

Diana gasped, grasping the import of the words for the first time. She had not even known George had children. How horrid that those children thought she had helped George poison their mother! Who else must think this, especially after reading the *Mirror*?

Edward shot her a sharp look, but continued: *"Under the circumstances, are you prepared to face the music and be married?"*

Diana bowed her head, unable to even look at Graham. "Under the circumstances," how sinister it sounded.

Edward finished reading: *"I want to do something quickly. Let me have something from you, my love."*

Edward carefully appraised Diana. "This is the only communication you have had from Mr.

Greenville?"

Diana nodded, still not looking up.

"And what of the proposal? Have you answered?"

"God, no. Of course not. Everything happened so quickly. And why George thinks I would entertain such a proposal..."

Edward held up his hand. "I would think the letter makes it quite clear why he thinks you would be susceptible to his influence. You did know him? The *Mirror* is correct?"

"Yes, I knew him, but not in the way..."

"And you did, as the earlier article suggested, accompany him to various London restaurants and clubs? Just the two of you?"

"Yes, but..."

"Then, young miss, the language of the letter is clear to any reader." The grandfather clock in the anteroom struck the hour causing Edward to examine his pocket watch before continuing. "The inquest will be held tomorrow. Are we to assume, Miss Vanderwell, that you wish to hire Smythe and Company to represent your interests in this matter?" He looked intently at Diana.

"Yes. Yes, please." Diana, having realized the full implication of the letter, was now desperate for such assistance.

"Very well. Ivy will work with you to draw up a mutually acceptable contract."

He frowned at Diana. "You received no communication requiring you to attend the inquest?"

"No. Certainly not."

"Then you must not appear. Graham, you will go alone to Brighton to observe the inquest. Take careful notes, but under no circumstances divulge the name of our client to the newspapers."

"Go! Go! We have much work to do." Edward clapped his hands, in a manner Diana found particularly irritating.

Before Diana exited the office, she overheard Edward instruct Graham, "While you are in Brighton, talk to that scoundrel Marshall Phillips. It appears quite likely the inquest will result in George Greenville being arrested and charged with the poisoning of his wife. Should that be the case, it is more probable than not Miss Vanderwell will be investigated as an accessory."

Edward rubbed his hands in glee. "Great opportunity for the firm!"

Diana gasped in horror.

Chapter Six

Carmagien Guild Hall, Brighton

Graham boarded the Brighton Belle for the price of five shillings. "A straight line: the quickest way to travel between two points" read an Art Deco advertising poster with an image of a green train traveling along the points of a compass, hanging at the entrance to the dining car.

The dining carriage, christened the Minerva, consisted of wonderful Edwardian marquetry and plush armchairs along with tables adorned with elegant glass, crisp linen, and beautiful flowers. Graham spied Marshall Phillips, seated near a window.

"Graham, my lad. Come over," called Marshall. Graham eased into a leather armchair. "How are you, my boy? A Glenfiddich, what?"

After ordering the scotch "neat," Marshall returned his attention to Graham. "So, young man, to what do I owe the pleasure of seeing you? Traveling to Brighton, what?"

"Somewhat the same matter as you, sir."

"Same matter as me? Why, that's impossible. I am…"

"Attending the inquest on the death of Mabel Greenville. Yes sir, as am I."

"Come to watch your old master in action, are you,

lad? That old dog Edward Smythe realized you could learn a few things, did he?"

"Actually, sir, the firm may have a client with—shall we say—an interest in the proceedings."

"Client with an interest, who my lad?"

"You promise not to disclose it to the papers?"

"Of course not, my boy. Goes without saying."

"Miss Diana Vanderwell, sir."

"You don't say. None other than the Tennessee Princess. One of Mr. Greenville's many—how shall we describe it—alleged interests. What does Miss Vanderwell say about Mr. Greenville's proposal, heh, my lad?"

"Afraid I am not at liberty to discuss that, sir."

"No, indeed. I imagine not." Marshall paused. "Well, perhaps after the inquest we should consider how our clients' causes may be related."

"Of course, sir," Graham politely agreed.

The rest of the trip passed companionably in legal gossip about the major cases at Old Bailey and the barristers maintaining chambers at Lincoln's Inn Fields. Both men steadfastly avoided any discussion of the Greenville matter, as they glided through the stunning scenery toward Brighton.

As the Brighton Belle pulled into its station nestled against the sea, however, Marshall gave Graham an appraising look. "Diana Vanderwell, indeed. You have heard, I imagine, that George claims he is most assuredly innocent."

"Yes, of course."

"But perhaps," Marshall continued, "you have not heard that, should he be found not to be innocent, he may contend he had an accomplice." He gazed at

Graham a moment. "Very interesting, what?" Marshall shook his head and quickly exited the compartment.

****

Graham overslept the next morning, forcing him to run the few blocks to Guild Hall where the inquest was to be held. Although this was only his second inquest, he was aware such proceedings were presided over by the coroner and determined by a jury of twelve men. Inquests occurred primarily in cases of violent or unnatural death or deaths of an unknown cause. Where—as in Mabel Greenville's case—the cause of death was unknown, the coroner would order a post mortem examination and, if the death was deemed suspicious, hold an inquest. In the present case, the presence of the arsenic discovered during the post mortem rendered the death suspicious. The jury would be charged with verifying the identity of the deceased, as well as the place and time of death. Most importantly, the jury would determine the manner of death.

The initial testimony presented at the inquest concerned the medical evidence. "Mabel Greenville's heart simply wore out," testified Dr. Morris. "I certified death as being due to valvular disease in the heart."

"When the body was exhumed, no trace of valvular disease was found." Dr. Batchelor, who had examined Mabel's remains, conversely testified. "The body was much too well preserved. I found between a quarter and a half a grain of arsenic. The cause of death was certainly not due to the valvular disease indicated on the death certificate."

Next, Sergeant Hodge Lewis read over his investigation notes. Of particular interest was Nurse

Nemeth's statement that "the last medicines Dr. Morris prescribed to Mabel contained bismuth and morphine." Sergeant Lewis also read notes memorializing Nurse Nemeth's statement that "George Greenville neglected his wife, the better to enjoy other female company."

Nevertheless, when Nurse Nemeth was called to give evidence she firmly denied the statements. Rather, she opined, "I am telling the whole truth. As a nurse of many years, I have had numerous cases like this. There was nothing unusual about this death."

Graham watched as the police sergeant and the coroner exchanged sour looks and glared at the nurse. He wondered if the nurse had changed her testimony upon receiving the marriage proposal from George Greenville.

Further testimony was elicited from Mr. Christopher Bland, manager of the Brighton office of the Bank of England. He stated, "George Greenville's income from the practice of law was chancy, even in a good year. His dead wife, now that was a different story. Mabel Greenville had between £700 and £800 a year in her own right. A not inconsiderable sum, if I do say so."

The final bit of testimony came from Mr. James Bell, the Brighton chemist. Mr. Bell testified, "George Greenville purchased two separate packages of Cooper's Weedicide, containing sixty per cent arsenic each, the week before his poor wife died. I remember it clearly."

The jury was excused to begin their deliberation on the cause of death. Graham reasoned that they could not fail to reach a conclusion of death from arsenic poisoning performed by George Greenville. His prediction proved accurate.

When Maxwell Jones, the jury foreman, led the eleven others back into the inquest room from their deliberations, he told the coroner in a loud voice, "We are unanimously of the opinion that the death of the deceased, Mabel Greenville, was caused by acute arsenical poisoning, as certified." Staring around and basking in the wave of the muttered acclamation rising from the public seats, he added dramatically, "And that the poison was administered by George Greenville!"

Shouting broke out, the populace of Brighton giving vent to its feelings. In Graham's view, those feelings bode ill for the man who had been in such haste to remarry that he had made two proposals and for the subjects of those proposals: Nancy Nemeth and Diana Vanderwell.

****

Riding the Brighton Belle back to London late that afternoon, Graham mulled over the case. It was certain the police would soon arrest George Greenville. Would Diana also come under suspicion? Diana lived by her own rules, but she was beautiful and desirable. He smiled, remembering their evening at the Savoy. He had never met a woman he wanted more. He longed to hear her deep southern voice, feel her silky skin, taste…His thoughts were interrupted as the Brighton Belle pulled into Victoria Station.

Graham hailed a taxi to chambers and found Edward and Ivy, as well as John and Hannah, enjoying glasses of sherry and a quiet conversation in front of a roaring fire. "Ah," he murmured. "A relaxing evening."

"Graham. Thank heavens you are here." Ivy leaped up as soon as she saw him. "We have been waiting for you, endlessly. You will never believe what has happened!"

"Bloody hell, now what?"

"Let the poor boy rest," Edward implored. "Rest and tell us about the inquest. Hannah, bring more sherry. John, stoke the fire!"

While Hannah and John attended to their duties, Edward and Ivy listened to Graham's account of the inquest. Several times they exchanged glances, but refrained from interrupting.

When he had finished, Edward summed up the group consensus: "It is certain the police will arrest George Greenville, given the outcome of the inquest."

"Yes…" Graham began.

"And they will have some interest in questioning Miss Vanderwell."

"Yes," Graham began again. "And on the Brighton Belle, Marshall Phillips volunteered that, although to date George has proclaimed his innocence, he may later contend he had an accomplice."

Graham ignored Ivy and Edward as they again exchanged glances and continued. "But I would not think an accusation from the defendant together with a self-serving marriage proposal would be enough to charge anyone as an accessory, particularly someone of Miss Vanderwell's background."

"Graham, you are naïve," Ivy broke in. "I have been researching the law. In the case of *Rex v. Jones,* the court described an accessory as someone who has knowledge that a crime is being, or will be, committed and assists by helping or encouraging the criminal in some way, or by failing to report the crime. The assistance may be of any type, including emotional assistance."

"But," Graham objected, "what evidence exists that Diana knew a crime would be committed, or encouraged it? More importantly, what possible motive could she have?"

"Motive is easy: the love and support of George Greenville if the marriage proposal is to be believed. Additionally, it appears Diana may have been more involved with Greenville than originally represented." Diana handed Graham the evening edition of the *Mirror*.

The headline screamed: *The Plot Thickens.*

Graham rolled his eyes.

"Read on," Ivy encouraged.

Graham cleared his throat and began to read from the *Mirror*:

"It has now been reported that Miss Diana Vanderwell, companion to solicitor George Greenville, has been seen about town wearing his late wife's jewelry. Of particular interest is a brooch of a unique Egyptian pattern inherited by Mrs. Greenville from her aunt, wife of renowned Egyptian explorer Henry Butler."

Graham paused, remembering the brooch Diana had worn to the Savoy. In a somber voice he continued reading:

"Also, a second letter has surfaced. Earlier today, the Mirror received a copy of correspondence to Miss Vanderwell from George Greenville. In the letter, Greenville claims that he would not have taken 'any actions' if not for Ms. Vanderwell's encouragement and again proposes marriage. The Mirror has been unsuccessful in reaching Miss Vanderwell for comment.

One must ask whether the police will have more luck. Perhaps a certain young barrister, seen in compromising positions with the Tennessee Princess at the Savoy several days ago, will be able to provide more information."

Graham cringed. "What does Diana say?"

"The *Mirror* was not the only party unsuccessful in trying to reach Miss Vanderwell. Father sent John to Rose Cottage, but her maid claimed Diana was out."

"This situation is becoming quite untenable." Edward sighed. "The *Mirror* knows more about our case and our client than Smythe and Company!"

"Perhaps not, Father." Ivy smirked. "The *Mirror* mentions the barrister seen with our client at the Savoy. Perhaps that barrister has more information. Graham?"

"Not at all. We must find Diana."

Chapter Seven

*Chimera Booksellers, Bloomsbury and
Rose Cottage, Chelsea*

Diana trudged forlornly past the British Museum, wearing cream silk trousers and a red swing coat with matching cloche. She was exhausted, having spent the day wandering the streets of London working up the courage to face Graham.

She had received the second letter from George Greenville by messenger the morning of the inquest. As with the first letter, it made no sense. There was nothing in her relationship with George which would justify his claims or his marriage proposal. She had intended to take the letter to Graham this morning, when she knew he would have returned from the inquest. She was confident Graham would believe in her innocence, particularly after the evening they had spent at the Savoy.

Diana smiled to herself as she thought of that evening: the stimulating conversation in the American Bar, the passionate embrace in the ascending room, the joy of dancing on the rooftop. She wanted Graham, and until she saw the late edition of the *Mirror* last evening, she had been confident she would have him.

The revelations in the *Mirror* as to the origins of the Egyptian brooch, as well as the contents of the second letter, had shaken her confidence. The brooch clearly had sentimental value to George's wife. She shook her head. George's wife, whom she had not even known existed. But who would have missed the brooch—if she had been alive at the time Diana received it. Diana shuddered. How was she to explain her relationship with George and—if she was honest—so many others, to Graham?

After perusing the evening edition of the *Mirror*, Diana instructed Mary to advise anyone who inquired of her whereabouts that she was unavailable and retreated to her room. This morning, unable to gather her wits sufficiently to face Graham, she had avoided a second inquiry from the clerk for Smythe and Company. This afternoon, she set out for Smythe and Company, but then remembered a poetry reading at Chimera Booksellers. Hoping to avoid Graham just a little longer, she detoured to Chimera.

Diana had fallen in love with the sprawling bookstore on her first evening in London. Opening soon after the war in the Bloomsbury neighborhood, near the British Museum and University of London, the Chimera benefitted from a close association with Leonard and Virginia Woolf's Hogarth Press. It was a favorite among a loose band of artists and writers, known as the Bloomsbury Group, and was managed by an appealing twenty-eight-year-old blond with soft features and little fortune, known simply by his surname: Garrett.

Diana adored Garrett, in a brotherly fashion, and regularly attended activities at the Chimera including poetry readings, writers' meetings, and tea parties. Its small, intimate bar, known affectionately as the Reading Room, was one of her favorites. She visibly relaxed as she entered the store. The Chimera boasted a heavenly labyrinth of narrow passageways lined by casually carpentered bookshelves, secret alcoves, and small rooms with whimsical names. Scavenged floorings included marble tiling stolen decades ago from a local cemetery and laid down in a mosaic around the store's wishing well.

Artists had painted their favorite epigrams above doorways and on steps. Diana proceeded to a room with the name "Blue Oyster Tearoom" stenciled above its door, accepted a cup of Earl Grey, and sank into a much worn gold baize settee. Her mind wandered again to Graham as she listened to the poetry reading already in session. He was working no doubt—his arms embracing dusty legal case books when he could be holding her, his sensuous lips pursed in thought when they could be brushing hers... Shutting her eyes, she abandoned herself to the fantasies that rapidly followed.

****

Graham rushed past the British Museum on his way to the poetry reading at his favorite bookstore, the Chimera. His day had been frustrating, to say the least. Despite repeated efforts, he had been unable to reach Diana. As her barrister, he was incensed. How could he possibly represent her, if he couldn't find her? As her friend, perhaps more, he was concerned. Had she come to some harm? How drab his life would be without her!

Graham paused as he reached the small half plaza in front of the Chimera. The bookstore's green and yellow façade welcomed him. The hand hewn signage with the chimera of Greek mythology—a fire-breathing female monster with a lion's head, a goat's body, and a serpent's tail—amused him. In English, the name of the bookstore referenced a thing wished for, but impossible to achieve. In Greek mythology, it referenced a fire-breathing female. Both, he thought wryly, might be considered applicable to his current love life.

Shaking the thought from his head, he entered the bookstore and headed down one of its winding passageways toward the Blue Oyster Tearoom. He could hear animated conversation and feared he had already missed the first reading. Carefully minding his steps so as not to trip on the ancient marble tiling or inadvertently fall into the wishing well, he was surprised when he raised his eyes to look directly into those of the woman he had been dreaming about.

"Graham! I was on my way to see you...I have been thinking of you...We need to talk." Diana took a breath. "But what are you doing here?"

"Trying to distract myself from the unfortunate fate of a barrister who has a client who refuses to speak to him, who may very possibly have lied to him, and who provides the *Mirror* with more information than those responsible for her legal defense." Graham glared at Diana.

"It's not like that. I wanted to see you. But you were in Brighton when I received the letter. And then the *Mirror*, it made everything sound so sordid. I was on my way to see you, truly. I only stopped here to muster my courage. It is my favorite place in London!"

"Mine as well." Graham smiled, in spite of himself. The room quieted, as the next reader was introduced. "Is there somewhere we can talk?"'

Now it was Diana's turn to smile. "Follow me. I know just the place."

She led Graham down a series of winding

passageways, then up a series of steps, until they reached a room that somehow appeared much older than the rest of the building. Above the doorframe, no longer square, was painted: "Be not inhospitable to strangers, lest they be angels in disguise."

"Marvelous, isn't it?" Diana whispered. "Have you been here? It's the used and antiquarian book section. Rumor has it that the owner insists this section must be located here, because the room is so romantic. The gaps between the shelves are intentional, so you can see and fall in love with a customer on the other side while you are reading Shakespeare's sonnets."

Graham nodded with appreciation. "This store has rooms like chapters in a novel."

"Exactly!" said Diana, surprising Graham by throwing her arms around his neck and pressing her body close to his. "Why are you so perfect? You understand everything!"

His mouth found hers. His hands untied the sash of the red coat and reached for the small pearl buttons on her silk blouse. She pressed closer, and he felt his body respond.

"We need to find somewhere more private." Graham whispered, remembering the mention in the *Mirror* of their evening at the Savoy.

"I know just the place."

****

The afternoon was still warm as Diana led Graham outside and into a taxi. She gave the driver the address for Rose Cottage. "Quickly, please," she added, glancing at Graham.

She snuggled into his embrace and eagerly sought his lips, nipping at them ever so gently. He responded instantly, running his hands over her hair, her neck, her breasts, her thighs. The ride ended all too quickly.

Arriving at Rose Cottage, Diana led Graham to her favorite location: the garden. The late afternoon sun cast a golden glow over the many colors of the borders, rockeries, and cutting beds.

"It's wonderful!" Graham laughed out loud.

"Sit," Diana ordered, pushing him into a hammock strung between two pear trees. Slowly she began to undress. First the hat, then the red coat, lastly undoing the pearl buttons of her blouse.

"Let me," Graham begged.

"No," Diana replied with a hint of a smile. "You must watch."

She removed her blouse and the chemise beneath. When she was wearing only the silk trousers and her shoes, she climbed into his lap. Straddling him.

"What of these?" Graham asked playfully, pulling on the trousers.

"These stay on, until I finish telling you about George."

Graham rolled his eyes.

"It's important!" Slowly, he ran his thumb around her nipples. She felt herself grow damp. "But I'll be quick."

Graham's thumb worked its way down into her trousers. "I think you had better."

Diana gulped. "We met through a mutual friend, from Tennessee actually. I never knew he was married. We went to dinner and dancing when he was in London. He gave me small gifts which, I admit, gradually became more extravagant. We never discussed marriage, seriously. We joked about what we

C. K. Charlotte

might do when we reached our dotage. But I—at least—was only being facetious. He told me he found the brooch in an antique store during a business trip to Paris. I have no idea why he is sending me these letters, truly." She slid off his lap onto the hammock next to him. "Oh Graham, everything is such a mess. Whatever shall I do?"

He slid his hands under her buttocks and brought her back onto his lap. "Hold me," he said.

She straddled his thighs, her head against his breast, and her legs—still in the cream silk pants—spread apart. Slowly, he finished undressing her. Kissing her everywhere, as he did so. Diana had never felt so alive. It was as though an electric current ran through her body. She closed her eyes and enjoyed the sensations. Each place he kissed came to life: her throat, her breasts standing erect in the cool breeze, her thighs as he laid her back against the hammock. "Now, Graham." She sighed. "I must have you now."

"Oh no, not yet. You began with teasing me," Graham responded. "My turn."

She opened her eyes and smiled at him, but his attention was elsewhere. He had reached into the grass beneath the hammock to pick wildflowers.

"What are these?" Graham asked, holding up the blue and purple flowers. "The flowers are attached to the side of a stem that resembles the tail of a scorpion."

"Viper's bugloss, sometimes called 'blueweed,' " answered Diana. "The stem uncoils as the flowers bloom. The name 'viper' is thought to derive from the shape of the plant's seed, which resembles a viper's head. 'Bugloss' is derived from the Greek word for 'ox tongue,' since the leaves resemble this part of the

150

animal's anatomy. We had them in our gardens in Tennessee, but they are native to Europe."

"Ox tongue, imagine." Graham returned to pleasuring Diana.

She laughed. "We used to weave them into bracelets, when we were children."

"This is much better," he said, as he threaded the flowers in the ebony hairs of her mound of Venus.

Slowly, his fingertips found her secret place, and she gasped as she climaxed at his touch. Just as she thought she might die from pleasure, the clouds opened and released a cold rain.

****

They raced to the cottage; Diana wearing only her shoes. Graham was chilled to the bone. Diana, clutching her clothing, appeared unaffected.

"It is Mary's night off, so we won't have any explaining to do," Diana explained. "But we will have to light our own fire, I'm afraid."

Graham followed her through the cottage, stepping over the uneven floorboards and weaving his way around the mounds of books. No wonder she loves the Chimera, he thought wryly.

At last they reached the parlor, and tossing a pile of books to the floor, Diana curled up on a rose chintz sofa and covered herself with a pale green cashmere blanket. Graham lit the fire.

"You are beautiful," he said wistfully, as he unwrapped the layers of cashmere and gazed at the folds of her body in the firelight.

"And you are soaked. Come, let's get you out of this clothing. I can't have all the fun."

"I should go," Graham said, surprising himself.

What is this about, he wondered.

"Are you sure? I could find my riding crop." She grinned mischievously.

Graham shook his head. Whether from the rain and cold, his recollection of his ethical duties toward a client, or Diana's revelations regarding George Greenville, Graham found himself curiously depressed.

Diana retreated under the cashmere throw. "Very well."

"We should speak about your case tomorrow, in chambers. Is ten o'clock convenient?"

Diana merely nodded.

"Bring George's latest letter, if you please."

Diana nodded a second time, as Graham headed for the door. Without turning back, he added, "And the brooch and any other items you may have received from the generous Mr. Greenville."

Chapter Eight

Smythe and Company, Lincoln's Inn Fields, London

Graham walked into chambers the following morning feeling the same general malaise of the night before. He wanted Diana; she excited him like no woman he had ever known. But her casual relationships troubled him, to say nothing of the fact she was a client.

Shaking his head to clear the cobwebs, he walked through the door to find Diana already present and speaking with John, Ivy, and Edward. God, she looked good today. She wore a blue silk skirted suit, the man's tailored jacket containing a collar of dyed fur, a blue cloche with a red feather, and red pumps. Despite the nature of her visit and the lateness of the hour at which he left her, she was animated and glowing.

"Graham!" Ivy sought his attention as he stood admiring Diana. "Diana brought the second letter and has been explaining the brooch. And, good news, she had no idea George Greenville was married!" The two had obviously bonded.

"He knows," Diana interrupted. "We discussed it last night."

"Umm." Ivy was momentarily and uncharacteristically speechless.

"*Harrumph.* Well, that being said," Edward said,

"perhaps we can get back to strategizing the case. Graham, Ivy, Miss Vanderwell, in my office. John, visit the metropolitan police, Old Bailey, and the *Mirror*. See what you can find out about the case against George Greenville."

The remainder of the morning was taken up with interviewing Diana on the facts of her interactions with George and her lack of knowledge about his wife and evaluating Diana's options. Together, the three barristers sought to provide Diana with an analysis of the advantages, risks, and chances of success of each option.

"As with all legal cases, a number of scenarios are possible, Diana," Graham began. "On the one hand, should George not be arrested, which is highly unlikely given the outcome of the inquest, or should George be arrested and tried, but found to be innocent, then there would be no basis to hold you responsible as an accessory to murder."

"That's good, then?" Diana looked to Graham.

"Yes. But on the other hand, if George is arrested and found guilty, it is possible you may be arrested as an accessory to murder."

"But I did not even know George had a wife!" Diana wailed. "How could I be involved in her murder?"

"Well," said Graham, warming to his legal hypotheticals and ignoring his client's distress, "a number of possibilities present themselves, actually. George could claim you did know about Mabel and his plan to murder her to marry you. Or other witnesses could be found to testify to those facts. Then there are the letters you received, as well as the presents from

George. And, of course, there is the gossip of the neighbors in Brighton."

"Stop. I have a headache! What nonsense the law is! Whatever am I to do? Where is justice?"

"Justice can only be found in the law..." Graham began pompously.

"Old George Greenville's been arrested and is locked in jail!" John, returning from his legal reconnaissance mission, interrupted.

"How is he pleading?" Ivy inquired.

"Not guilty."

"Good," said Edward, thinking of their prior conversation and seeking to reassure Diana. "What other news?"

"Very little, sir. The clerks at Old Bailey estimate it will only take two months to come to trial, the courts in Brighton having so many fewer cases than those in London. It is expected Greenville will remain in jail the entire time. Bets are two to one the old man will be found guilty. I took a piece of that action myself!" John confessed, ignoring Edward's frown. "The *Mirror* plans to run an article in the evening edition about the case but doesn't have much new to report." He stopped to reconsider. "Oh, but there is one bit of news. The nurse who tended to Mabel Greenville—and has since taken a romantic interest in George—also received jewelry belonging to his wife. Just like the miss here." He nodded toward Diana.

"Ahem!" Edward cut him off. "Has the nurse," Edward paused to recall her name, "Nancy Nemeth, been arrested?"

"No sir, only questioned."

A quick knock at the door preceded Hannah.

"Chief Inspector Fox to see you, sir."

"That's the other thing!" John smacked himself on the forehead. "Chief Inspector Fox said he would stop by to chat about the case. No harm he says in discussing it, it being handled in Brighton and all."

****

"Good day, Mr. Smythe, Mr. Wetherington, Mrs. Henderson." Fox bowed slightly. "Or is it Lady Henderson, now that you are married to the Honorable Bryan Henderson? Titles always confuse me so."

Fox is exceedingly polite today, thought Graham, his suspicions immediately aroused.

"And this must be the renowned Miss Vanderwell." Fox executed a low bow in Diana's direction. "Chief Inspector Fox of the metropolitan police."

Diana nodded pleasantly and offered her hand but focused a perplexed look on Graham.

"So pleased you are present," Fox continued. "I am so very curious about your involvement with George Greenville."

"See here!" said Edward.

"I will not allow her to answer," added Graham.

"Indeed," Fox calmly responded. "Perhaps your client would rather be transported to Brighton to answer questions."

"Have you a warrant? Cause for an arrest?"

"Perhaps."

"Just a moment," Edward broke in. "Let us start again. Exactly why are you here, Chief Inspector?"

"To be honest, Mr. Smythe, the blokes at the Brighton station—understanding you represent Miss Vanderwell—requested I visit and ask a few questions."

"Regarding?"

"Well, as you know, Greenville has been arrested and will be tried shortly. We—the police that is—need to ascertain any knowledge Miss Vanderwell may have related to his guilt." Fox paused. "And, sir, seeing Miss Vanderwell is sitting right here, I thought I might as well ask her."

Graham was outraged but with great difficult held his tongue. He knew Ivy and Edward had worked successfully with Fox when Bryan Henderson had been charged with murder.

Ivy looked at her father, who nodded for her to continue.

"Chief Inspector Fox," Ivy began politely. "It would probably be most appropriate for us—as the barristers—to answer any questions you might have for Miss Vanderwell."

Well done, thought Graham. Totally avoids the issue of whether Fox has the authority to question Diana on behalf of the Brighton police.

Fox hesitated.

"Miss Vanderwell is, of course, present," Ivy added. "We can obtain information from her as needed."

Fox sighed. "Very well, that will do for now. But please understand that neither I nor the Brighton police relinquish our right to question Miss Vanderwell, whether in London or Brighton, should we deem it necessary."

Graham shot a quick look at Diana to see her reaction. Her visage had visibly paled.

"So," Edward said. "What questions might you have?"

An hour later, it was established that: Diana knew George Greenville, accompanied him to various locales in London, and accepted gifts from him during their relationship. It was further established that Diana had received two letters proposing marriage and the much publicized brooch from Greenville following his wife's unfortunate demise. Graham watched Diana grow ever more somber.

"Have you ever been to Brighton, Miss Vanderwell?" Fox unexpectedly leaned forward and began directing his questions to Diana, rather than Edward.

"No, I don't…"

"Did you ever meet Mrs. George Greenville, also known as Mabel?"

"No. I never even knew George was married!"

"Truly?" Fox asked. "It never came up in conversation? You never thought to ask?"

"No. I…"

"Move along, please," interrupted Edward. "She has answered that question."

Fox raised his eyebrow, then changed his line of questioning. "Have you ever had reason to purchase arsenic?"

"Certainly not, I…"

"Anyone ever purchase arsenic on your behalf?"

"Of course not, I…"

"Intend to marry Mr. Greenville, did you?"

Graham could not contain himself. "Really, Chief Inspector, I hardly think…"

But Edward waved away his objection. "Allow her to answer."

"Wise decision," Fox responded sternly, causing

Edward to glance up sharply.

"Miss Vanderwell," continued Fox. "Please answer the question. Did you plan to marry George Greenville?"

"No! He would mention it from time to time. I never thought he was serious. It was never more than a casual relationship." She paused, then brightened as if finding the proper word. "A friendship."

Fox's eyebrow rose higher; Graham stifled a wince. I wonder if that is how Diana would classify our relationship, he thought, a friendship.

"A casual relationship, Miss Vanderwell? A friendship? Do you have a number of casual male friends," he paused for emphasis, "whom you accompany to private dinners and dancing? Male friends who regularly provide you with expensive gifts? Gifts of jewelry stolen from their wives?"

Diana looked to Graham, her eyes seeking solace or, perhaps, answers to the questions. It was apparent to Graham, in that instant, that Diana had a number of such male friends. It was equally apparent Fox considered such relationships not only highly unusual, but also highly inappropriate. Graham suspected that a Brighton jury might agree.

The unanswered questions hung in the air.

Diana looked to Graham a second time, and Edward leaped into action. "That will be enough for today. Miss Vanderwell is clearly exhausted. Please contact Smythe and Company, if you should have any further questions Chief Inspector."

Fox turned when he reached the door. "Please do not leave town, Miss Vanderwell."

****

Diana sat frozen in shock. "Could they really force me to go to a police station to answer questions?"

Graham looked pointedly at Ivy and answered, "Yes."

"Could they force me to testify at George's trial?"

"Yes."

"About everything?"

"Everything you know about George Greenville, your relationship, his wife's death…"

"Will it be reported in the newspapers?"

"Perhaps."

"What if my father hears of it? What will he think? Whatever will he do?"

"That is the least of your concerns," Graham said sternly.

Graham's tone, as much as his words, caused Diana to reconsider her position. It was clear the Chief Inspector was skeptical of her answers. The British could be so stuffy. She wondered how a Brighton jury would react to her dilemma. "What is the greatest of my concerns?"

Graham's silence assaulted her. Was it possible? Could she end up in jail?

Chapter Nine

Carmagien Guild Hall, Brighton

The next several months passed quickly for Graham. Ivy spent more and more time with Bryan at his family's estate in Oxfordshire, and Graham inherited many of her clients. Neither Chief Inspector Fox nor the Brighton police made any further attempts to question Diana. Edward ordered Graham to attend Greenville's trial and requested he limit his contact with Diana to legal consultations.

A blanket of fog hung over Brighton, as Graham disembarked from the Brighton Belle on the first day of trial. Greenville, surrounded by mounted police, was taken the short distance from the jail to the Guild Hall. The streets echoed with the baying of an angry crowd of onlookers.

Graham was aware, from conversations with Marshall Phillips, that Sir Michael Darling—the presiding judge—would be hearing his last murder case after a long and distinguished judicial career. The seventy-three-year-old jurist was slight of build and rather stooped, but of colossal intelligence. The jury was composed of twelve men: seven farmers, one merchant, and four professional gentlemen.

Graham also knew the first several days of trial would be dedicated to presentation of the prosecution's case. After a weekend recess, the jury would reconvene to consider Greenville's defense. The prosecution contended Greenville had placed weed killer in a bottle of Burgundy, quaffed by his wife Mabel over lunch on the ill-fated day of her death. Marshall, as defense counsel, contended this was impossible for the Crown to prove.

Sir Edward Marley, on behalf of the prosecution, began the trial with the testimony of Dr. Batchelor. As at the inquest, Dr. Batchelor testified the death certificate completed by Dr. Morris listed valvular disease as the cause of death. When the body was exhumed, however, no trace of valvular disease was found. Rather, it was discovered the remains held between a quarter and a half a grain of arsenic.

Sir Marley next proceeded with the testimony of Mr. Bell, the Brighton chemist. Again, similar to the inquest, Mr. Bell testified Greenville had, on two separate occasions, purchased an arsenical compound containing sixty per cent arsenic and marketed under the brand of Cooper's Weedicide.

Then the case got down to the nitty-gritty. Sir Marley requested all witnesses ordered from the court, save for medical experts. Graham, like many of the lawyers in the courtroom, sat riveted with attention.

Once the witnesses were excused, the prosecution informed the court it would later introduce evidence in the form of testimony from Eileen, the Greenville's maid. As an offer of proof, Sir Marley advised the court Eileen would testify that on the day of the fateful Sunday lunch Greenville had ample opportunity to place the weed killer in the bottle of Burgundy.

Sir Marley then called the Crown's medical expert,

Dr. William Cox, to the stand. Dr. Cox opined that the two purchases of weed killer were more than sufficient to kill Mrs. Greenville. Further, if dissolved in the Burgundy, neither taste nor color would be noticeable. Finally, Dr. Cox gave as his expert opinion that Mabel Greenville's death was due to heart failure consistent with prolonged vomiting due to arsenical poisoning.

Having introduced Dr. Cox's expert testimony on death due to arsenical poisoning, Sir Marley called Eileen. The maid declared on oath that George Greenville spent half an hour in the pantry before lunch on the fatal Sunday and he, alone, decanted and served the wine.

As to motive, Sir Marley began with Mr. Bland, manager of the Brighton office of the Bank of England. Mr. Bland testified that George Greenville was dependent on his wife's money. Greenville's own income from the law, according to Bland, was chancy even in a good year. His dead wife, however, received between £700 and £800 a year in her own right.

Sir Marley concluded his case in what Graham considered a brilliant move: the testimony of Brighton matron Henrietta Copperway concerning George Greenville's enjoyment of female company other than his wife's. "In other words," Sir Marley asked of Mrs. Copperway, "Mr. Greenville was physically fit and virile?"

"Oh my, yes sir." Mrs. Copperway tittered.

Laughter wafted through the courtroom. Judge Darling struck his gavel.

"And poor Mabel Greenville had been a sick woman for some time?"

Mrs. Copperway lowered her head. "Yes, sir."

"And Mr. Greenville was known to, shall we say, seek comfort from women other than his wife? Is that a fair statement?"

"I would say so, sir. Yes, indeed." Mrs. Copperway tittered again.

"In addition, Mr. Greenville was eager to enjoy the fruits of matrimony again, despite the fact that these had withered in his marriage to Mrs. Greenville? Is that true?"

"I...I guess so, sir."

"So much so that within weeks of the unfortunate Mabel's death, he made not one but two offers of marriage?"

"Objection!" Marshall complained.

"Withdrawn," Sir Marley responded. "No further questions."

Thus, Graham mused, jury deliberations were recessed for the weekend with the prosecution having painted a very vibrant picture of the means and motive for George Greenville to murder his wife.

****

While Graham occupied himself with the trial of George Greenville, Diana sat pretending to read one of the many books in the drawing room of Rose Cottage. The months away from Graham had only made Diana want him more. Absence does make the heart grow fonder, she thought. She had tried amusing herself with her male friends, members of the Society of the Bright Young People, but to no avail. She longed for Graham's agile mind, to say nothing of his body.

"Anything I can bring you, miss?" Mary entered the drawing room.

"Something to shorten time?" Diana requested

wistfully. "Oh, I wish I could see Graham."

"You are meeting him tonight, are you not, miss? After he returns from the trial?"

"Yes. In the Reading Room at the Chimera."

"The *Mirror* is full of nothing else but details of the trial. 'Murder of the Century' they are calling it. So exciting." Mary shivered, then catching a glimpse of her mistress's expression, added, "But very difficult for you, I know, miss."

How little you know, thought Diana, reflecting on the discussions at Lincoln's Inn Fields. If George is found guilty, I may very well be arrested as an accomplice. She shook her head, in an ineffectual attempt to dispel the thought, and went to dress for the Reading Room.

Chapter Ten

*The Reading Room, Chimera Booksellers
Bloomsbury*

Diana dressed carefully for her rendezvous with Graham. Sleeveless, V-necked, low-backed, and above the knee, her dress alternated black and nude strips of silk with gold threads and was tied at the waist with a gold sash. Gold Mary Janes and a gold tiara with a black feather completed the look. She chose her gold embroidered evening coat to keep out the chill. She wanted Graham to want her as much as she needed him. She was conscious of several appreciative male glances as she exited the taxi in front of the Chimera, confirmation that she had chosen her outfit wisely.

She entered the Chimera and made her way down the narrow passageways lined with bookshelves and secret alcoves to come at last to the Reading Room. The epigram painted above the doorway was another of her favorites: "Most bars exist for drinking; this one to foster thinking."

The Reading Room was a romantically, if poorly, lit diminutive black box open only on weekend evenings. In excess of three thousand books, arranged according to color—from black to white—lined the handcrafted bookshelves. Velvet chesterfields, overgrown brocaded chairs large enough for two, and tufted ottomans graced the singularly civilized salon. The Reading Room, known for its literary cocktails, was perfect for sipping a cocktail and carrying on a conversation.

Diana perused the prose-inspired menu printed as a bookmark. Each cocktail paid homage to an author. Diana's favorite—the "Dorian Gray"—was infused with rose water, spiked with *eau de vie*, and garnished with an orchid in honor of Oscar Wilde. She imagined Graham would want the "Final Problem," a green chartreuse and Scotch cocktail honoring Sir Arthur Conan Doyle.

A jazz trio played on the minuscule stage. Seated nearby—at a small table with a stunning blonde sheathed in a cream-colored dress and salmon-hued heels—was Prince Said Fusani. Diana had last seen the well-known Egyptian playboy the evening she had met Graham at the Savoy. As usual, he cut a striking figure. Diana speculated on the whereabouts of his Parisian wife.

The prince's table was strewn with tiny umbrellas and several rainbow-hued cocktails, various chess pieces—although it was clear no game was in progress—and a pristine copy of *War and Peace* by Tolstoy. Certainly not the inspiration for the rainbow-hued cocktails accompanied by the tiny umbrellas, thought Diana.

Prince Fusani caught Diana's eye, nodded, and rose to greet her. Encircling her waist, he held her close and favored her with a much too familiar kiss. Diana rejected the impulse to object; it felt too good to be appreciated.

"Diana, what may I get you?"

"Good evening, Said. A Dorian Gray," she requested, naming the Oscar Wilde concoction she adored. "But don't let me interrupt your evening,"

"Don't be silly, my darling. Just a small diversion. I had no idea I would be so lucky as to enjoy your company tonight."

"Actually, I'm meeting…Oh! There he is now."

****

The Brighton Belle had been delayed; Graham rushed from Victoria Station to the Chimera to meet Diana at the prearranged time. The prosecution's case against George Greenville greatly concerned him. On the basis of the evidence presented, it appeared certain George would be convicted of murdering his wife. If that were the case, it was entirely possible Diana might be arrested. He did not feel confident she fully understood the seriousness of her position; he loathed to be the one to explain it to her. Perhaps it would have been better to have Ivy meet with Diana in chambers. But no, he had to see her. The need was so great he could almost…

Entering the Reading Room, he stopped abruptly. A woman who was surely Diana was in the process of being kissed quite passionately by a dark, well-dressed man. As they separated, Graham realized it was Diana and the man was the Egyptian she had been so familiar with at the Savoy: Prince Fusani. He frowned as he remembered Chief Inspector Fox's questioning of Diana. Was this perhaps another one of Diana's casual male friendships?

He watched as Diana, registering his presence, said goodbye to the prince and glided across the room to meet him. His hands clenched as the prince's eyes tracked Diana's movements, traveling down her back as though he were undressing her. Definitely not the behavior of a gentleman, thought Graham. He wanted Diana, but he wanted her exclusively. He refused to share.

Reaching him at last, Diana pecked Graham lightly on the cheek.

"Not quite the greeting the prince got," Graham said in a low voice. He wrapped her in his arms and placed his lips on hers, teasing them open with his tongue, then kissing her deeply.

Diana responded by clutching his body close to hers and whispering in his ear, "I have missed you, so very much."

"It did not appear so, a few moments ago."

"Oh, the prince, he's merely a…"

"Yes, I know, a friend. Let's find a quiet corner where we can talk. I am afraid I need a cocktail; we have much to discuss."

Seated in one of the hidden corners of the Reading Room, Graham nursed his cocktail honoring Sir Arthur Conan Doyle. Diana amused him by regaling him with her adventures since he had been immersed in the trial. He enjoyed the time to relax and to observe Diana. So beautiful, so animated, he simply could not imagine his life without her. The thought forced him to attend to the purpose of the meeting—the trial and its ramifications for Diana, as his client.

"Diana?" She focused her violet eyes upon him. "We must talk about the trial."

"I know." She sighed and placed her hand over his.

"It is not good," he blurted out.

"Oh, Graham, let's talk about something else. I

cannot bear it."

"You must. We must. Diana, it is almost certain that George Greenville will be found guilty of murdering his wife."

"Poor George!"

"Diana," Graham said through gritted teeth, "you must understand, if George is convicted there is a high likelihood you will be arrested."

"No."

"And you may be tried as an accomplice."

"I cannot. I will not…" Diana withdrew her hand.

"Diana."

"Let's talk of something else, something pleasant."

"I would do anything for you, Diana, you know that, but this is beyond my powers. We must…" Graham ran his fingers over her hair and softly kissed the crevice at the base of her throat. In the dim atmosphere of the Reading Room, he heard a soft moan.

"Will you come home with me tonight?"

Graham felt his body react to the invitation; it took every ounce of his willpower to control it. "I can't, Diana. I promised Edward we would have only professional interactions until the case is resolved. It's not appropriate." He paused. "And, in addition, there is the matter of your male *friends* to resolve."

Diana shook her head, radiating sadness. "Walk me out then. I am suddenly very tired."

"We'll talk tomorrow, in chambers."

Diana looked solemnly at Graham. "As you wish."

****

I have never lied to Graham before, thought Diana as she sat alone in the back of the taxi. How sad it is that I should do so now, at what perhaps will be the last time I ever see him.

Reaching Rose Cottage, she entered and called for Mary. "Come quickly. I must pack."

"Pack, miss? It's the middle of the night. Where are we going?"

"I am going to Paris. I must leave before daybreak."

"Alone? Paris?"

"Yes, alone. You must stay here. Stay and tell anyone who asks that you have no idea where I am. That I left this evening for the Chimera and never returned. Quickly now, my bags."

"But miss, why?"

"I learned tonight that George Greenville will most likely be found guilty of murder, and I might soon be arrested."

"Arrested, miss?"

"That's what Graham Wetherington implied this evening. I have always had whatever man I wanted, Mary, and I have never wanted a man more than I want Graham. But I cannot be confined to a Brighton jail. I will not. This is all a horrible misunderstanding. I must go to Paris and hope it blows over. If not, I must return to Tennessee."

"But where will you stay, miss? Paris is so foreign."

"I have friends in Montparnasse, on the left bank of the River Seine. Many of them are virtually penniless painters, sculptors, and writers. But they have come from around the world to bask in the creative atmosphere of post-war Paris. In the cafés and bars of Montparnasse, ideas are hatched and mulled over."

"Truly, miss?" Mary's eyes were wide and unbelieving.

"Absolutely, it's wonderful in its own way. In cafés such as Le Dôme, and La Coupole, starving artists can occupy a table all evening for a few *centimes*. If they fall asleep, the waiters do not wake them. If they cannot pay their bill, the proprietors accept a drawing or a poem, holding the works of art until the artists can afford to pay. In some cafés, the walls are littered with collections of artworks. Someday, Mary, the curators of the world's greatest museums will drool with envy thinking of Montparnasse."

Diana stopped, took a deep breath, and tried desperately to dispel her longing for Graham. "I will be happy in Paris, Mary. I must be happy."

Chapter Eleven

Carmagien Guild Hall, Brighton

The following Monday morning, Graham found himself once again on the Brighton Belle headed south. He was in poor spirits, for several reasons. First, Diana had never shown up for their agreed upon appointment on Saturday. Despite repeated trips to Rose Cottage and discussions with her maid Mary, he had been unable to determine her whereabouts. He feared she had fled London. The irresponsibility of such flight infuriated Graham. Not only did it violate the Chief Inspector's orders, it suggested she might be guilty after all. To date, Graham had steadfastly believed in Diana's innocence, but it was becoming increasingly more difficult.

The second reason for his low spirits was the reconvening of the jury in the trial of George Greenville. After a weekend recess, the jury would this morning consider George's defense to the charges against him. The prior week, the prosecution had presented convincing evidence that Greenville had killed his wife. Graham was doubtful that Marshall Phillips, as defense counsel, could successfully rebut the prosecution's case.

Thus it was with a heavy heart that Graham walked to the Guild Hall on the morning of trial. Rain descended in sheets, and like the prior week, the streets echoed with the shouts of angry onlookers as Greenville was escorted from the jail to Guild Hall.

Having clerked for Marshall, Graham appreciated his reputation as a formidable orator. He had successfully defended so many citizens accused of notorious murders, he was known as "The Great Defender." As Graham well knew, Marshall's law clerks performed the legal research and brief writing needed for his cases. Nevertheless, Marshall had a talent for exploiting emotions, and he approached each new jury as an audience waiting to be won. One of his techniques was to begin his defense argument with the defendant's questionable attributes. Then, one by one, deny that they played any role in the charges leveled against him.

It was with this technique that Marshall began his defense of George Greenville. "My client, Mr. Greenville is not on trial for being a poor provider with a struggling law practice," he told the jury. "Nor is he on trial for being a less than attentive husband, frequently enjoying the company of other women while his longsuffering wife waited at home. He is not even on trial for making two marriage proposals to two different women, shortly after his wife's death." He paused. "Although he certainly might be on trial had he married both women." The courtroom, including several of the jurors, chuckled appreciatively.

Judge Darling glared. Marshall waited for the laughter to pass, then continued. "No, George Greenville is on trial for murdering his wife with arsenic by utilization of weed killer in a bottle of Burgundy. And, gentlemen of the jury, none of his shortcomings as a husband are in the slightest way relevant."

By exposing his client's shortcomings, Marshall had manipulated the jury into believing the defendant truthful, even contrite. And indeed George Greenville sat before the jury looking innocent of murder and regretful of his shortcomings as a husband. The courtroom was so quiet, Graham thought, one could hear a pin drop.

Having successfully countered the prosecution's argument regarding the defendant's interest in other women, Marshall next moved on to the motive of financial gain. He called as a witness Mr. Geoffrey Toll, a London solicitor who had prepared the estate documents of Mabel Greenville's late father. Toll testified that, as a result of Mabel Greenville's death, George Greenville had lost by far the major part of his income. His wife had been only a life tenant of her father's estate. On her death, the income had passed in equal shares to her children, whose trustees controlled it. In short, Toll concluded, "Mr. Greenville simply couldn't get his hands on any capital. Mrs. Greenville's death left him unable to live in the style to which he had become accustomed."

A second technique of Marshall's was to annoy the presiding judge to the point that the judge would snap at him. Marshall would appear humbled, making all of the judge's subsequent objections appear to be motivated by personal dislike, rather than an appropriate point of law. By creating the impression the court was prejudiced against his client, Marshall often manipulated the outcome in his client's favor.

Marshall made use of this ploy now. "In your view,

is this an important point to bear in mind when considering motive—or lack of it?" he asked Toll.

"Objection!" Sir Marley interjected on behalf of the prosecution.

"Sustained!" Judge Darling agreed. "The question is stricken, the witness ordered not to answer, and counsel for the defense sanctioned."

Marshall feigned surprise but bowed to the court in submission. Sir Marley snorted. But the unanswered question hung in the air, influencing the jury. What reasonable man would kill a wife who was his only reasonable means of support—particularly when he enjoyed the freedom to entertain other women while she was alive?

Graham begrudgingly admired Marshall's skill. Can't un-ring that bell, Graham thought to himself.

Having established that the defendant had no motive to kill his wife, Marshall moved on to the origination and manner of delivering the arsenic. He recalled Dr. Morris to the stand.

"Dr. Morris, the prosecution sought to show that the two purchases of weed killer from Mr. Bell were more than sufficient to kill Mrs. Greenville. Also, if dissolved in the rubicund Burgundy, neither taste nor color would be noticeable."

"Is the respected counsel for the defense asking a question or testifying?' Sir Marley inquired.

"Please pose a question, Mr. Phillips," Judge Darling responded.

Marshall once again smiled at the jury. Turning to Dr. Morris, he inquired, "Could you have made a fatal error by administering Fowler's solution of arsenic, instead of bismuth, to Mabel Greenville?" He pointed out, in his trenchant manner, a photograph of the doctor's surgery showing bottles containing both mixtures standing side by side.

Dr. Morris was uncertain and contradicted himself. At one point he insisted the pills were bismuth, at another morphia. He could not produce his prescription book, and the exact nature of the pills he had given his patient remained in dispute.

Marshall called as his poison expert a Colonel Toobad. The colonel stated that Mabel Greenville died from morphia poisoning, following acute gastroenteritis set up by eating gooseberry skins. Apart from the vomiting, he said, there was no evidence of arsenical poisoning.

Further confusing matters, Dr. William Griffiths, also for the defense, argued that a quarter of a grain of arsenic in a body was not conclusive evidence that it had caused death. He pointed out that a living body could contain two and a half grains of arsenic without any ill effects.

With the medical evidence on the cause of death so obviously in conflict, the public benches were overrun with whispering. Judge Darling banged his gavel and looked at Marshall with disdain. Marshall responded by bowing deeply to the judge, but Graham noticed several of the gentlemen on the jury hid smirks behind their hands.

Having cast doubt on the cause of death, Marshall now sought to disparage the prosecution's claim that the existence of the arsenic was hidden in the Burgundy. The Greenvilles' maid, Eileen, had testified during the prosecution's case that George Greenville was the individual who had decanted and served the wine; even more incriminating, he alone had been in the pantry during the decanting.

Marshall now called Suzanne, the Greenville's daughter, as his witness. Suzanne said she had drunk wine from the same bottle as her mother during the fateful Sunday lunch and "had not felt even the slightest bit queasy." Moreover, she had drunk two glasses to her mother's one. In Graham's view, her evidence demolished the prosecution's case which was built almost entirely upon the administering of the Burgundy by an alleged poisoner.

During his summing-up, Mr. Justice Darling warned the jury against any show of bias. "It is your duty to concentrate wholly upon the guilt or innocence of the prisoner," he told them.

The jury was absent for two and a half hours before the foreman delivered their written verdict to the judge. Judge Darling read the verdict aloud: "We, the jury, are satisfied on the evidence of this case that a dangerous dose of arsenic was administered to Mabel Greenville. But we are not satisfied that this was the immediate cause of death. The evidence before us is insufficient and does not conclusively satisfy us as to how and by whom the arsenic was administered. We therefore return a verdict of not guilty."

Graham sat in silence as the jury filed out. The verdict left any number of pertinent questions unanswered, but the acquittal of George Greenville meant Diana would never be arrested. It was impossible to be charged as George's accomplice, now that George had been acquitted.

Turning to leave, Graham observed George and Nancy Nemeth in a passionate embrace. The nurse's left hand ruffled George's hair, and a large diamond ring sparkled in the lights of the courtroom. It appeared that either George was innocent, as the jury found, or if he had indeed had an accomplice, it was Nancy Nemeth. The thought brightened Graham's spirits immensely.

Graham had a duty to report the verdict to his partners at Smythe and Company. But what he really wanted was to find Diana. Being so close to losing her had made him realize how much he wanted her.

****

Several hours later, Graham burst into chambers. Ivy and Edward immediately broke into applause. "Hannah, the champagne!" yelled Edward.

Graham grinned. "Clearly, the news has preceded me."

Ivy laughed. "John retrieved the news from the blokes at the *Mirror*, as he calls them. They are even now preparing a special edition on the verdict. Marshall is quite the topic of every conversation in every chambers in Lincoln's Inn Fields."

"And rightly so," added Edward. "Although his success has ended a wonderfully juicy case for us before it even had a chance to begin."

Graham slowly exhaled. "Yes. I must find our client and share the good news."

"Plenty of time for that. After all, it was the client who disappeared. Quite cheeky actually. Good thing George was acquitted, or she would be sitting in jail."

"Father." Ivy sighed in exasperation. "Graham has feelings for…"

"Feelings?"

Ivy put her hand on her father's arm. "Shush, I

have news. I know where Diana is hiding."

"How? Where?" Graham was already on his feet.

"I went to visit Mary at Rose Cottage. I thought a heart-to-heart might be helpful."

"Ivy, you are wonderful. Was it?"

"I have an address in Montparnasse." She held out a note, just out of Graham's reach. "But I promised Mary your intentions were honor—"

Graham grabbed the note and was out the door, before Ivy could finish her sentence.

Chapter Twelve

Le Boeuf sur le Toit et Le Mistral Hôtel, Paris

Her promises to Mary to the contrary, Diana was anything but happy in Paris. All she could think of was Graham. She longed for his embrace, his kisses, even his lawyerly sensibilities. No matter what entertainment she engaged in, she could not enjoy herself. Tonight was no exception.

Diana found herself at a celebrated Parisian cabaret: The Ox on the Roof or Le Boeuf sur le Toit, as it was known it French. Le Boeuf was the gathering place for the *avant garde* arts scene after the Great War. Pianists played tunes by George Gershwin and Cole Porter. The audience often included artists such as Pablo Picasso and performers such as Maurice Chevalier.

Jazz musicians from other Paris clubs would show up at Le Boeuf after hours and play long into the night. Jazz, first introduced to Paris by the members of the United States Army during the Great War, was immensely popular on the left bank. Tonight, Diana watched as the American Josephine Baker—wearing only a loincloth of bananas—performed a suggestive dance at a Charleston tempo. Her act met with wild enthusiasm. The French people wanted to forget the war and catch up on the four years that they had lost.

Paris—and Le Boeuf—was at the heart of it all.

But Diana could not forget Graham. She sat in Le Boeuf at a *petite* wrought iron table covered by a white cloth. Having consumed a late meal of *soupe a l'oignon* made with cognac and gruyère cheese melted onto a baguette, she now sipped a champagne cocktail.

Diana caught sight of her reflection in a floor to ceiling mirror with Art Deco etchings. She wore a gown of purple silk, which matched her eyes. A white fur stole graced her slender shoulders and a diamond tiara, adorned with a white feather, encircled her ebony curls. Her chandelier earrings caught the light, creating patterns across the ivory skin of her exposed neck and her translucent pearl necklace. I look much better than I feel, she thought wryly.

Beside her sat Prince Said Fusani, who magically appeared at every cabaret she visited in Paris. "Beautiful, but so distant," the prince purred, as his fingers teased the miniature chandeliers. "Have you brought your riding crop? Your saxophone? What entertainment may I envision tonight?"

Diana widened her eyes as his hand moved up her thigh. Oh Graham, she thought, where are you?

****

Graham left Folkestone Harbor aboard the Southeastern Railway Company's steamship to Boulogne. The railway company operated a fleet of steamships with connecting train-ship-train services between London and Paris. Once in Paris, he hurried to the address provided by Mary, but the residence was dark and the bell went unanswered.

Disheartened, Graham checked into Le Mistral, a hotel named for the strong northwesterly wind that blows from southern France and is rumored to bring good luck. A seventeenth-century edifice on the left bank, it provided access to a number of clubs and restaurants and featured an indoor swimming pool, an outdoor dining terrace, and tranquil courtyard gardens. Despite the indignities the hotel had suffered during the war, the lift to the second floor was in operation and Graham was soon enjoying a bottle of Côte du Rhone in a room dominated by an antique mahogany sleigh bed. *Diana Vanderwell will soon be in this bed beside me,* he swore to himself.

Graham changed into his dressing gown but could not relax. *This is ridiculous,* he thought. *I am in the most charming city in Europe. I should enjoy myself.* There was a cabaret Graham remembered from his time in Paris, immediately after the war: Le Boeuf sur le Toit. Replacing his dressing gown with a Saville Row suit, he exited the hotel and made his way through the streets of the left bank toward Le Boeuf.

****

Diana sat as though paralyzed. Josephine Baker sang "J'ai Deux Amours," and Prince Fusani's hand made its way up her thigh in slow, circular motions. She wanted to object but could not find the energy. She closed her eyes and dreamed of Graham.

"Diana!" Her eyes still shut, she fancied she heard Graham's voice. *Amazing what the imagination can conjure,* she thought. A strong hand suddenly grasped her arm; she bolted upright. Staring into Graham's blue-green eyes, she gasped.

"Graham! Whatever are you doing here?"

"Looking for you. May I sit down?" His voice dropped several degrees. "Or are you otherwise engaged with this…" He paused and looked directly at Said Fusani. "…gentleman?" Graham stood glaring at the prince, until he withdrew his hand from Diana's thigh.

"Actually, I was just leaving. Please take my seat." With a low bow, Prince Fusani disappeared.

Graham took the prince's seat and assumed his position, placing his hand on Diana's thigh—albeit slightly higher. "Is this about right?"

Diana leaned into his touch and reached up to caress his face. There was so much she needed to tell him.

As if reading her mind, he kissed her. A soft, seductive kiss. His tongue teased her lips until they opened, then gently slipped between her teeth; his hand fondled her breasts, stroking her nipples. Without breaking the kiss, his hand rode up her leg above her stockings and garters to stroke her inner thigh. She placed her hand in his lap and felt his passion growing against the fabric of his trousers.

"Graham, we need to find somewhere…"

Much to her dismay, he chuckled and removed his hand. "Do you not want to hear about the trial? Are you not curious about your fate?"

Diana sighed. The moment of truth had come. She had tried everything to escape from the trial and the abominable George Greenville, but it appeared she could not. Rather than the evening of passion she envisioned, she must learn about the law and her imminent arrest as an accomplice to murder. Was this justice? Diana removed her hand from Graham's lap.

****

Graham intended to draw out his rendition of

Marshall's defense, withholding the jury's acquittal of George Greenville as long as possible in order to punish Diana. He wanted her to experience remorse for fleeing London, for being cavalier in her approach to the justice system, for becoming involved with Greenville in the first place, and for her continued "friendships" with men such as Prince Said Fusani. Finding her with the prince had aroused his jealousy, but also his passion. Diana was a woman who would never bore him; he had met his equal. And he would begin treating her as such. It was time for Diana Vanderwell to grow up.

"Your flight from London, particularly after Chief Inspector Fox specifically forbid it, is quite serious." Graham sat back in the uncomfortable wrought iron chair. He firmly placed both of hands on the table, in order to avoid the temptation to touch her.

"I understand. I was very frightened; I am sorry."

"You could face very serious consequences."

"Yes, I know. It was a mistake."

"A serious mistake in judgment, as was your involvement with George as a *friend*."

"I do realize now…George and my other male acquaintances…but I don't need them anymore, don't want them." Diana looked plaintively at Graham. "I have you."

Graham took her in his arms and brought her close; he could not punish her any longer. "It's over, Diana. Truly over. Bloody George Greenville was found not guilty and acquitted. He—and you—are free."

Diana brought her violet eyes to his. "Thank heavens; now can we find somewhere private."

God, I love this woman, Graham thought.

****

C. K. Charlotte

Diana would cherish her memories of the remainder of the evening forever. The taxi ride back to Le Mistral seemed endless. It was almost beyond her powers to sit quietly next to Graham. She so longed to touch him. Once inside the hotel, she quickly sought to locate the lift to his room—remembering the sensations generated by a similar ride at the Savoy.

Much to her dismay she found that other American guests—rumored to be a novelist and his wife—had eliminated the waiting time for the lift to reach their third floor room by rigging its door open with a belt. She and Graham entered the stairwell but found they could only make it up a few steps before they needed to stop. By the second step, he had unzipped her dress; by the fourth step, she had unzipped his trousers. By the time they opened the stairwell door to the second floor, they were, for the most part, undressed.

Entering Graham's room, they were beyond reason. Latching the door, Graham finished undressing Diana. He ran his hands over her naked body, causing it to tingle and tighten. He began stroking her throat, then her breasts. Slowly, he circled her nipples, first with his thumbs, then his tongue. As she softly moaned, he moved his hands to the soft black curls of her mound of Venus, stroking her until she was damp and writhing. He knelt down, licking her until he felt her reach orgasm. When she cried out in ecstasy, he picked her up and carried her to the sleigh bed where he had envisioned her earlier that evening. Laying her on her back, he repeated the process of running his hands over her body. When he again lowered his mouth to pleasure her with his tongue, she called out a single syllable: "Now!"

186

"Now, are you sure?"

Diana mewed and thrust her pelvis toward him in longing. Smiling, he entered her, laughing as they climaxed together.

Diana awoke the next morning to find Graham gazing at her. She reached out to caress his most intimate parts. He kissed her passionately but stilled her hand.

"We must return to London."

"Now? Truly?" She nuzzled up to him. "Couldn't we stay a few more days?"

"We have many things to attend to, Diana," he smiled, "but there is no reason we cannot continue this in London."

"If you say so, my love," Diana said, surprising herself.

"Forever?"

"Yes, my darling, forever." She paused. "If I can have you now." She ran her hands over Graham, feeling him harden. Then rolling over, she gently lowered herself until she felt him throbbing inside her.

Diana was happy.

Chapter Thirteen

Rose Cottage, Chelsea

Diana remained true to her promise to return to London; later that afternoon, Diana and Graham boarded the Calais Express. The train—composed of four sleeping coaches, a restaurant coach, and two baggage cars—was of Art Deco design. The carriages sparkled in their navy and gold livery.

Diana and Graham dined on oysters, soup with Italian pasta, turbot with green sauce, fillet of beef with *château* potatoes, chocolate pudding, a buffet of cheeses, and a bottle of—surprisingly—Burgundy. Thereafter, they retired to their private cabin, where Diana found the swaying of the carriages along the tracks from Paris to Calais increased her pleasures in new and wonderful ways.

"We must make many more train trips," said Diana, after one particularly satisfying episode of lovemaking.

"You are a vixen," Graham teased. "Will you bring your riding crop?"

****

The following day found Diana and Graham at Rose Cottage, in a driving rain. Running through the front garden and pushing open the door, they found the house cold and dark.

"Wherever is Mary?" asked Diana.

Graham held up a note. "It appears, not knowing when you would return from Paris, she has gone to visit her sister."

"We shall have to lay the fire and prepare dinner ourselves." Diana began to pout, then brightened. "But we shall have the evening to ourselves."

"Capital," responded Graham. "I know just how to enjoy it."

A short time later found them lying on a white leopard rug in front of a roaring fire, wearing the pale green cashmere blanket—and nothing else. Graham regarded the rug ruefully. "Is this rug, perhaps, the remains of the creature brought to the Savoy by Prince Fusani, the first time I was so fortunate to lay eyes on him?"

Diana laughed. "I am afraid not. It, as all the furnishings, came with the cottage. I agree, it is an unfortunate choice."

"But very soft," said Graham, gently moving Diana to a reclining position. He stroked the beautiful curving globes of her buttocks. With subtle movements, his hand brushed the folded warmth of her secret places.

"You are exquisite," he whispered, as he stroked.

Except for the beating of the rain, there was silence. Diana weaved her fingers through the hair at the root of his belly. "This is lovely here." She reached up to the vase of daisies Mary had left on a nearby table. Grinning, she threaded the flowers through his love-hair.

Graham laughed, remembering his first visit to Rose Cottage and the viper's bugloss. I would sacrifice my career, my reputation as a barrister, all of it if necessary, to have Diana, he thought.

As if reading his mind, Diana raised her violet eyes to his and sighed. "I love you, only you. I would do anything for you. Love demands nothing less."

"Do you mean it, Diana? Forever?"

"Of course. Forever."

"Then I suppose we must soon be sailing to America to make the acquaintance of a certain publishing magnate in Tennessee. I have something very important to ask him."

"I suppose we must," agreed Diana, abandoning her weaving and pulling Graham close. "I wonder if transatlantic ocean liners are as much fun as trains."

"Vixen," murmured Graham, as he bent to kiss her. "Don't forget the riding crop."

Love and the Pursuit of Redemption

by

C. K. Charlotte

Prologue

Paris, France, November 1917

"What delights may I provide you this afternoon?"
Margarite Hagen inquired of her British lover James
Arthur, the second Duke of Donovan.

The two were enjoying a light luncheon at Les
Ambassadeurs in the Hotel de Crillon. The hotel,
originally designed by Louis XV as a government
building in 1758, had been transformed into a hotel in
1909.

James's view was of the Place de la Concorde,
where Louis XVI and his queen Marie Antoinette were
guillotined during the French revolution. But James
only had eyes for Margarite. Petite with a fair
complexion, Margarite—a well-established courtesan—
wore her blonde hair in ringlets, and her large hazel
eyes missed nothing. She was dressed in a pale green
creation by Messieurs Paquin, one of the leading
couturiers in Paris, and her stylish gown was
complemented by a collection of rubies and pearls.

James found Margarite compellingly attractive. He
could never look at her without remembering the first
time they met. Margarite wore a black top hat, black
silk stockings, a black garter belt, extremely high heels,
a garnet necklace, a chemise of burgundy silk crepe de
Chine—and nothing else.

James was introduced to Margarite on St. George's Day, Monday the 23rd of April 1917. Having received a week's leave from his wartime duties, he drove his new Rolls-Royce coupe to Paris. He installed himself, with his valet, in the hotel Meuric—a comfortable establishment in the Rue de Rivoli. That evening he was escorted to a private suite at the Hotel de Crillon by his best friend and fellow British officer, the Honorable Frederick Henderson—for the purpose of meeting the infamous Margarite Hagen. He was shocked, but delighted, by her appearance in the burgundy chemise. James and Margarite immediately retired to the boudoir where they remained for most of the week.

For the last seven months, James had spent every moment he could steal from the war with her. Margarite was a beautiful woman, excellent company, and highly skilled in the arts of her profession. Her apartment, where he now stayed whenever he was in Paris, was conveniently close to the Bois de Boulogne. James and Margarite would invariably enjoy a morning ride. Lunch was at Les Ambassadeurs, or a similar establishment, and ended at about three o'clock. Afternoons were kept free for their liaisons. Dinner was often in the Bois in one of the lamp hung restaurants such as Au Pre Catalan or the Chateau de Madrid. In the evenings, they might attend the cinema or visit a Montmartre nightclub. Although wartime restrictions required licensed premises to close early, they were not disappointed—for the closures left ample time for a second round of lovemaking.

Now, however, it was November and the XIVth Army HQ—including James—was to be dispatched to Italy. He had not yet shared the news with Margarite, for he did not wish to spoil their time together. But it was time to break off the relationship, and his deployment to Italy provided the perfect opportunity. She was a Parisian courtesan, a *demi-mondaine*. He was a British landowner, son of Earl Victor Arthur, grandson of the first Duke of Donovan, and one of the wealthiest men in England.

He broke from his reverie to gaze fondly at Margarite. "I wish to experience all of your delights this afternoon, my darling. Every single one."

"We had best be going then, my love." Margarite laughed and caressed him discreetly as she rose to leave the table.

****

"I hate you. I hope you are shot in Italy!" Margarite hurled her silver hair brush, a gift from another British admirer, at James.

"I have no choice. My country demands it. I must go. It is my duty." James ducked, and the hairbrush shattered the mirror hanging opposite her bed.

Despite her anger, Margarite took a moment to admire her lover's fractured reflection: tall and muscular, he enjoyed ice blue eyes and stylishly cut hair the color of *café au lait*. His voice was deep and sonorous. She found him irresistible.

"And when the war is over? You will return to me?" Margarite stood naked, hands on hips, eyes narrowed, lips pursed.

"You know I must return to England. To my family, my responsibilities…"

Margarite screamed and reached for the silver hand mirror on her chest of drawers. It hit the door, as James softly closed it behind him.

Chapter One

The Provencal Hotel, Knightsbridge, London
June 1927

Carrying packages from Harrods and Cartier, Margarite Fusani nee Hagen strode past the large green copper lions guarding the corners of the pavilion roofs and entered the newly installed art deco doors of the Provencal Hotel. A frequent visitor of the hotel since the end of the Great War, Margarite enjoyed its prime London location. Situated in Knightsbridge, the elegant property offered twenty-four deluxe rooms, twelve luxury suites, and six fully furnished and serviced apartments as well as proximity to some of London's finest shopping. Margarite also appreciated the hotel's evocative confluence of various Parisian architectural traditions. Its arcade echoed the ground floor of the Place Vendrome and the Riu de Rivoli, while its tall windows and wall panels resembled those of the residence originally built for French statesman Jules François Camille Ferry on Rue Bayard.

Waving off assistance from the hotel staff, Margarite entered the lift and slowly made her way to the fourth floor and the Provencal's luxuriously furnished apartments. Margarite and her husband, Prince Said Fusani, leased Apartment 402 for the month of June. Its entrance was formed by a double set of carved, mahogany doors. Inside, a marbled bathroom was found immediately to the left. To the right lay a short corridor leading to two bedrooms. Each had a double bed covered in silk tapestries and embroidered pillows. Straight ahead lay the drawing room complete with French antiques, including a delicate Louis XIV writing desk. The well-appointed chamber also boasted a working fireplace and a fully stocked bar. Beyond it was a small terrace.

Entering the blissfully empty apartment, Margarite kicked off her pumps and released a sigh of relief. Her marriage to Egyptian millionaire Said Fusani was not all that she had hoped. That morning they had come to blows, not for the first time in their marriage. She was forced to ask her maid, Aimee, to cover her bruises with makeup before she could leave her suite. She was grateful for the opportunity to avoid her husband for a while longer.

Margarite first met her husband in Paris. Said was making his annual tour of Europe taking in Paris, Biarritz, and Monte Carlo. Margarite, ten years older than Said, was fascinated by the young Egyptian. Delighted by his obvious infatuation with her, she began to envision the possibilities of a life she had only read about in *A Thousand and One Nights*. She was wooed by his passionate words of love and promises of vast wealth. They had married in Egypt in an extravagant civil ceremony, later followed by a restrained religious one.

Margarite could not help but smile when she thought of her wedding at Shepheard's Hotel in Cairo. Built in the 1840s, Shepheard's was famed for its grandeur and opulence. During the Great War, it served as British Headquarters in the Near East. On the night of the civil ceremony, it was packed with fifteen hundred guests. A jazz band belted out the latest favorites, "Ain't We Got Fun" and "I'm Just Wild About Harry." There was barely dancing room under the great chandelier, decorated in cascades of bougainvillea. At midnight the lights were dimmed, and two dozen white doves were released from the balcony, while bags of white confetti were emptied on the heads of the onlookers. In the early morning hours, the newlyweds and their entourage departed for a romantic journey out of town to gaze upon the pyramids by moonlight.

But as Margarite quickly learned, life with Said had an undesirable dimension. The young Egyptian was handsome and extremely rich. From the day he came into his inheritance, he was found to be immensely attractive by any number of women. Since their marriage, Margarite was aware that he had engaged in affairs in Egypt, France, and elsewhere.

Margarite tensed as a key turned in the lock.

"Madam. Are you at home?" Aimee's voice echoed with concern as she entered the apartment, having traveled from the eighth floor where she shared accommodations with another guest's maid.

"In here, Aimee," Margarite called from the drawing room.

"Is there anything you need, madam?"

"A new husband," Margarite churlishly replied. Then she brightened. "But I am feeling much better since shopping." She held up her purchases.

"Prince Fusani left word he would be spending the afternoon and early evening at his club, but he will meet you downstairs in the dining room for a late supper."

"The restaurant here is so stuffy." Margarite pouted.

"It serves a lovely Yorkshire pudding," Aimee attempted to placate her mistress.

"But the orchestra is beyond sedate; they are simply melancholy. And the clientele, they are a crowd of well-dressed non-entities. I would prefer the Savoy."

"Prince Fusani did not offer any alternatives."

"Of course not," Margarite observed wryly. "But the Savoy Grille is much more lively. Personalities from the theater are likely to dine there."

Aimee paused to choose her words carefully. "I am afraid it was not a request, madam."

"Very well. Perhaps we might visit the Savoy ballroom for dancing afterward." Margarite exhaled. "I must rest now, Aimee."

Margarite retired to her bedroom. Undressing, she removed the small pearl-handled pistol hidden in her garter and gently placed it under her embroidered pillow.

****

James Arthur, the second Duke of Donovan, was enjoying a late night dinner at the Provencal with Lily Pomerville, one of his many female companions. Just as he raised his first glass of wine to toast the beautiful Lily, a shriek broke out.

"Who was that woman you were talking to when I entered the restaurant? One of your fancy women no doubt!" a woman sitting behind James yelled, her French accent familiar.

"A whore you mean," an accented male voice

retorted. "Certainly you could be expected to recognize one."

"Be quiet! Or I shall break this bottle of wine over your head!"

"Do so and I will return the favor, my love!"

James and Lily paused in mid-toast and stared at each other in amazement.

"What on earth..." James turned in his chair to determine the cause of the disturbance. He paused in mid-sentence, unable to believe his eyes. An elegant, bejeweled blonde in a pale blush satin Chanel gown stood holding a wine bottle over the head of her youthful white-tie-and-tailed Middle Eastern companion.

James blinked several times to clear his vision, but it did not change. The woman was Margarite Hagen. He had not seen her for almost ten years, but he still thought of her almost every day.

Lily was amused. "Do you know who that is?"

"Do you?" James raised his eyebrows.

"Prince and Princess Said Fusani." She smiled sarcastically. "Loving newlyweds."

"P-P-Princess?" James stuttered.

"Actually, he is not really a prince, but he does little to discourage the use of the title when he is away from Egypt. Filthy rich, I understand. His family made a fortune on cotton during the war."

"They are truly married?"

Lily laughed. "Do you never read the *Mirror* or the *Herald*? It must be over a year now."

James nodded absently.

"Do you know what they say about her?"

James feigned ignorance.

Lily bent closer and whispered, "They say she was a high-class Parisian hooker and notorious gold digger. She had affairs with some of the wealthiest men in Europe during the war, hoping to snare a rich husband."

James winced. A vision of Margarite in a chemise of burgundy silk crepe de Chine—and nothing else—flooded his memory. He blushed.

Lily continued, "As for the prince, he is considerably younger than she. A rich Egyptian playboy, who is besotted with her and intensely jealous. It is said they are forever clawing and scratching each other, biting and kicking."

James took another look behind him. Margarite and Said, apparently calmed by the efforts of the head waiter, were bent over the table in intense conversation. Frowning, not touching, bodies rigid, it was clear the conversation was not a romantic one. He watched, fascinated. The prince reached across to touch the still exceptionally beautiful Margarite. She raised her small hand, as if to stroke his cheek, then suddenly scratched him—drawing blood. James gasped as the prince grabbed her roughly by the arm. Fortunately, the head waiter chose that moment to intervene.

James returned his attention to Lily, to find her staring at him with concentration. "You are very pale. It is as though you have seen a ghost."

James sighed. The relationship he shared with Lily was not one which would accommodate a discussion of his affair with Margarite Hagen while stationed in Paris during the Great War. Margarite was the most exciting woman he had ever known; the most desirable even in this room. Try as he might, he could not forget her.

Because of Margarite, no other woman—even the

lovely Lily—could hold his attention. He was devastated to find she had married, particularly to a man such as Said Fusani. Turning to glance their way once again, James smiled ruefully. Apparently, Margarite enjoyed so many lovers she does not remember me, he mused.

Several glasses of wine later, movement caught James's eye. The Fusanis were leaving the dining room. Slowly Margarite made her way toward the exit, her eyes downcast. Just as she passed his table, James felt her hand touch his knee. As she removed it, she left a calling card of creamy vellum. Discreetly turning it over, James read a hand-written message:

"My love,

Meet me at the Gargoyle Club tomorrow afternoon at one o'clock. I must see you.

Yours always, M."

Chapter Two

Black's Club, London

James awoke from a dream of a chemise-clad Margarite to sunlight streaming into his sleeping chambers at Donovan House. Donovan House, the official residence of his family in London, stood at Hyde Park Corner and faced east toward a busy traffic roundabout.

Even more than Preston Place, his family's estate in Cheshire, James loved Donovan House. It enjoyed an excellent location in the heart of London. More importantly, it contained his grandfather's—the first Duke of Donovan—world renowned collection of paintings, porcelain, silver, and sculpture.

James's favorite work of art was Antonio Canova's marble nude of Napoleon, as Mars the Peacemaker, holding a gilded Nike in the palm of his right hand. The sculpture stood guard in the grand hall to welcome all who entered Donovan House. In contrast, James's compatriots at Black's Club most enjoyed the eighty-three paintings acquired by the first duke in 1813 after the Battle of Vitoria. The paintings had been in Joseph Bonaparte's baggage train and were part of what the club members commonly called "the biggest loot in history."

James's favorite room in Donovan House was the

drawing room with its apsidal end—a semicircular recess covered with a hemispherical, semi dome painted in sky blue and gold leaf. His companions at Black's Club again had a different view, however. They much preferred the double height Waterloo Gallery, occupying the entire length of the first floor of the eastern side of the building. Designed in an opulent gilded Louis XIV style, it boasted seven mirrored window shutters inspired by the Galerie des Glaces at the Palace of Versailles. Black's Club members had whiled away many interesting evenings within the red damask walls of the Waterloo Gallery.

"Plans for today, sir? Will you be wanting breakfast?" James's ruminations on Donovan House were interrupted by the arrival of his butler, Johnathan, with the morning tea.

Johnathan carefully deposited the tray on the small mahogany table facing the floor to ceiling windows looking out on the roundabout.

"Actually, I shall be breakfasting at Black's Club this morning—with Bryan Henderson. We have several things to discuss. Later, I shall be lunching at the Gargoyle."

"Ah. The Honorable Bryan Henderson." Johnathan smirked. "Still eluding arrest, is he? The beautiful young barrister he married has something to do with that, I dare say."

"Johnathan, enough," James warned, with a knowing smile. He took a sip of tea and began to dress.

****

James approached Black's Club in good spirits. His father and grandfather had both been members of Black's Club, one of the oldest and most exclusive gentlemen's clubs in London. The club was well known for its aristocratic members as well as its hijinks. Recently gambling aristocrats had left a member lying on the pavement outside the club during a thunderstorm, rather than abandoning the bets they had placed on whether he could rise of his own accord. James found it a welcome respite from his daily duties as the second Duke of Donovan.

James also enjoyed his weekly breakfasts with the Honorable Bryan Henderson. Bryan was the younger brother of his former best friend, Cambridge roommate, and fellow officer, Frederick Henderson. It was Frederick who first introduced James to Margarite, when both young men were posted to Paris during the war. Following Frederick's death while stationed in Italy, Bryan became heir to the Hendersons' considerable estates. He also became one of James's closest friends.

James grinned as he considered Johnathan's earlier inappropriate remarks regarding Bryan and his wife, Ivy. Several years ago, while still single and an active member of London's society of bright young people, Bryan was accused of murdering several prostitutes. He was ultimately found innocent and released but not before falling madly in love with Ivy Smythe, the beautiful barrister charged with defending him. Ivy and Bryan married soon thereafter and appeared to have the perfect union. Ivy still practiced law with her father, Edward, and another of James's fellow officers during the Great War, Graham Wetherington.

James was particularly anxious to meet with Bryan this morning, prior to his lunch with Margarite at the Gargoyle. He was in need of a discreet sounding board for the appropriate forms of release for his admittedly amorous feelings toward his former lover.

Passing a bow window jutting out from the ground floor, James entered the club and proceeded to the dining room. "Good morning, my fine fellow," he greeted Bryan, who was perusing the morning papers. "What is new in the world? How is the lovely Ivy?"

Bryan stood, shook his hand, and pulled out a chair. "So good to see you, James. Ivy is wonderful, thank you for asking. Her law practice continues to prosper. Smythe and Company will be turning away clients before long.

"As to the news"—Bryan's eyes returned momentarily to the paper—"let's see. The most amusing story is running in the *Herald* in Ruby Sharp's column. It appears Prince and Princess Fasuni were involved in another altercation at the Provencal last night."

"You read the gossip columns?" James raised his eyebrows in surprise.

"On occasion, old chap, on occasion. Plus, this particular post is of special interest to me. You may remember that my brother Frederick, God bless his soul, was an acquaintance of Princess Fusani, formerly known as Mademoiselle Margarite Hagen."

"Yes, I remember. All too well."

"I am sorry, old chap." Bryan grimaced. "Of course. I had forgotten, you were quite smitten with Mademoiselle Hagen during the war yourself." He paused. "A good deal of time has passed. Have you seen her since you left Paris for the Italian front?"

"Not until last night."

"Last night?"

"At the Provencal, scene of the scandalous altercation reported by the *Herald*."

"You were there?"

"Only as an observer. I had taken Lily to the hotel restaurant for dinner."

"Pray tell, did Margarite truly threaten to bean the prince with a wine bottle?" Bryan leaned forward in anticipation.

"I am afraid so. It was quite sad." James shook his head.

"I cannot imagine what enticed her to marry that savage." Bryan sighed. "Did Margarite recognize you?"

"I thought not. But when the happy couple left the restaurant, she handed me this." James pulled the rumpled note from the pocket of his impeccable Saville Row suit and passed it to Bryan.

"*Meet me at the Gargoyle Club.*" Bryan read aloud. "Are you going?"

"I don't rightly see that I have much choice."

"Of course you do. You are one of the wealthiest men in London, a duke. You own the most beautiful house in London as well as one of the finest country estates. You are involved in untold worthy causes and business ventures." He stopped to take a breath. "You knew this woman—albeit in the Biblical sense—a long time ago, in another country. A woman who made her living during the war as a courtesan. A woman who is now married to a violent foreigner, no less. Why in bloody hell…?" Bryan stopped in midsentence. "Oh, I see."

"Right." James smiled ruefully. "I am afraid that I am still smitten."

"That smitten? After all this time? Given all the

differences that remain between you? What do you intend to do?"

"I honestly do not know," James confessed. "I just know I still have feelings for her…strong feelings. Do you have any advice?"

Bryan drew in a sharp breath and appeared to utter the first thought that entered his head. "Abort the mission."

"Abort the mission?" James was amused.

"Before the prince kills you, old chap. Before the prince kills you."

Chapter Three

The Gargoyle Club, London

Margarite sat before the petite dressing table in the larger bedroom of the Provencal suite, preparing for her luncheon at the Gargoyle Club. Carefully, she dabbed makeup over the bruises on her face and arms. The argument with Said in the Provencal's dining room the prior evening had escalated once they reached the apartment. Marriage had changed Said from a generous, creative lover to a jealous, violent fiend.

"How wrong I was to believe I could find security in marriage," she said aloud.

"Yes, madam," answered Aimee as she inspected and carefully stored Margarite's purchases from the day before. "Prince Fusani has changed since we first met him in Paris."

"I was destitute as a child," Margarite continued.

"Yes, madam," agreed Aimee who had heard this story many times.

"My father was a cab driver, my mother a scullery maid."

"Yes, madam."

"I was very young when I became a cabaret singer, then a dancer at the Follies Bergeres. I was pleased when important men showed an interest in me. Delighted to have nice things, a lovely place to live."

"I understand, madam."

"I was one of the most accomplished and sophisticated courtesans in Paris during the war. It was an honorable way to make a living. I harmed no one." She paused and allowed herself a small smile. "I pleased many."

"I know, madam."

"So how have I come to this? To be ridiculed and insulted by a man who promised to love and protect me? To be assaulted?" Margarite touched the bruise still visible beneath her eye, despite her best efforts.

She turned from the looking glass to face Aimee. Aimee, eyes averted, merely shook her head.

Margarite rose to inspect the contents of her wardrobe. "I will not tolerate this situation any longer. Today will be different." She removed an expertly tailored skirted suit in a deep shade of jade green which complemented her hazel eyes and emphasized her figure. "I shall wear this with the Hermes scarf I purchased yesterday, Aimee. What do you think?"

Aimee tilted her head as she inspected Margarite's choice. "Where shall you be wearing this, madam?"

"The Gargoyle, for lunch. I am meeting an old friend."

Aimee shifted her gaze from the jade suit to Margarite. "The duke?" She grinned. "I saw him enter the hotel last evening; he is an exceptionally attractive man. It has been a long time since he was with us in Paris, madam. But I remember him fondly." Her face darkened. "What of the prince, madam?"

"I am a married woman, and unlike my husband, I honor my vows. I am only going to talk with an old friend and hopefully obtain a much needed reference."

Margarite eyed her sternly. "But Aimee, the prince must know nothing of this."

"A reference, madam?"

"I must protect myself. I wish to speak to a London solicitor about divorce."

Aimee drew in a sharp breath and articulated the fear foremost in Margarite's mind. "The prince will kill you, madam!"

****

On his way to the Gargoyle Club to meet Margarite, James reflected on their last afternoon in Paris during the war. How could he have treated her so cruelly? He was young, but that was hardly an excuse for his behavior. At least not in hindsight. She had truly been the love of his life; he had never met another woman to compare with her.

James's reverie was broken as he rounded the corner onto Dean Street and viewed the Gargoyle Club. The Gargoyle, a chic nightclub, was home to the bright young people—the nickname given by the tabloid press to the group of youthful bohemian aristocrats and socialites currently fascinating London. Bryan Henderson had once been counted among its members; James had many friends among their ranks.

In the evening, fashionable young men in dinner jackets and flappers in cloche hats dominated the Gargoyle, dancing the Charleston, champagne glasses in hand. But during the daytime, it was a refuge for writers, painters, poets, and musicians who were sold good food and wine at affordable prices. The artist Henri Matisse, a member of the Gargoyle Club, had designed the Moorish interior mirrored with pieces of eighteenth century glass. The ghost of Charles II's mistress, Nell Gwyn, was rumored to haunt the premises although James had never glimpsed her.

James entered the club and waited impatiently for the rickety lift. Exiting the gilded cage on the first floor, he perused the ballroom, bar, coffee room, and drawing room searching for Margarite. He found her seated at a small table in the drawing room, nursing a champagne cocktail. She looked stunning in a jade suit with a fashionably short skirt. He had forgotten she was rumored to have the most attractive legs in Paris. Margarite smiled, and the room noticeably brightened.

"Am I late?" James kissed her on both cheeks in the European fashion.

"No, I am afraid I am unfashionably early." Margarite frowned. "My apartment at the Provencal has become unbearable."

James sat beside her and grasped her hand. "It is so good to see you. You look as marvelous as ever." He touched her cheek.

Snatching his hand, she winced. "Perhaps not as young, or as carefree."

James was taken aback, but decorum prevented him from asking the questions that were most on his mind. "What have you been doing since I saw you last?" He chose what he hoped was an innocuous inquiry.

"Well, as you see I have married. It has been more than a year now."

"Do you have children?"

"No, not yet. Perhaps never."

"Are you happy, Margarite?"

"I was in the beginning. It was as though a fairy tale had come true. But lately…" Margarite looked down, and a single tear stained the white linen tablecloth.

James could not bear to see her unhappy. "Come, let's order lunch, and I shall amuse you with my adventures from the war."

The waiter brought a decanter of Pinot Noir with two Waterford glasses. "A toast"—James raised his glass—"to our reunion."

A luncheon of oysters, braised chicken with asparagus and boiled potatoes, and flavored ices followed. True to his promise, James regaled Margarite with stories of his wartime assignments in Italy, his return to England, and his re-assumption of duties as the second Duke of Donovan.

"And your wife, the duchess?" Margarite asked.

"I have never married, Margarite."

"The woman who accompanied you to dinner last evening?"

"Lily? One of many companions."

"Your position in society does not require you to marry? To produce children? 'Issue' is how I believe you referred to your future heirs when we were last together in Paris."

"Did I?" James gulped.

"Indeed. I remember the moment exactly. The gist of the conversation being that our relationship must end with your posting in Italy because your position in society required you to marry and produce *issue* with a woman of a similar class. 'An aristocrat rather than a courtesan' is how I believe you expressed it."

"Did I?" James repeated himself and poured a second glass of wine.

Margarite raised an eyebrow but remained silent.

"I…I…" James stuttered, then tried again. "England has changed since the war. The pressure to marry and produce an heir is not as intense. My mother barely mentions it."

"Is that so?" Margarite's eyebrow inched ever higher.

"Well, of course I will marry eventually. I…I…I simply have not met the right woman." James finished with a flourish, throwing out his hand and sending his crystal goblet crashing to the carpet. Hopefully that will end this conversation, he thought.

As the waiter replaced the goblet and poured more wine, James decided it would be wise to change the subject. "Was there something you wished to speak with me about besides old times, Margarite?"

Margarite's silence in response was deafening. James thought perhaps she might not have heard him. At last she asked, "Why did you never contact me, after the war?"

James sighed. "I wanted to. Truly I did. But it seemed unfair. The only relationship I could offer you was the one we had, with you as my mistress. I cared for you. I wanted you to have more."

"And so I have: a handsome and wealthy young husband, homes in Paris and Cairo, luxury apartments in London and Deauville, race horses, speed boats, motor cars, priceless jewels, and designer gowns." She rose, as if to take leave.

"And a black eye," James blurted out, surprising himself.

"Yes, and a black eye." Margarite sat back down. "And a broken spirit."

"Margarite, how can I help you?" James

whispered, leaning forward and grasping both of her hands.

"I am considering divorce, but my husband is very influential." She paused. "You perhaps have connections in London, a solicitor I could speak with privately."

James was thoughtful. "Of course. I will be glad to make inquiries."

"It must be confidential."

"Yes, I understand. But the prince…" James took a deep breath. How could he express the fears raised by Bryan this morning without alarming Margarite? His discretion proved unnecessary.

Margarite looked him directly in the eyes. "If my husband discovers I have inquired about divorce, he will most certainly kill me." She paused. "And you, as well."

Chapter Four

The Provencal Hotel, Knightsbridge, London

The following evening found Margarite once again at her dressing table camouflaging her bruises. Aimee stood behind her, reflected in the mirror, working to fasten a string of translucent pearls about her neck.

"You look beautiful tonight, madam."

"Thank you, Aimee." Margarite beamed.

"These pearls glow as if from the moon herself. I have not seen them for a very long time."

"No, I have not worn them for many years." Margarite sighed. "Too many memories." She glanced up and caught Aimee's expression in the mirror.

"*Mon dieu!*" Aimee gasped, suddenly remembering the provenance of the pearls.

"I see you remember the gentleman who gifted them."

"The duke, Paris, 1917." Aimee gazed solemnly at her mistress in the mirror.

"I have recently had reason to revive his memory." Margarite's smile was now bittersweet. "Come Aimee, help me finish dressing." Margarite stood and turned to face Aimee. Dressed only in her stockings and chemise, the small pearl-handled pistol was visible in her garter.

"Of course, madam." Aimee obediently slid the black sequined gown over Margarite's outstretched arms. Fashionably short, it fell seductively over her voluptuous figure. Its low-cut neckline revealed her snow-white breasts and showcased the pearls.

Margarite admired herself in the mirror, then turned and hugged Aimee.

"Madam, what of the prince? What will he say about the pearls?"

"I pray he will not notice, Aimee."

"But he is accompanying you to the Cavendish tonight, is he not?"

"Yes. In fact, it was his idea. But given his beastly behavior lately, I needed a talisman to remind me of happier times."

"And do you expect to see the duke at the Cavendish, madam?" Aimee frowned.

"I do not know. If I should, he will know I am thinking of him."

"Madam…" Aimee began to protest.

"Please let the prince know I am dressed and prepared to accompany him." Margarite abruptly silenced her loyal maid with an upraised hand.

Aimee frowned as she left to locate the prince.

****

"I hear you are ready for a wonderful evening, my dear. How delicious you look." Said Fusani leered at his wife, standing in the suite's spacious drawing room.

I must try and make this marriage work, Margarite thought. She gazed at her husband's reflection in the mirror above the Louis XIV desk, where she had been admiring her appearance. She turned with outstretched arms, intending to embrace him. The lights from the Waterford chandelier overhead illuminated the pearls; sparkles of brilliance danced in the opulent room.

The prince's countenance darkened. "Another new necklace, my love? I have not had a request for approval from Cartier's."

"It is old. I have had it for many years." Margarite sighed.

"I am sure I would remember such an exquisite necklace, my dear." The prince stepped forward and fingered the pearls. Suddenly his hands tightened on her neck.

"Come, Said. Let's not argue. Our friends will be expecting us at the Cavendish." Margarite loosened his grip and stepped back.

"You dare to order me about. You! A harlot wearing another man's gift, payment no doubt for services rendered." The prince moved menacingly in Margarite's direction, his hand raised as if to slap her. "I think not."

Instinctively, Margarite's fingers brushed the pearl-handled revolver through the fabric of her gown.

The prince smirked. "What have you there, Margarite?" He stepped closer, within striking distance. "Your gun perhaps?" He put his hand on her cheek and looked into her eyes. His hand moved lower, until it rested on her thigh and the pistol. "Will you shoot me?" As he spoke, he grabbed the gun through her gown and pulled it from her garter.

With a cry, Margarite stepped back against the antique desk. Said dropped the pistol. It clattered to the floor.

"You wench!" Chuckling, the prince reached down and retrieved the small pearl-handled gun. "I have always thought this quite an attractive item. Which one of your lovers is this from? You never did tell me."

"It is mine, Said. Another item I have had for years, from before the war." She held out her hand. "Please, return it to me."

The prince turned the gun over for a more careful review. "I think not, my dear. Who knows what damage it might cause? I think I must keep it." He raised his arm and aimed the pistol at her heart. "It may come in handy."

"You fool!" shouted Margarite. Reaching for the gun, her heel caught in the oriental carpet. She fell forward into Said. The weapon discharged.

Laughing, the prince turned toward the wall where the bullet had lodged. "You must be more careful, my dear."

"I despise you, Said!" Margarite grabbed the pistol from his hand. "I will shoot you one day! I promise!"

****

Fleeing the suite, Margarite nearly collided with the night porter. Known only as "Clive," he hovered scandalously close to the door of Apartment 402.

"May I help you, Princess Fusani? Is something amiss?" Clive's eyes strayed to the small pistol clasped in her hand.

"No. Nothing." Margarite moved the gun behind her back. "It is just that I am in a terrible hurry."

"No doubt, Princess. No doubt."

Margarite looked at him sharply and hurried down the hall. She paused to deposit the pistol in her evening bag, before ringing for the lift. She turned back to find Clive eyeing her cautiously as he commenced knocking on the door to the Fusani apartment.

"Prince Fusani, is everything satisfactory?" Margarite heard Clive yelling through the heavy mahogany doors. "A guest has reported a gunshot, sir. And"—Clive paused and returned his gaze to Margarite, as she rang a second time for the lift—"a woman's voice threatening to shoot you. Promising to shoot you, Prince. Please open…"

Margarite leapt onto the lift without waiting for it to come to a complete stop. Clutching her evening bag, she closed her eyes and sank to the floor. The lift slowly descended to ground level. Clive's voice echoed in her ears: "a woman's voice…promising to shoot you, Prince."

Chapter Five

The Cavendish Hotel, London

"The Cavendish Hotel. Please hurry." Rudely bypassing the valet, Margarite jumped into the first waiting taxi in the Provencal's motor court.

The scene with Said upset her greatly. The Cavendish was the only place she could think of to go. James was the only man she wanted to see; she did hope he would be there.

The taxi ride from the Provencal to the Cavendish seemed endless. She was not accustomed to examining her feelings, but suddenly she was drowning in them.

On the one hand was Said. They had marvelous times together when they were courting and during the first few months of their marriage. She had loved him, very much. Even now, when she feared for her life almost daily, she did not seriously wish to harm him. She only wished to be free of him.

On the other hand was James. Spending the last few days with him had brought back the wonderful times they had shared in Paris. She had relished the morning rides in the Bois de Boulogne, the long lunches at Les Ambassadeurs, the dinners in the lamp-hung restaurants in the Bois. She smiled. She had especially enjoyed the long afternoons kept free for their liaisons; James was an imaginative lover. Even more, he was a valued friend and confidant.

"My marriage is over," she murmured, reaching a decision. She pulled the small gun from her evening bag and eyed it sadly.

"Pardon, madam?" The driver sought to catch her eye in the rearview mirror but caught sight instead of the pearl-handled pistol. Margarite pulled up the hem of her gown and replaced it in her garter.

****

Margarite adjusted her frock and concealed her weapon as the taxi pulled up to the unassuming brick front and large plain doorway of the Cavendish Hotel. Even outside, the music was exceedingly loud.

"The Cavendish has the best jazz in the city," the driver confided.

Margarite exited without comment and entered a drawing room crowded with bright young people, as well as too much furniture. Slowly she maneuvered around red plush settees and morocco leather chairs, estate maps, archery targets, croquet mallets, and polo sticks, all mixed in with photographs of men on horseback and yachts in full sail.

"Margarite! Princess!" A group of the most fashionable members of London society called out to her. She plastered on her brightest smile as she made her way to her friends.

"Margarite, where is Said?" Lady Katherine Bolyn, a great admirer of the prince, asked breathlessly.

"Oh Kate, I am so sorry. H-h-he's not feeling well this evening." Margarite stuttered as she struggled for a reply. "So v-v-very tiresome. And how very much I would enjoy a champagne cocktail to lift my spirits." Her hand shook as she reached to grab the desired concoction from a passing waiter's tray.

Taking a sip, she began to sway. Just as she feared she might collapse, she felt a muscular arm encircle her waist.

"Allow me, please," a deep voice whispered in her ear. Turning her head, she gazed into the ice blue eyes of the second Duke of Donovan.

"James! Oh, how glad I am to see you!"

"How beautiful you look! I would know those pearls anywhere." He grinned, but a troubled look clouded his eyes.

"What is it?" Margarite asked, hypervigilant.

"The pearls, they bring back so many memories." His hand caressed the pearls, then her neck, dropping slowly to a spot near her cleavage.

His touch caused a thrill to run though her. Images of their passionate afternoons in her Paris apartment near the Bois de Boulogne flooded her imagination. She shook her head. "James, I must…"

"My dear Duke, what a pleasure." Lady Katherine, living up to her reputation of being ever on the lookout for attractive male companionship, descended upon them. She paused, appraising them. "I see you two have met." A frown crossed her otherwise pleasing countenance, followed by a cough. "Of course, the war. I remember now. Please excuse me." She winked at James. "I am sure you have much to discuss. But save a dance for me."

"Insufferable woman," muttered James. "I wish I had never met her. She…"

"James, I must speak with you," Margarite interrupted, not to be deterred. "There has been an altercation. Said…" She moved closer to James, standing on tiptoe to whisper in his ear.

****

The scent of Lanvin, the brush of blonde hair against his cheek, the warmth of Margarite's voluptuous body pressing against him flooded James with memories. He stiffened as he remembered his introduction to Margarite in Paris. Whatever had become of the burgundy silk chemise, he wondered.

"You are breathtaking." James's hand caressed her cheek. "How did I ever leave you? Why did I ever leave you?"

"You had other obligations, the war, your country, your family, the estate." She sighed and looked away. "I do understand now. But oh! How I wish I had been born in another place, another time…a place and time where we could be together."

"Margarite." James reached over and turned her head until she faced him. He slowly traced her open lips. Then he gently slipped his tongue between her teeth. His hand moved down to fondle her breast. He felt the heat in his groin. He stroked her nipples. His member rose. How he wanted her; his position and responsibilities be damned.

****

Margarite closed her eyes and leaned into his embrace. But her mind raced. She was, after all, still a married woman. One whom had always honored her marriage vows, despite the actions of her playboy husband.

"James." She opened her eyes and pulled away. Taking a deep breath, she returned to their earlier conversation. "I nearly killed Said this evening."

"Killed him? Divorce I understand, but murder?"

His hands dropped to his sides.

She smiled in spite of herself. "He's fine. You can relax." Lowering herself into a red plush settee, she continued, "We tussled; the gun went off. He laughed at me. I told him I would shoot him, someday."

James groaned and joined her on the settee. "This simply cannot continue. A gun." He paused shaking his head. "Wherever did it come from?"

"Paris." Smiling wryly, Margarite discreetly raised the hem of her dress to reveal the pearl-handled pistol.

"My God!" James yanked the gown down.

Shivers of pleasure shot through her as his fingers touched her thighs. Leaning forward, she allowed her lips to brush his.

He sighed and reached for her. "I want you."

"And I you. But first, I must return to the Provencal and speak to Said. You are absolutely correct, this cannot continue."

"I'll accompany you." James stood.

"No, I must do this alone."

"He will kill you."

"I am not afraid." Margarite patted the pistol now hidden within her gown. "We shall see who has the last word." She strode to the door.

****

"A penny for your thoughts?" Lady Katherine stroked James's arm affectionately.

"So beautiful," James murmured as he watched a distraught Margarite disappear.

"Thank you, kind sir." Lady Katherine performed a mock curtsy.

"Right." James, realizing his mistake, slowly began removing his arm from her grasp. "Kate, I…"

"How have you been, James?" Lady Katherine simpered. "One hears so much about you these days. Your estate, your title. 'Duke' suits you well, I must say." She grasped his arm tighter, cutting off his escape.

"Kate, I…"

"All you are in need of is a duchess, I understand. A member of the gentry." She moved in closer, stroking his cheek. "An aristocrat without a past. One who has never married, of course."

James could tolerate her advances no longer. Nasty woman; so different from Margarite. How could he have let Margarite go to face Said alone, without support? Bollocks, how could he have left Margarite go, ever? Her past be damned. She was the woman he loved.

"Kate, I…" More brusquely than he intended, he removed himself from Lady Katherine's clutches. "I must go."

"So soon? We have just begun to reconnect."

Bloody hell, thought James. Outwardly he graciously kissed her hand. "I have pressing business to attend to."

Without further explanation, he moved toward the door of the Cavendish. His last impression was of Lady Katherine staring after him, open-mouthed.

Chapter Six

The Provencal Hotel, Knightsbridge, London

It had been an exceptionally hot day in London. By the time Margarite returned to the Provencal, there was almost continuous thunder. Exiting the lift on the fourth floor, Margarite entered Apartment 402 and moved toward the darkened drawing room. The suite was illuminated only by intermittent flashes of lightning.

Switching on the Waterford chandelier, she nearly screamed. Said sat behind the Louis the XIV desk, twirling the evil looking Egyptian dagger he used as a letter opener. Made with a cast gold blade, the knife contained thirty-two ounces of pure gold. Said claimed it was an exact replica of the gold dagger found in King Tutankhamun's tomb, opened by the British several years earlier. The knife never failed to unnerve Margarite.

"I have been waiting for you, my love." Said continued toying with the dagger.

"I must speak with you, Said. Please put that ghastly thing down."

"And I you. Where have you been?" Said rose, twisting the knife.

"The Cavendish, as we had originally intended. Lady Katherine inquired of your whereabouts."

"The lovely Kate." Said advanced, still holding the

dagger.

"And what did you do this evening?"

Said smirked. "I went to the West End—Piccadilly to be precise."

"In this weather? In full evening dress? For what purpose?"

"Oh, there are many interesting people there."

"Prostitutes you mean."

"Speaking of harlots." Said snorted. "I see you are still wearing the pearls." He reached out and touched her neck with his free hand.

Margarite tensed. "Said, I cannot go on this way any longer."

"And what way is that, my darling?" His hand stroked her neck.

Margarite shuddered. How I have come to hate his touch, she thought. How I wish it was James's. She looked up to see the hatred in Said's eyes as she felt his hand tighten around her neck.

"Which part of your life is so unbearable, Margarite? The lavish homes in Cairo and Pairs? The apartments in London and Deauville? The motorcars? The speedboats? The jewels? Perhaps it is all that shopping that has you so depressed? Come my dear, do share what makes you so unhappy."

Margarite found it difficult to breathe as her husband tightened his grasp. "We are both unhappy." She gasped. "Doing things we regret, things that are unworthy of us. The other things, the material things, ultimately they do not really matter, Said."

"Don't they, my dear?" Said loosened his grip and returned to stroking her neck. "You will be perfectly happy without the material things, as you so dismissively refer to them?" His hand reached down to stroke her cleavage.

Feeling ill, Margarite involuntarily took a step back out of his reach. "Said, please, we must…"

"We 'must' my dear?" Said frowned and took a step forward. His hand sought out her cleavage. "As your husband, I decide what we 'must' do. And my love, at the moment what I 'must' do is…" His cold, reptilian eyes focused upon hers. "This." His hand traveled lower, roughly grabbing at her most intimate parts.

"I hate you, Said!" Margarite reached up and scratched his cheek, drawing blood.

Said howled in pain, before landing a resounding slap against the side of her head.

Slightly dizzy, Margarite heard a knock at the door as she sought to return the blow.

"Be still!" Said ordered as he returned the knife to the desk. With a fierce warning look in her direction, he moved gracefully toward the door of the apartment where the incessant pounding continued.

As he opened the door, Margarite heard Clive's Cockney accent. "Good evening, Prince Fusani. Is everything satisfactory?" He paused. "I am sorry, sir, but there have been more complaints about the noise."

"I see." Margarite could hear the barely controlled anger in Said's voice. "I fear things are less than satisfactory, Clive. Look at my face!" His voice rose. "Look at what my wife has done! I am bleeding! My dear wife, so soon after threatening to shoot me, has now physically assaulted me."

"I do regret such an incident, Prince Fusani." Margarite thought that Clive's reply showed little

229

interest in Said's injury. "Nevertheless, I must ask you to quiet down. I am afraid you are disturbing our other guests quite frequently tonight."

In response, Margarite heard only the slam of the door and Said's cursing as he traversed the hallway to return to the drawing room. Fearing the worst, Margarite retrieved the pistol from underneath her gown.

Still cursing, Said entered the room. He walked directly to the small ornate desk and grabbed the dagger. Grasping it in his palm as though intending to use it as a weapon, he turned to face Margarite holding the pistol at her side.

"What have we here, my dear?" Said's eyes narrowed. "I knew I should have kept this little item when I had the chance, earlier this evening." He reached out his free hand for the gun, while continuing to clutch his weapon in the other. "Give it to me, Margarite."

Margarite shook her head. "Said, I am telling you for the last time: put down the dagger."

He struck her so fast, she did not have a chance to react. "You will learn to be a proper wife. You must never question my authority. Never!" Said crouched and hissed as he grabbed at the pistol she was still holding by her side. "I will teach you to obey me!"

Her head reeling, Margarite stepped back and raised the small pearl-handled gun. There was a sudden flash of lightning, followed almost immediately by a tremendous clap of thunder.

Said sprang forward, grabbing her by the neck. A shot rang out.

****

The knocking commenced almost immediately. "Prince, Princess, you must open the door. Now, please." Margarite recognized Clive's panicked voice, as she bent to pick up the pistol from the blood-stained Oriental rug.

Said lay slumped against the desk, muttering. Blood flowed freely from the wound on his temple, from which splinters of bone and brain tissue protruded.

"*Qu'est-ce que j'ai fait*? What have I done?" Margarite screamed.

"I am using the passkey, Princess," Clive yelled to Margarite as he opened the door.

"What have I done? What have I done?" Margarite repeated as she fell into the night porter's arms, tears running down her cheeks, her gown stained with blood. Looking up into Clive's lined face, she continued, "I have been married only a short time. It has been torture for me. I have suffered terribly. But this is a mistake, an accident." Her voice broke. "You must believe me, please. Oh, what have I done?"

The night porter gently sat her on a brocaded bench. "Stay where you are, Princess Fusani. Do not touch anything." He noted the pistol, still in her hand. "But please, hand the gun to me."

Grasping the weapon, Clive returned to the outer hallway and the service telephone. Margarite overheard his directions to the hotel receptionist. "Send for an ambulance!" He took a deep breath. "Call the police!"

****

James cursed himself on the entire trip to the Provencal. He was a fool to have let Margarite return to the hotel alone. Anything could happen.

"There is an emergency of some sort at the

231

Provencal, sir." The taxi driver echoed his worst fears. "The avenue is closed."

James looked up to find the way blocked by an ambulance. Two attendants accompanied a figure on a stretcher, shrieking in pain. "Whatever is that language the patient is screaming?"

"Arabic, sir," responded the driver. "I served in Egypt, during the war."

James shook his head in dismay and reached for his wallet. "I'll walk from here. Thank you."

Sprinting past the man on the stretcher, James was shocked to find his face covered with a white cloth stained with blood. "The patient? The cloth?" James asked the doorman, seeking to determine the identity of the figure on the stretcher.

The doorman sniffed. "Sir, I am only allowed to say that at the Provencal cases of violence are kept confidential and bodies removed surreptitiously."

James shook his head for the second time in as many minutes and sprinted to the fourth floor. The door to Apartment 402 was ajar. James, giving a quick knock, entered.

"Margarite?" James called, as he proceeded down the hall to the drawing room.

"James!" he heard Margarite cry.

James entered the room to find it occupied by two men and a distraught Margarite. The first man was dressed in a hotel uniform; his badge identified him as "Clive Martin, Night Porter." The second man wore a rumpled suit and a brown fedora. In one hand he held an umbrella; in the other, he grasped Margarite's small pearl-handled pistol.

"James! I am so relieved to see you!" Margarite

rushed toward him.

"Please, Princess." The man in the rumpled suit placed the gun in his lap and reached out his hand to restrain her.

"And who might you be, sir?" He turned to James.

"I might ask you the same question," James acrimoniously replied.

"Chief Inspector Fox of the Metropolitan Police," was the immediate reply. "I will be asking all of the questions from here on out, if you please. Now, your name sir."

"James Arthur, Duke of Donovan."

"And your business here?" Fox was clearly unimpressed.

"I am a friend of the princess."

"Indeed. I see. And of the prince as well?"

Margarite began to sob, successfully deflecting the Chief Inspector's insensitive question.

James took the initiative. "What happened here?"

"Exactly what I intend to find out," Fox responded. "If you will allow me, sir." He shot a warning glance toward James.

"Princess, I think it best if you accompany me to the station," the Chief Inspector continued, turning to Margarite.

Margarite looked to James.

"Is that really necessary, Chief Inspector?" James could not bear to think of Margarite at the mercy of the Metropolitan Police. "Is she under arrest?"

"I have not yet had an opportunity to question her," Fox replied, clearly agitated.

"Chief Inspector, the princess has had a harrowing evening. I just passed her husband being taken to the hospital. Clearly she will want to accompany him. Would not tomorrow morning be a more appropriate time for her to give a statement?" James paused for emphasis and in his most commanding voice added, "I will bring her to the station myself."

Fox hesitated.

He is aware of my position after all, thought James.

Eventually the Chief Inspector drew himself up to his full height, sighed heavily, and said, "Suppose we begin by finding out what happened here. Princess Fusani?"

Margarite wiped away tears. "I returned from the Cavendish a short time ago. My husband and I argued. He threatened me with a dagger. We struggled." She again broke down in sobs. "It was an accident."

"Indeed." Fox raised his eyebrows. "Your husband, he did not accompany you to the Cavendish?"

"No-o-o." Margarite involuntarily glanced at James. "We had a row before I left."

"A row, about what subject, Princess?"

"It was nothing. My necklace, my pearls."

The Chief Inspector looked sternly at Margarite.

"We fight about everything. We…"

"It is true," interjected the night porter. "Everyone at the hotel has heard them."

Fox eyed him curiously, before continuing, "And the gun, Princess?"

"I have had it since the war." Margarite shot another furtive glance toward James. "For protection. I…"

"I saw it!" interrupted the night porter for a second time. "It was in the princess's hand both times I saw her this evening."

"Indeed." The Chief Inspector regarded the night porter more seriously and checked his notes. "Clive Martin, is it? I will also need to speak with you."

"Chief Inspector, please. The princess must get to the hospital." James impatiently paced the room. "She cannot wait for you to interview the night porter. I give my word that I will bring her to the station to give her statement tomorrow morning. Shall we say about eleven o'clock?"

"Harrumph." Fox, clearly displeased, cleared his throat.

James continued, "She has told you everything. And by tomorrow, when the prince is available and can give his statement, there may be nothing further to investigate."

"I will need to take her dress and pearls with me. And the gun, of course." Fox insisted. He picked up the dagger lying on the carpet, near the desk. "And this, I suppose."

Margarite visibly paled. James rushed to her side. He shuddered as he noticed the blood that speckled her dress. "Please Chief Inspector," he implored, "allow the princess to leave. She herself may need medical care."

Fox narrowed his eyes suspiciously. "After she changes, so I may take the dress with the other items."

James turned to assist Margarite to her dressing area, but the Chief Inspector's next words pulled him up short. "I must advise you, Princess, you may not leave London until this matter is resolved to the Crown's satisfaction."

Chapter Seven

Donovan House, London

Shortly after dawn the next morning, James, remembering the glowing description given of Ivy and her partners at Smythe and Company, telephoned Bryan Henderson. The parting comments of Chief Inspector Fox the prior evening had left James with the impression that it would be prudent to speak with legal counsel before the eleven o'clock meeting with the Metropolitan Police.

Once roused and brought to the telephone, Bryan proved himself irritatingly amused by the situation in which James now found himself. "Hah, old chap, sounds as though, like many of us, Margarite will need a barrister."

James heard Bryan ask Ivy, "Darling, do you know a good barrister? One who has experience defending socialites and aristocrats on murder charges? One who has perhaps bested Chief Inspector Fox, not once but twice?"

Murder? Thought James.

"Bryan, what on earth?" James heard Ivy respond. There were several moments where he heard only whispers. He surmised Bryan was explaining Margarite's plight to Ivy.

Suddenly Ivy was speaking into the telephone.

"James? Please come to Smythe and Company at nine o'clock today. Bryan can give you the address." She paused. "And arrange for Madame Fusani to arrive a half-hour later. My father and I will want to speak with both of you."

James was nonplussed. "Do you really think all of this is necessary? I promised to take Margarite in to give her statement to the police at eleven o'clock. Moreover, it may turn out to be nothing. The prince may be released from hospital and all forgiven."

There was a long moment of silence, before Ivy responded. "I am afraid James that it is quite necessary. Please read the morning papers before you arrive."

James stared perplexedly at the telephone, as Ivy rang off.

****

Racing down the heavily carved, semi-circular staircase of Donovan House, James called for his butler. "Johnathan, the newspapers please!"

Johnathan, frowned at him from the floor below. "The morning papers are arranged at your place at the table as usual, sir."

"Have you read them?"

"Of course not, sir. Whatever…"

"There is something about Prince and Princess Fusani…"

"Oh that, yes sir." Johnathan nodded knowingly. "The murder. The staff can talk about nothing else. It seems Elsie in the kitchen has been fraternizing with Clive at the Provencal and…"

"Murder!" James cut off Johnathan's rendition of the downstairs' alliances. "Whose murder?" He rushed into the dining room. "By whom?"

237

"Why Prince Fusani by his wife, that French courtesan." Johnathan scowled. "A sordid story it is, sir."

James looked up in shock from his task of shuffling through the newspapers. "Murdered? Said Fusani?"

"Indeed, sir." Johnathan looked curiously at James. "The *Herald* reports he died after being shot by his wife in a fight over her newest lover. Clive was able to give quite an accurate description of the man involved with the princess, although the *Herald* does not include his identity."

"Rubbish!"

"No sir, look." Johnathan gently pulled the *Herald* from James's astonished hands. As he held up the front page, James read the garish headline: *Prince Said Fusani Murdered at the Provencal Hotel in Dispute over Princess's Newest Lover.*

"I simply cannot believe it."

"Yes, sir. It is all here, sir. Even the lover's description." Jonathan read aloud from the now crumpled newspaper: "*tall, muscular, brown hair, blue eyes, aristocratic bearing…*" Johnathan stopped and looked appraisingly at James. "Amazing. If I didn't know better, sir, I would say it was you."

James collapsed into one of the dining room's many Chippendale chairs.

Johnathan's eyes widened. "Sir, are you unwell?"

James waved away his obvious concern. "What else does the *Herald* report?"

"Ahem." Johnathan cleared his throat and began to read:

" *'What have I done?'* The voice of Princess Fusani echoed through the halls of the fourth floor of *the Provencal Hotel very early this morning.*

"The Provencal Hotel opened in 1899. It has been no stranger to scandal. Nevertheless, it has remained the popular place to stay for celebrities and royalty visiting London."

James rolled his eyes. Johnathan continued reading:

"Prince and Princess Fusani arrived at the Provencal earlier this month. Said Fusani was not actually a prince but encouraged the use of the title. The young Egyptian met his bride Margarite in Paris, and they were married shortly thereafter in Cairo. Margarite Hagan Fusani was an infamous French courtesan during the war and was considered by many to be a flirtatious gold-digger."

"Not so!" objected James.

"Oh sir, wait there is more." An oblivious Johnathan continued reading:

"After only a few days in London, it was apparent that all was not well within the marriage. A meal in the hotel restaurant was disrupted by a vicious argument. Moreover, the prince appeared in public with scratches on his face, and the princess was seen with ill-disguised bruises."

"Scandalous," murmured Johnathan.

James sank lower into the Chippendale chair and waved him on. Jonathan continued:

"Last evening the theatrics began again. Provencal night porter Clive Martin disclosed to the Herald *that several guests at the posh hotel reported hearing voices raised in argument and a gunshot emanating from the Fusani suite, Apartment 402. Upon investigating, the night porter observed the princess, carrying a small*

pearl-handled pistol, exit the fourth floor apartment and enter the lift. Confirming that no one had been injured, Clive returned to his duties.

"Several hours passed, and he was again sent to investigate complaints about shouting in Apartment 402. For a second time, Clive confirmed there were no serious injuries and returned to his duties, attempting to put the disturbing encounters in the back of his mind.

"A short while later, however, the night porter heard a shot ring out on the fourth floor. Entering Apartment 402, he found the princess carrying the small gun he had observed earlier in the evening. She kept repeating, 'What have I done?' Clive told the Herald. The intrepid night porter called for an ambulance and the police.

"The police arrived, followed by a gentleman..."

"Yes, yes. You can skip that part, Johnathan," James said irritably. "I was there. Move on to Said Fusani's death, please."

Johnathan released a small gasp, but continued reading:

"The prince was taken by ambulance to Charing Cross Hospital, where he expired at approximately four o'clock this morning. The Metropolitan Police have not yet issued a statement."

"That's the end of it, sir. You were there?" Jonathan stared at James in disbelief. "When do you think the police will be arriving, sir?"

James groaned. "Not before I make my escape, I pray." He left an astonished Johnathan to dress for his appointment with the barristers of Smythe and Company.

Chapter Eight

Smythe and Company, Lincoln's Inn Fields, London

James strode purposefully through the London drizzle toward Smythe and Company, the prior evening's thunderstorm having given way to a cold rain. The partners of Smythe and Company—Ivy and her father, Edward, together with Graham Wetherington—had all trained at Lincoln's Inn, one of London's four Inns of Court. The firm maintained chambers in Lincoln's Inn Fields and was renowned for its expertise in criminal law, an area in which James had never expected to need assistance.

James approached the red lacquered door and raised the lion's head knocker. A small brass plaque next to the door commemorated the building's construction in 1641. As he passed into the reception area, he could see the venerable edifice still retained its mahogany paneled walls, floor to ceiling bookshelves, brass sconces, and marble fireplaces.

An attractive woman with bobbed chestnut hair and blue eyes rushed out to meet him, her hand outstretched. "Ivy Smythe Henderson," she introduced herself. "Bryan has told me so much about you, Your Grace."

"Please, call me James." He kissed her hand, rather

than shaking it. Ivy grinned.

"And I am Edward Smythe." An older distinguished gentleman held out this hand to James. This time, James shook it.

"Where is the illustrious Graham Wetherington?" James looked around the offices for the third member of the firm. "I don't know if Bryan mentioned it, but Graham and I served in the Great War together."

"Nashville." Ivy smirked.

"I beg your pardon?" James was puzzled.

"Graham Wetherington is in Nashville, Tennessee, spending time with the Vanderwells, his new wife's family."

"Right." James grinned. He had read about Graham's defense of Miss Vanderwell, who had been considered a person of interest in the untimely death of the wife of Brighton solicitor George Greenville.

"Quite an interesting case, if I do say so," Edward opined.

"With a happy ending," Ivy chimed in. "But James, we have not much time. Tell us about the Fusanis. The morning papers are consumed with the story. What an unfortunate incident." Ivy shook her head as she brought out the morning editions of the *Herald*, the *Times*, and the *Mirror*.

"The pertinent question is: what can we, as barristers, do to assist you, James?" Edward brushed the newspapers aside. "It seems abundantly clear that Madame Fusani is responsible for her husband's death. Motivated by her interest in her new lover, no doubt. The new lover described by the *Herald*…"

"Father," Ivy began cautiously.

Thank God! Bryan must have provided Ivy with

the full history of my relationship with Margarite, thought James.

Edward appeared to ignore Ivy as he rifled through the *Herald* looking for the description. "Ah here it is: *tall, muscular, brown hair, blue eyes, aristocratic bearing.* It all sounds quite familiar, actually..." Edward suddenly stopped reading and looked at James. "Oh, quite. I see now."

"As usual the newspapers are not altogether accurate, sir. I do admit, however, that my past relationship with Margarite and Bryan's advice to seek counsel"—he nodded toward Ivy—"is what brought me here."

Edward's eyes took on a faraway glaze. "Lover to Margarite Hagen, heh my boy? Why I've heard..."

"Father!" Ivy spoke sharply, turning abruptly when the lion's head knocker rapped once again, and the door to chambers slowly opened.

****

Margarite walked haltingly through the rain on her way to meet James at Smythe and Company, reliving the events of the past five hours. Said had passed from this life by the time she arrived at the hospital. Chief Inspector Fox had escorted her back to the Provencal, repeating his earlier admonition to appear for questioning in the morning.

Devastated, she had retreated to her bed. But shortly thereafter, she was awoken by Aimee with a directive from James to meet at the offices of Smythe and Company. She had immediately burst into tears. "Oh, Aimee," she had wailed. "What have I done? I loved Said when I married him. I thought we would be happy. Our lives were straight from *The Arabian*

243

Nights. We fought, often. But I never meant to harm him."

Dressing, she had continued her diatribe. "Now the Chief Inspector has my pistol. How sinister it must appear to him. How can he understand what I have suffered? What it was like to be hungry, cold, and alone in Paris; first as a child, then during the war."

Now, arriving at the red lacquered door of the barristers' chambers, Margarite straightened her shoulders and took a deep breath to clear her head of the painful memories. Passing into the reception area, she faced the curious appraisal of an elderly gentleman whom she assumed to be the barrister, Mr. Smythe. Behind him stood an attractive young woman with bobbed hair, and James.

"Margarite!" James grasped her by the arm and kissed her gently on the cheek. Shivers of pleasure ran up her spine, despite the circumstances of the meeting. "Please make the acquaintance of Mr. Edward Smythe and his daughter, Ivy."

Margarite nodded and handed Ivy her handbag, as she turned toward Edward. Ivy stiffened and dropped the handbag on the floor.

James continued, "Ivy and Mr. Smythe are both well-known barristers in the area of criminal law. If we are lucky, they will agree to represent you."

"A woman barrister? Is that legal?" Margarite asked, not realizing her pun.

"It certainly is," Ivy answered coldly.

"Well," said Edward, "having settled that, shall we get down to business? Please come into my office."

Moving toward the back of chambers, Edward called out loudly, "Hannah, some tea, please."

"I simply could not survive without that woman." Edward confided to James and Margarite. "She has been with me for over twenty-five years."

"Another barrister?" asked Margarite sarcastically as Hannah, dressed in her traditional black and white uniform, entered the room with the tea tray.

"No, no, my housekeeper, err, office assistant." Edward sought to explain Hannah's presence.

Ivy narrowed her eyes at Margarite, then turned to James. "May I be so bold as to inquire as to the nature of your relationship with this"—her voice was icy—"woman? Bryan was a little unclear."

Margarite felt her face grow hot. "Although I cannot imagine it is any of your concern, James and I are friends."

"If Smythe and Company is to represent you, everything is our concern," Ivy retorted. She continued, "Friends? Not lovers?" She regarded James. "Might you be a subject of the investigation as well?"

James shook his head. "Until a few days ago, we had not seen each other for ten years. Our few recent meetings have been quite public. I did not arrive at the Provencal until after the police had secured the scene."

"Good. Very good," Ivy responded, arms crossed.

"But a long time ago, in another place, another time…" Margarite began wistfully, but was interrupted by the unexpected entry of Chief Inspector Fox.

****

James plastered a smile on his face and reached out his hand. "Chief Inspector Fox…"

"Good morning, Your Grace, Princess, Ivy, Edward, good to see you." Fox dropped his dripping raincoat and brown fedora over the nearest chair.

"To what do we owe this pleasure, Chief Inspector?" Edward asked, his tone conveying somewhat less enthusiasm.

"As the princess and the duke may have told you, we have an appointment at headquarters shortly. Nevertheless, upon learning the group had congregated in your chambers, I thought I would pop over." Fox paused. "Particularly as matters changed so dramatically overnight."

"Changed?" Edward harrumphed. "In what way, Chief Inspector?"

Fox released a sly smile. "In the nature of the charges, which are now murder rather than assault."

"Murder! That's absurd," burst out Ivy. "It was an accident."

"Indeed," responded Fox. "You seem to know a great deal more about the case then I was able to learn in the short time the princess deigned to speak with me last evening."

Fox regarded Margarite. "Perhaps you would like to explain exactly how this accident occurred, Princess?"

Ivy again interrupted. "Now is really not the time. We have not had an opportunity to consult with Madame Fusani."

Fox repeated his wry smile. "And will the story change after that, Counselor?"

"Certainly not!" Ivy responded, visibly insulted.

"I don't mind speaking to the Chief Inspector," Margarite interjected.

Ivy rolled her eyes.

Edward intervened, "Assuming Madame Fusani has no objections, you may question her in our presence, Chief Inspector. But we reserve the right to instruct her not to answer."

"Very well, we can revisit those questions upon her arrest." Fox shrugged.

"Arrest?" Margarite asked, eyes wide.

"Really Chief Inspector," Edward interrupted, "that is a bit unnecessary. Perhaps we should hear the story before rushing to conclusions."

"Very well. Exactly what did happen last evening, Princess?" Fox seated himself and crossed his legs, revealing carelessly darned socks.

Margarite briefly recounted the events of the prior evening. James nodded encouragement as she spoke. Not even the Chief Inspector can doubt the prince's death was an accident, he thought. Margarite finished and turned her gaze to her lap.

"As you see, Chief Inspector, the prince's death was quite clearly an accident. Nothing for a man of your stature in the Metropolitan Police to be concerned about…" Edward began.

"Just a moment, please Counselor. A few questions, if I may." Fox cleared his throat. "Princess Fusani…"

Margarite visibly flinched. She was very pale.

"The pistol was discharged on two separate occasions last evening, is that correct?"

"Yes, but…"

"The first time was a result of an altercation over"—Fox pulled the still lustrous pearls from the pocket of his well-worn tweed sports jacket—"these?"

"Yes, but…"

"And where did you get—" Fox paused and looked at James.

James, imagining the Chief Inspector was about to inquire into the provenance of the pearls, felt his own visage pale.

"—the gun?" Fox smiled.

"My garter," Margarite answered literally.

Edward, obviously shocked began to object, but Fox continued, "Indeed Princess, do you always carry your firearm in your garter?"

"Since the war." Head still downcast, Margarite was oblivious to the sarcasm in the Chief Inspector's tone.

"I see. Quite irregular that. I imagine a London jury will be intrigued."

Edward frowned and cleared his throat. "Let's move along, Chief Inspector."

"And the gun went off?" Fox continued unfazed by Edward's rebuke.

"My husband grabbed the weapon and pointed it at me. I demanded it back. Reaching for the gun, my heel caught in the carpet, and I fell against him. The pistol discharged."

"No one was harmed?"

"The bullet lodged in the wall. My husband laughed and told me I must be more careful."

"And your response to his concern was to grab the weapon from him and promise to shoot him with it?"

"I...I...I..." Margarite put her hands to her temples. "I was upset. I was not serious."

"Right. And what did you do next?"

Margarite looked sideways at James, who shut his eyes. "I went to the Cavendish."

"Alone, with the gun?"

"Yes. I returned it to my garter."

"Of course." Fox smirked. "The Cavendish is a nightclub, is it not? Why would a loving wife retreat alone to a nightclub following such an incident?"

"I like it there." Margarite bristled.

"Right." Fox looked at his notes. "And others saw you there?"

"Yes. Many people; James included." James tensed as Fox turned to him.

"The duke? Had you planned to meet him?"

James shook his head.

"No," Margarite answered, somewhat hesitantly.

"But you were acquainted with the duke, prior to last evening?"

"Yes, many years ago in Paris during the war, we were…" Margarite's voice trailed off.

"Friends," Ivy firmly filled in.

"Right, I have heard that." Fox's smirk returned. "Ultimately, you returned to the Provencal?"

"Yes."

"Alone, except for the gun."

"Yes."

"Where you encountered your husband. Where was he in the apartment?"

"In the drawing room, at the desk, opening correspondence."

Fox's expression visibly brightened. "Really? Opening letters? With this?" Fox once again reached into the pockets of his tweed sport coat. He retrieved the Egyptian knife with a gold blade.

Bloody hell, thought James. Is he carrying all of the evidence with him?

"Y…Y…Yes." Margarite shivered.

"And what occurred next?"

"We argued. My husband approached me. He was holding that…" Margarite eyed the knife. "That dagger as a weapon."

"So you shot him?"

"No! I scratched him. He howled. The night porter came to the apartment to complain about the noise."

"Where was the gun?"

"In my garter. I removed it when my husband went to answer the door—for protection."

"And then?"

"My husband returned, still holding the dagger. He slapped me; demanded the gun. I refused. He crouched and hissed, grabbing at it."

"So you shot him?"

"No! I stepped back, raising the gun. He sprang forward; the pistol discharged." Margarite sobbed. "It was an accident!"

"Quite." Fox sounded significantly less convinced than James had hoped. "You admit you pointed a pistol—" Edward cleared his throat as if to object, but Fox held up his hand. "—at your husband, who was holding a letter opener. The gun fired and struck your husband, who died, after you had promised to kill him only a few hours before."

Margarite buried her head in her hands. James looked on helplessly, wanting only to comfort her.

"That is quite enough for today, Chief Inspector." Edward rose.

"You are only prolonging the inevitable." Fox turned as he reached the door and regarded Margarite. "The analysis of the evidence will be completed shortly; an arrest is assured." The Chief Inspector bowed slightly before leaving chambers.

Chapter Nine

Deauville, France

It was still raining when James, firmly supporting Margarite, left the chambers of Smythe and Company. "Damnable weather," he muttered as they climbed into a taxi.

Margarite was quiet; tears streaked her cheeks.

"There, there." He put his arm around her shoulder. "Things are not all that dark. Ivy and Edward will do a fine job representing you."

"They are dark, James. An English jury will never understand what I have been through." She breathed deeply. "I simply cannot spend time in an English prison. Imagine…" Her voice trailed off, as she began sobbing in earnest.

"Here, my love." James handed her his handkerchief. Why was it a woman never had a handkerchief during a crisis he wondered but was astute enough not to inquire.

"Thank you." Margarite was silent for several minutes.

James spent the time looking over the damp streets of London and reminiscing about his time with Margarite during the war. How he wished he could return to 1917 and the Hotel de Crillon!

As if reading his thoughts, Margarite suddenly

looked up. "James, we must get away!"

"Now?" James sputtered. "Wherever would we go?"

"I don't know..." Margarite's face darkened. "Anywhere away from here, away from London."

"I do not believe Chief Inspector Fox..." James began.

Margarite interrupted. "I know! We will go to Deauville! I have an apartment there!"

"Prince Fusani had an apartment there, you mean," James responded drily.

"It is my apartment, as well." Margarite sniffed.

"It simply cannot be done." James groaned. "I have my estates, my responsibilities. I cannot abandon them. In addition, Chief Inspector Fox specifically forbid..."

"Do you remember our times together in Paris? During the war?"

"Yes, of course. Fondly. I was just reminiscing..."

"Then what is stopping you, my love?" Margarite snuggled closer.

James grimaced. "As I have just said, I have responsibilities I cannot abandon."

"Nothing has changed. You do not love me." Margarite pulled away.

"I do love you, Margarite!" James sighed. "I have always loved you. But I have a life here."

"What of me? How can you contemplate a life in England when I will be tried for murder?"

"Ivy and Edward will think of something; they most always do." James moved closer. The scent of Lanvin was intoxicating. He wanted nothing more than to bury himself in it...in her. He shook his head to clear it; this was madness. He tried again. "Margarite, the

Chief Inspector has forbidden you from leaving the country. He will follow you to Deauville and arrest you, if you flee."

"I will soon be imprisoned in any event, if one listens to Chief Inspector Fox." She stroked his thigh, sending electric currents through his body. "Please? We would return before the tests on the evidence are completed." Her hand strayed to his inner thigh. "No one will know we are gone." With a discreet look at the driver of the taxi, she moved her hand higher. "We will enjoy many pleasures in Deauville," she whispered.

James closed his eyes. He could resist no longer. Margarite climbed onto his lap, moving her hips against him. She kissed him, her tongue tantalizing him with what was to come. Taking her in his arms, he surrendered.

****

Arriving after a six-hour train ride from the Trouville-sur-Mer station in Paris, Margarite was, as always, struck by the glamour of Deauville. Located in the Calvados department in the Normandy region of northwestern France, Deauville was a well-known playground for the aristocracy. Developed by the first Duke of Morny, half-brother of Emperor Napoleon III, Deauville boasted a race course, harbor, grand casino, and sumptuous hotels. It was regarded as the queen of the Normandy beaches and had long been home to French society's finest resorts. Margarite's favorite was La Terrasse, which included a complex for hydrotherapeutic baths as well as an eighteen-hundred meter promenade along the water. She also enjoyed the shopping, particularly Coco Chanel's boutique.

Her apartment in Deauville was located at the

Hotel Normand, built in 1912. Decorated in blue and white with oriental accents, it had a magnificent view of the sea from every vantage point—particularly the four-poster bed. Margarite had envisioned the delights she would bestow upon James in that bed during the entire six-hour train ride from Paris.

****

James had been in Deauville during his posting to Paris in 1917, but never with Margarite. He found the experience exhilarating. The first day of their stay they leased an open Rolls Royce from the hotel and drove twelve miles for lunch at the Auberge de Guillame le Conquerant, a world-famous restaurant. Afterward they drove to Caen, a city of great beauty with half-timbered medieval houses, stone guildhalls, and great Norman churches. Another day they toured the unspoiled fringes of the Seine estuary, visiting Touques and the fishing port of Honfleur.

Evenings were equally delightful. During the war, the prefect had roped off the promenade, closed the casino bar, forbidden the playing of baccarat, and banned the tango. All were considered symbols of decadence. But James was delighted to see that entertainment had now returned to pre-war levels.

Their second evening in Deauville, James and Margarite enjoyed baccarat, followed by dancing and a late supper at the casino. They then retired to the promenade, where they sipped Whizz-bangs and Bulldogs, alcoholic delights served by Charlie the casino's "King of Cocktails."

Margarite placed her drink on the promenade railing and began to dance to the soft strains of jazz emanating from the casino. Amused, James placed his cocktail next to hers and joined her in the Slow Waltz. The moon reflecting on the sea highlighted her short silver frock as she swayed against him.

He kissed her gently. Her hand slid down his chest. His kiss became more urgent. She molded herself against him; her hand strayed below his belt. Her touch set him afire. He pressed in on her, sliding his leg between hers while continuing the sensuous dance. A growl emanated from the back of her throat. His hand slid to her thighs. She flung one leg around his waist and clamped her body to his. Slowly, she unzipped his trousers and released his throbbing manhood.

Maintaining the slow dance, he placed both hands on her buttocks and lifted her onto the promenade railing. She pulled him closer and continued swaying to the music. The silver dress brushed against him, arousing him further. She reached out and guided him to her innermost parts. Groaning with pleasure, he grabbed her hips and plunged. She shuddered with delight.

Suddenly a group of good-time girls and their dates exited the casino, laughing wildly. "Perhaps we should retire to the room for the remainder of our activities?" Margarite suggested, straightening the short skirt of his now-favorite gown.

"Giddy up!" A naked woman unexpectedly came running from the Normand Hotel in hot pursuit of a dinner-jacketed man, whipping him with her rope of pearls.

"Ohhh! I have a marvelous idea." Margarite laughed, leaping down from the railing and grabbing James's hand.

****

Margarite squinted against the morning light and moaned. "James, I have hardly slept. It cannot be time to wake already."

"Do not be difficult, my love. It is a beautiful day. We must go to the beach."

"No." Margarite covered her head with the satin sheet.

"Yes!" James insisted as he pulled her from the bed.

Despite her initial resistance, Margarite enjoyed the day. Dotted with lively colored umbrellas and bathing huts, Deauville boasted a charming beach. All manner of well-known Europeans were observed by Margarite and James as they reclined in their beach chairs sipping Whizz-bangs. Of particular amusement was the Countess of Bremond, who wore black-and-white spotted bathing apparel matching the coat of her Dalmatian.

The sunshine and sea air left Magarite tired but relaxed, as she and James retired to the apartment. "What a capital day!" Margarite exclaimed as she discarded her bathing attire. Turning to James, wearing only her pearls, she gently kissed him on the cheek.

James eyed her critically, not the reaction she had been expecting. "You are quite sunburned, my darling."

Margarite crossed her arms over her breasts. James turned her around slowly for inspection, frowning.

"Lie down. Please."

"Why?" Margarite asked with a mischievous grin.

"On your stomach. I will be back in a moment."

James returned shortly carrying a crystal bottle filled with golden liquid. He began pouring it into his hand.

Margarite lay down on her stomach, as directed. James applied the liquid; rubbing it into her back and thighs. Margarite buried her face in her satin pillow. James poured more liquid into his hands and kneaded her neck and shoulders. Slowly he massaged her buttocks. Margarite whimpered.

"Turn over." James's voice was firm.

Margarite did as she was told. Her eyes were firmly closed, but a smile played about her lips. For a few seconds, James was still. Margarite discreetly opened one eye to watch as he added more of the golden liquid to his palm. He gently rubbed the oil onto her neck and arms. Margarite purred when James reached her breasts. He massaged them, then lowered his head to capture each nipple between his lips. Margarite grabbed the sheet beneath her with both hands and pushed her pelvis forward.

"I have not finished." Dribbling oil on her stomach, James massaged her breasts, her stomach, and her legs. Slowly his hands brushed her mons, using slow circular motions.

Margarite could wait no longer. She put her own hands on her breasts. Her palms slid down along her sides. Out of the corner of her eye, she saw James finally remove his own bathing attire. "At last." She arched her back just as a loud pounding commenced at the door.

****

"What the bloody hell!" James exclaimed. He reached for his robe, as the pounding continued. "Whatever in God's name do you want?"

"Police, sir."

Margarite groaned and pulled the coverlet over her

head.

"Everything will be all right, Margarite," James reassured her as he squared his shoulders and opened the door. How I wish that were true, he thought.

"Chief Inspector Fox!" James gulped in surprise. He looked askance at the English inspector and the uniformed French gendarme in the hotel hallway. "Whatever is the meaning of this? You have no powers on French soil." He drew himself up to his full height. "As you are well aware I am a man of some influence!"

"Indeed, Your Grace. A man of considerable influence, traveling with a fugitive." Fox frowned. "A fugitive whom I intend to arrest."

"No!" Margarite and James responded simultaneously.

"Stand aside, sir, *s'il vous plait*." ordered the gendarme.

"I will do no such thing!" James turned to the Chief Inspector. "We intended only to take a holiday. We will return, when necessary."

"It is quite necessary, now. I have a warrant for the princess's arrest." Fox eyed the pile of bedclothes. "Will the princess come peacefully?"

"Non!"

James and Fox exchanged glances. "Give us a moment of privacy, and we will accompany you, Chief Inspector," James finally replied.

"Very well. We will wait in the hall."

"I will not go. They cannot make me. I refuse." Margarite emerged from under the coverlet as Fox left the room.

"You must, Margarite. Come, get up. Get dressed. We cannot let the Chief Inspector see you like this."

"It is over now, James. Everything. Us. My life. What could have been. This is the end." Margarite stood, her oiled body gleaming in the sunlight.

"No, Margarite…" James began. But the firm knock of the Chief Inspector brought him back to reality. His statement hung in the air unfinished.

Chapter Ten

Old Bailey, London

The first morning of Margarite's trial found James rushing toward the Central Criminal Court, better known as the Old Bailey. It was his first visit, and he was surprised by the formidable appearance Old Bailey presented. A grim and grimy structure, it was faced with unpolished Cornish granite and gray Portland stone from the Newgate Gaol which formerly occupied the site. Above the main entrance was inscribed the admonition: "Defend the Children of the Poor & Punish the Wrongdoer." On the dome above the court stood a bronze statue of Lady Justice holding a sword in her right hand and the scales of justice in her left.

Courtroom number one, where the trial was to be held, was located one floor above ground level. James walked somberly up the large marble staircase and turned to the right down a long hall decorated with colored mosaics representing Labor, Art, Wisdom, and Truth.

Entering the oak-paneled courtroom, he found most seats already taken and many people standing at the back and sides of the room. In front of the judge's dais and beyond the seat of the court clerk stood the treasury table holding exhibits. Nearby sat a number of police officers. Behind them, in counsel's row, sat the principal prosecuting counsel known as the Treasury Counsel, Sir Percival Bonde. Bonde was a tall, thin, colorless man with a dour expression. Ivy and Edward were crammed into counsel seats for the defense. Opposite the lawyers, on the other side of the courtroom, were two empty benches awaiting their complement of twelve jurors.

High above the barristers, in the public gallery, James could see the spectators. Reporters were seemingly everywhere, balancing their notebooks wherever they could. A continuous line of policemen, journalists, and members of the bar not associated with the case streamed into the courtroom. James took the seat directly behind Ivy. He felt fortunate she had reserved it for him.

The competing conversations in the courtroom were abruptly silenced by three sharp knocks heralding the arrival of the judge. James, together with everyone else in the courtroom, stood at attention. Mr. Justice Michael Harrod, wearing scarlet robes trimmed with ermine, entered court, followed by the sheriff.

"Oyez. Oyez," cried the usher. This time-honored reference referred to the process of hearing and determining issues at trial. Mr. Justice Harrod bowed to counsel. He then settled himself in the chair, which James thought much resembled a large throne, standing beneath the sword of justice.

"Margarite Fusani!" The Clerk of Arraigns solemnly intoned.

James turned in his seat to see another small procession make its way up to the dock. Margarite had been transported from Holloway Prison, where she was taken after her arrest. She wore a black tailored suit trimmed with mink and a black cloche hat with a wide brim and a short veil. *She is dressed for mourning*, thought James.

Standing in front of the dais, Margarite swayed slightly, despite the wardress holding her arm. The clerk read the indictment, "The prisoner is charged with one count of murder."

"*Non coupable*, not guilty." Margarite responded to the indictment without emotion.

James cringed as she took her seat, expressionless, then closed her eyes.

Immediately, the doors swung open and the gaggle of citizens summoned for jury service made their way into the packed courtroom. The jury was composed of ten men and, somewhat surprisingly, two women jurors. They noisily made their way to the benches beyond the lawyers.

"Ahem!" The Clerk of Arraigns brought the crowd's attention back to the front of the courtroom. Facing the jury, he again read out the indictment. He concluded by adding, "The prisoner Margarite Hagen Fusani has pled not guilty. As jurors, it is your charge to say whether she be guilty of murder or not."

****

Margarite, upon hearing her name, slowly opened her eyes and gazed at James. *How I love him*, she thought, before turning her attention to what she understood to be the prosecuting attorney's table. A tall, thin man with a dour expression rose. Margarite watched as the judge nodded to him. The prosecuting attorney immediately straightened his robe and adjusted his wig.

"I am principal prosecuting counsel, Sir Percival

Bonde." The prosecuting attorney addressed the twelve jurors in what Margarite could only describe as a dry monotone. "I will present the Crown's case against the prisoner."

Margarite listened as the formidable case against her was set out by Sir Bonde. The opening argument lasted less than an hour and was delivered in the same monotone as his introduction. The tone contrasted sharply with his portrayal of her extravagant lifestyles in Egypt and France, the rage and passion she exhibited in London, and the actions resulting in the violent death of her husband.

Prosecuting counsel emphasized to the jury that the post mortem report, the exhibits, and the witnesses were consistent with the Crown's contention that she had murdered her husband in cold blood. "From her own lips, it is known that she caused the death of her husband," Sir Bonde told the visibly shaken jury.

"The prisoner and her husband fought frequently, often violently. You will hear several witnesses testify to their arguments throughout the time they were in London, including the night Prince Fusani was shot. Early in the evening in question, those witnesses will testify, they heard quarreling, a gunshot, and the prisoner threaten to shoot her husband. Much later in the evening they again heard quarreling, a gunshot, and a high-pitched scream.

"The prisoner will claim that during this latter argument her husband advanced toward her threateningly with this"—he retrieved the Egyptian knife from the exhibits' table—"a curio Prince Fusani used as a letter opener. She will further claim she was so frightened by her husband's behavior, she pulled out her pistol." Sir Bonde picked up the pearl-handled pistol. "A gun, ladies and gentleman of the jury, which she admits she carried on her person for years. Carried"—he paused—"in her garter, no less."

Prosecuting counsel smirked as laughter rippled through the courtroom. Mr. Justice Harrod rapped his gavel sharply, demanding silence.

"The prisoner says she only intended to frighten her husband, but he continued to advance toward her," Sir Bonde continued. "She claims he pounced on her, they struggled, and the gun discharged. She contends she does not remember pulling the trigger. She further contends she was surprised the gun went off because it discharged earlier in the evening, and she therefore thought it was unloaded." He paused once more. "But remember this, ladies and gentlemen, when the same weapon was fired earlier in the evening the prisoner told her husband, 'I will shoot you.' " Sir Bonde brandished the small gun before the eyes of the jury, then added softly, "And shoot him she did."

Margarite hid her face in her hands. Sir Bonde had successfully portrayed her as a hard, greedy, ambitious, pistol-packing woman with a violent temper.

Prosecuting counsel opened his case with the coroner who testified as to the cause of Said's death. Chief Inspector Fox then testified on his arrival at the scene of the crime at the Provencal Hotel, his viewing of Prince Fusani's body in the mortuary of Charing Cross Hospital, and his investigation and arrest of Margarite Fusani. He also identified the Egyptian knife and the small pearl-handled pistol now resting on the exhibits' table.

"Was that pistol the cause of Prince Fusani's

death?" Sir Bonde asked.

"Quite definitely," the Chief Inspector responded.

On cross examination, Ivy pursued this line of questioning. "You have testified that this pistol was the cause of Said Fusani's untimely demise?"

"Yes," Fox answered. "The prisoner's weapon caused her husband's death."

Ivy unperturbed, smiled at the jury. "And did you find her fingerprints on the trigger?"

Fox sighed. "No."

"No?" Ivy raised her eyebrows.

"No," Fox gruffly replied.

"I see. Did you find Said Fusani's fingerprints on the trigger?"

"No."

Ivy's smile broadened. "Did you find anyone's fingerprints on the trigger, Chief Inspector Fox?"

Fox closed his eyes and frowned.

"Chief Inspector, I asked whether..."

"Yes. Yes. Only my own prints and those of the Provencal's night porter were found on the weapon."

Murmurs filled the courtroom as Ivy returned to defense counsel table. "No further questions," she told the judge.

Sir Bonde next presented two guests of the hotel who testified regarding the constant fighting between the Fusanis, the firing of two shots on the fatal evening, and Margarite's threat earlier in the evening to shoot her husband.

Margarite found the witnesses less than satisfactory. Their testimony conflicted on the number of shots. One testified to hearing two shots, but the other changed his testimony to three shots upon cross-examination by Ivy. Likewise, neither could state with certainty when questioned by Ivy that the voice they heard was Margarite's.

Clive Martin, the Provencal's night porter, was the last witness of the day. Clive was a neutral witness with "no axe to grind" as Sir Bonde explained it to the jury. He approached the witness box warily but soon warmed to his star witness status. He appeared to take great delight in describing the constant complaints the Provencal's guests lodged against the Fusanis.

Focusing on the night of the shooting, he testified at length regarding his three visits to Apartment 402. The first when, responding to reports of a gunshot and threats, he found Margarite in the hallway holding a small pearl-handled pistol. The second when, again responding to complaints, he was met at the door by the bleeding prince contending his wife had physically assaulted him. The third when he heard the fatal gunshot and found Margarite holding the pearl-handled pistol.

"And what did the prisoner say to you when you came to the apartment following the gunshot?" asked Sir Bonde.

" 'What have I done?' " Clive responded. "She kept repeating, 'What have I done?' "

Ivy barely cross examined this witness. She had warned Margarite that the only thing to do in the face of damning testimony was to ignore it and hope the jury did likewise. She did however have one important question.

"Mr. Martin, you have heard Chief Inspector Fox testify that your fingerprints were found on the weapon?"

"Yes," Clive replied, eager to explain. "The princess was holding the gun when I came to the door. I took it from her."

"You also heard Chief Inspector Fox testify that neither of the Fusanis' fingerprints were on the trigger?"

"Yes." Clive looked confused.

Ivy made eye contact with the jury. "Did you shoot Said Fusani, Mr. Martin?"

Prosecuting counsel rose to object. Ivy quickly withdrew the question.

With Clive's testimony and Ivy's cross examination echoing in the jurors' ears, Mr. Justice Harrod adjourned trial for the evening. The jury retreated to the Manchester Hotel, their enforced home for the duration of the trial.

Margarite, preparing to return to Holloway Prison, exchanged glances with James. Oh to be back in Deauville with my love in my arms, she thought.

****

The second day of trial dawned wet and windy. The jurors were assembling in the jury box, as James slid into his seat behind Ivy. He stood as the Clerk of Arraigns called the court to order and the judge took the bench. He sighed as Margarite, escorted across the dock by the wardress, fell listlessly into her assigned chair.

In James's view, the most important witness of day two of the trial was the firearms expert. John Churchill, a leading expert on firearms, had test-fired Margarite's pearl-handled pistol.

"In perfect working order" and "not in the least liable to accidental discharge," the burly witness told Sir Percival Bonde.

"Is it a weapon that continues to fire when the trigger is pressed or does the trigger require pressure for each shot?" Sir Bonde inquired.

"The trigger has to be pulled for each shot. The weapon is automatic loading, but not automatic firing," was the ominous response.

Churchill went on to testify that, with the clip in place, the gun could be primed by pulling back the sliding breach cover which laid over the barrel and then releasing it. This required "some experience of the weapon" according to the witness.

"Is this the sort of weapon that might discharge accidentally?" asked Sir Bonde.

"Highly unlikely," Churchill responded. "This pistol has a three-fold safety provision: the magazine has to be in place, the normal safety catch needs to be pressed, and the butt safety grip must be squeezed by the palm of the firer's hand as the trigger is pulled."

"Is it likely that the prince pulled the trigger himself during the course of the struggle?"

"Highly unlikely." Churchill snorted.

James glanced at Margarite. Eyes downcast, shoulders hunched, she looked as forlorn as he felt.

"Is it *possible* that the deceased pulled the trigger himself during the course of the struggle?" Ivy asked on cross examination.

"Anything is possible." Churchill sniffed.

The Crown's case closed with additional police evidence mostly of a formal character, with no significant disputes. Margarite, sobbing, was led from the courtroom by the wardress.

James, distraught, turned to Ivy. "I must see Margarite."

****

Margarite followed the wardress into the small windowless room where she regularly met with Ivy to discuss her defense. She tried to concentrate, but all she could think of was James. How she longed to feel his arms around her, his lips on hers, his…

"Margarite!" James unexpectedly entered the cell.

Margarite leapt up to embrace him. Her eyes shone despite her dismal surroundings and desperate circumstances.

"How are you holding up?" James smiled sadly. "Ivy arranged for us to have a few minutes alone, before the two of you discuss the defense."

Margarite molded her body to his and smothered his words with a fierce kiss. She explored his mouth with her tongue and ran her hands over his body. His lips were so sweet, she wanted more. He sought to break the embrace; she nipped at his bottom lip.

Ivy suddenly entered the room. Margarite reluctantly stepped back.

"Margarite, the wardress is ready to return you to Holloway," Ivy began breathlessly. "We must discuss the defense. There is no doubt that your pistol, a weapon you carried on your person for many years, discharged during a struggle with your husband, resulting in his death. Only you can give real force to the gamut of our allegations that you drew the gun because you felt threatened, that you never intended it to go off. You must testify."

Margarite shook her head. "*Non.*"

"Then I am afraid"—Ivy sighed—"all is lost."

Chapter Eleven

Old Bailey, London

A distraught James entered the courtroom on Monday morning for the second half of the trial: the presentation of the defense. Since Deauville, James's feelings for Margarite had haunted him. His position, his estates, his title—all were meaningless without her by his side. How terrible that he had only realized this now, when it appeared likely she would be convicted.

As they explained to the jury, Ivy's and Edward's theory of the case was twofold. First, Margarite had been consistently mistreated by Said and was in fear for her life. Second, she had only intended to scare Said; the weapon discharged accidentally.

Their first witness was Dr. Gladstone, who examined Margarite at Holloway Prison following her arrest. Dr. Gladstone, a rotund, jovial man, in contrast to his employment, testified that he examined the prisoner at the time of her incarceration and found severe abrasions on her person.

"Abrasions, doctor? Where?" Ivy feigned surprise.

"On the prisoner's neck."

"Only one?"

"No. There were several, three I believe."

"Do you know what caused them?"

"Based on their size, shape, and intensity, I believe

they were caused by a man's hand."

"Intensity?"

"Yes, they were horrible purple bruises."

One of the female jurors covered her mouth with her hand, the other eyed Margarite with concern. Margarite hung her head.

Ivy next called Detective Inspector Collins, a retired fingerprinting expert from Scotland Yard. Chief Inspector Fox had testified earlier that neither the fingerprints of Said nor Margarite Fusani had been found on the trigger of the pistol. Detective Inspector Collins testified that while his examination of the pistol showed many blurred and unidentifiable prints, the only ones clearly defined were those of the Chief Inspector and the hotel's night porter.

"How might this have happened?" Ivy innocently inquired.

"I imagine no attempt was made to examine the revolver for fingerprints until it had been handled by several people."

"Had proper precautions been taken, might the fingerprints of the deceased been found on, or near, the trigger?" Ivy asked.

James leaned forward, anxious for the response.

"Certainly!" Detective Inspector Collins confidently replied.

The third witness for the defense, Mr. Arthur Stupp, was one of the country's leading firearms experts. Mr. Churchill had testified for the prosecution that the pistol was neither automatic firing nor subject to accidental discharge. Mr. Stupp was called to establish that once the pistol had been primed by pulling back the breach cover and releasing it and the weapon fired, another bullet would automatically enter the chamber.

"So," Ivy inquired, handing the pearl-handled pistol to her witness, "someone might think they had cleared the barrel of this pistol when it discharged, but in reality, another bullet would automatically fill its chamber?"

"Yes," Stupp responded, holding the pistol outward toward Ivy with his finger on the trigger.

Ivy suddenly turned toward the exhibits' table, grabbed the dagger, and sprang toward her witness. Stupp jumped and pulled the trigger on the gun with a resounding click that echoed throughout the courtroom. A collective gasp escaped from the spectators.

"And that second bullet having automatically filled the chamber could be subject to accidental discharge?" Ivy continued undeterred.

"Objection!" yelled Sir Bonde. "Counsel for the defense's theatrics are prejudicial."

"Objection sustained," agreed Mr. Justice Harrod. "The Court is in recess!"

James stifled a laugh. The jury would not soon forget the ease with which Stupp had pulled the trigger when startled by Ivy.

****

Ivy and Margarite briefly left the courtroom during the recess. Upon returning, Ivy gave James a thumbs up.

"As our next witness, the defense will call Madame Margarite Hagen Fusani, My Lord," Ivy informed Sir Justice Harrod. The press and spectators murmured amongst themselves. James grimaced.

The start of Margarite's evidence was delayed by

legal wrangling during which the jury was sent out of court. Sir Bonde informed the court he intended to cross examine Margarite as to the nature of her life in Paris. Ivy argued that such an argument would prejudice the jury and that she had not contended Margarite was a woman of moral character.

Mr. Justice Harrod noted that since 1898, when a prisoner had first been allowed to give evidence on his own behalf, an accused had been shielded from questions about character and background. Therefore, the jury should not be told about Margarite's eventful past.

The jury filed back in and were told that they were now to be deprived of newspapers for the duration of the trial as the papers would report the substance of the legal arguments.

Margarite was then called upon to give evidence in her own defense. James watched worriedly as she made her way to the witness box.

Margarite began her testimony with some very brief personal details. Then the pace began to heat up. Margarite's musical voice carried well as she answered questions on her marriage: the numerous quarrels and the physical abuse. Now and then she shrugged a shoulder. Occasionally her gloved hands toyed with a monogrammed silk handkerchief.

Eventually, Ivy passed the pearl-handled pistol to Margarite. She took the weapon in her hand with a strained face.

"Come, take hold of the pistol. It is harmless now, Madame Fusani," Ivy reassured Margarite. "Have you ever intentionally fired this pistol at your husband?"

Tears welled in Margarite's eyes.

273

"Would you like a recess, madam?" the judge inquired. James held his breath. Margarite dried her eyes and shook her head no.

"Never!" she answered Ivy's question.

James exhaled with relief. This paved the way for the pivotal evidence concerning the night of the shooting.

"Returning to the night in question, why did you pull out the pistol not once but on two separate occasions?" Ivy asked.

"I was afraid. I thought I would frighten my husband with it."

Ivy proceeded to inquire regarding the events the first time the gun went off during Margarite and Said's altercation over the pearls.

"What did you think was the condition of the pistol after it had been discharged the first time, madam?" she asked, watching the jurors.

"The cartridge having been fired, I thought the pistol was no longer dangerous."

"And the second altercation, can you describe for the jury what happened?"

James averted his eyes as Margarite broke into sobs.

"Please, madam," the judge implored.

Margarite took a deep breath and straightened her shoulders. "We argued. My husband threatened me with his dagger. He struck me, and I scratched him. The night porter came to the door of the apartment to complain about the noise. When my husband went to the door, I took the opportunity to retrieve my pistol."

"Why?" Ivy interrupted.

"I was afraid. Afraid of what he might do to me."

"And what happened next, madam?"

"My husband re-entered the room and retrieved his dagger, grasping it as if he intended to use it as a weapon. He saw the gun and demanded it. I refused. He struck me. Then crouching and hissing, he grabbed at the pistol at my side. I stepped back and raised the gun. He sprang forward, grabbing me with one hand behind my neck, the other reaching for the pistol. A shot rang out."

Margarite resumed sobbing. "He was lying on the carpet. It was horrible."

Margarite spent four hours in the witness box before the prosecuting counsel began cross examination. James wondered if Sir Bonde could sense the mood of the jury and was aware of the change in the atmosphere since his opening argument several days before.

"Were you afraid the prince was going to kill you that night?" Sir Bonde's first question appeared to strengthen the defense's case.

"Yes, very afraid," Margarite responded.

Sir Bonde then blundered through a number of questions related to Margarite's background until Mr. Justice Harrod reminded him of the court's earlier rulings on reputation evidence.

"Were you very ambitious to become Prince Fusani's wife?" Sir Bonde tried a new tactic as a last attempt to impress the jury.

"Ambitious? No." Margarite wiped her cheek. "Before we were married, I loved him very much and wished to be with him."

"What did you do while he was being so cruel?"

"What could I do?" Margarite offered a sad smile.

"Once I boxed his ears in public, but he beat me so much that I never dared do it again."

James found her answer consistent with the poignant response of an abused widow. He wondered if the jury perceived Sir Bonde's questions to be as callous as he did.

****

Margarite listened carefully as Mr. Justice Harrod took pains to deliver a stern caution to the members of the jury at the close of the proceedings. "The prosecution has demonstrated that the prisoner killed her husband. It is an act which the law considers deliberate murder, unless the defense is able to prove otherwise."

Observing James's solemn expression during the charge, she shivered with fear. The jury's deliberation lasted no more than an hour. As they quietly returned to the courtroom and took their seats, she caught James's eye. Her heart stopped.

"Is the prisoner guilty of murder?" The clerk stood to ask their verdict.

Margarite was unable to breathe. She closed her eyes.

"Not guilty," the foreman of the jury answered.

The spectators in the court began to cheer and applaud. Sir Justice Harrod banged his gavel to call the court to order. "Madame Fusani, the jury has found you not guilty. You are acquitted of the charges brought against you. You are free to leave."

Margarite opened her eyes; James was gone.

Chapter Twelve

Donovan House, London

James stood outside courtroom number one, staring down the long hall decorated with colored mosaics. Overwhelmed with fear that he would lose Margarite, he had fled rather than suffer the verdict. Now, cheering and clapping emanated from the oak-paneled room. He was stunned. Surely no one would cheer the conviction and hanging of a woman. He began to force his way past the reporters and spectators.

"James! Wait, please!" Ivy restrained him. "Where have you been? As soon as Margarite was acquitted…"

"Acquitted?" James was incredulous. "Acquitted! Where is she? I must see her." He had waited so long to be with Margarite. He had so much to tell her. He so wanted to redeem himself. He envisioned her face when he surprised her with…

"It is best if you return to Donovan House," Ivy interrupted his thoughts. "There are legal matters to attend to. Father and I will deliver Margarite to you, in good time."

James uncharacteristically did as he was told. He had learned that it was best not to cross Ivy.

****

Arriving at his London townhouse, James entered the grand hall, passed Antonio Canova's marble nude of Napoleon as Mars the Peacemaker, and proceeded to the drawing room with its apsidal end. There he sat at his grandfather's desk and began to plan his evening with Margarite.

"Johnathan!" he called to his butler.

"What does Your Grace require?" Johnathan magically appeared.

"We must plan a marvelous feast!"

"A feast? In honor of Madame Fusani's release, I imagine." Johnathan smiled. "The news of the princess's acquittal has traveled quickly. When will this feast take place?"

"This evening."

"This evening, sir?" Johnathan raised his eyebrows in surprise. "For how many guests?"

"Margarite and myself."

"I see, sir." Johnathan's smile grew wider. "What would you like included on the menu?"

"Champagne."

"Of course, sir."

"Oysters, then a soup course with sherry, followed by a fish course with white wine, mutton cutlets accompanied by potatoes, vegetables and Burgundy, venison served with traditional game chips and claret, followed by fruit and nuts with port."

"Will that be all, sir?"

"Do you think more is required, Johnathan?" James eyed his young butler skeptically.

"No, sir. Where shall this feast be held?"

James paused before answering. In my bed, he wanted to respond. But he frowned and said, "The Waterloo Gallery, of course."

"Right, sir. The Waterloo Gallery." It was

Johnathan's turn to pause. "Might the gallery be a bit large, sir?"

"Not at all." James envisioned the double height gallery, occupying the entire length of the first floor of the eastern side of the building. With its seven mirrored window shutters inspired by the Hall of Mirrors at Versailles, it was perfect for what James had in mind. "And music, a pianist."

"Jazz?"

"Classical. And flowers. We need orchids. And…"

"Sir." Johnathan cleared his throat. "Perhaps I should be on my way if we are to accomplish this by evening."

"Of course, but one more thing: a frock."

"A frock, sir."

"For Madame Fusani. Something wonderful to make her forget everything that has happened. And relish what is to come."

Johnathan sighed as he left the room. James returned to his planning. The evening must be perfect; so much depended on it.

****

"I could sleep forever." It was late when Ivy, Edward, and Margarite left the chambers of Mr. Justice Harrod. Margarite's suit was wrinkled and dirty. She was exhausted.

"But we must go directly to Donovan House. I promised James. He is so anxious to see you!" Ivy on the other hand was full of energy and high spirits.

"I simply cannot." Margarite looked down at her bedraggled appearance.

"Oh, don't be silly. Of course you can. It will be good for you."

279

Margarite was too tired to argue. But what good can become of this, she thought. James has his title, his estates, his responsibilities. It would be foolish for me to become involved with him again. I am already much too in love with him. It would be better if I just…

"Here we are at Donovan House, my dear," Edward interrupted her thoughts. "Have a wonderful evening with the duke." He kissed her hand.

Margarite exited the taxi on the busy roundabout at Hyde Park corner and faced Donovan House. As she gazed in wonder, the intricately carved door of the massive town home opened.

"Madame Fusani, *entrée s'il vous plait*." A smiling young man in his gentleman's black suit and tie beckoned to her.

Margarite entered the grand hall and found herself welcomed by a huge statue of a nude man holding a gilded goddess in his right hand. Behind the statue rose a semi-circular staircase. "I never imagined…" she whispered.

"It is a pleasure to meet you, Princess." The young man bowed. "Please, call me Johnathan. If you will allow me, I will escort you to your bedchamber. The duke will meet with you at dinner."

Margarite proceeded up the staircase and down the long hall, musing on the meaning of separate bedrooms. She gasped as she entered her room. Laid across the pink satin coverlet of the canopy bed was a straight and slender silk gown with a lace overdress in a most delicious shade of celadon green. Holding it against her pale skin, Margarite gazed into the looking glass to find the butler's smile reflected behind her. "Green is my…"

"Favorite color," Johnathan finished the sentence

for her. "Yes, Princess. The duke has often commented on how it complements your eyes. He requests you wear the dress this evening with these." He held up a set of exquisitely cut emerald earrings which he set on a nearby chaise next to a pair of silver slippers, before quietly leaving the room.

Margarite carefully placed the gown on the chaise, before collapsing on the bed. Closing her eyes, she dreamt of James.

****

James sat at the small table in front of the fire set with Waterford crystal and fine Spode china. The pianist played softly in the background. The glowing candles and white orchids on every surface reflected into infinity in the mirrored shutters.

Still the beauty of the room was nothing compared to the vision in celadon silk before him. Blonde hair piled atop her head, emerald earrings catching the light of the candles, hazel eyes missing nothing, Margarite pensively sipped her Dom Perignon. How could he begin to tell her what she meant to him?

"You are still the most beautiful woman in the world, Margarite. My feelings for you…"

"Your lust you mean." Margarite sat up straighter, her eyes burning a hole in his heart.

This was not the reaction James had expected. He reached across the table for her hand, which she quickly withdrew.

"Margarite, I love you, truly." He reached again for her hand.

"James, I appreciate everything you have done for me, but…" Margarite stood, causing her reflection in the mirrors to flicker. She took a deep breath. "I cannot,

I will not, continue as your courtesan."

"Margarite…" James looked at her imploringly. "Please sit. I am trying…"

"No. You are not trying, James. Your estates, your responsibilities, your title," she all but spat the last word at James, "are of importance to you. From me you want only one thing, and I am done providing it." James ducked as she threw her crystal goblet against the marble fireplace, barely missing his head.

James rose. "You may go," he said to the young pianist, staring at him in amazement.

Bolting the door, he advanced toward Margarite and caught her in his arms. He lifted the silky dress over her head, then turned her so she stood in all of the mirrors reflected only in her chemise.

"I love you," he confessed to her reflection. "With all that entails, I want to marry you. You will be my duchess."

Humming, he twirled her about and began to waltz with her down the length of the gallery. As they danced, he felt her body relax until she was molded against him.

****

Pausing for breath at the end of the gallery, Margarite kissed him. The emotion-filled kiss caused them to reel apart, trembling. Slowly Margarite removed James's tuxedo jacket, his white bow tie, his waistcoat, and his white shirt trimmed with lace. James stood before her, his torso bare. She stroked the muscles rippling across his chest. How she had missed him during the long nights in Holloway Prison!

"Another dance, madam?" James's mouth curled into a sly grin. Without waiting for her to answer, he again began to twirl her through the reflected candlelight of the Waterloo Gallery.

"James?" Margarite asked as she watched his perfectly formed body move from mirror to mirror.

"Um?" He held her closer and kissed her neck.

"Were you serious?" Her hand stroked the downy hair on his chest and moved to the front of his trousers.

"Serious, my love?" James's tongue moved from her neck to her cleavage.

"About your love for me?" She stroked his growing erection through the luxurious cloth of his trousers. A low growl escaped his lips. "Is it really possible for us to marry?" She worked the flat fall of the tuxedo pants to release his pulsating member.

He lifted her and laid her on a velvet settee. "Absolutely, my love." He removed the chemise.

"And shall we have issue?" Margarite ran her hands over his body.

"Many, my duchess." James's lips brushed her nipple.

Margarite gasped and threw her thighs over his legs. Slippery and soft, she was ready for him. She laughed with pleasure as he entered her. The smell of orchids filled the air; the flickering candles twinkled in the multitude of mirrors, and the *galerie des glaces* reflected them as one.

Chapter Thirteen

Preston Place, Cheshire, England

Margarite awoke the next morning in James's massive mahogany bed. She stretched and gazed into the ice blue eyes of the second Duke of Donovan. "My Duke," she said playfully, "what is your pleasure?"

"You are my pleasure…" He paused adding softly, "Duchess."

"You were serious then last evening?" Margarite's hand strayed from James's cheek to his chest.

James ran his hands over her breasts and lightly brushed her mons. Margarite moaned. James intensified his touch. "Very serious. I…"

Margarite pulled him to her. "I," she said, "cannot wait." She wrapped her arms around him, pulling him in. He rose on his knees, surged, and entered her. Margarite felt delicious ripples of pleasure surround her.

James collapsed upon her. "I want to stay here all day, love, but we must get up. We have a busy day."

Margarite lay naked on the bed, too satiated to move. "Why? Where are we going?"

"Are *you* serious? About wanting to marry?" James stood. "There are many responsibilities for a duchess."

Margarite sat up. Not trusting herself to speak, she merely nodded.

"Capital! Because I cannot live without you." He kissed her on the forehead. "Which is why you simply must get out of bed and prepare to come to Preston Place"—Margarite stopped breathing—"to meet my mother."

****

On the drive to Cheshire, James explained the history of his ancestral home to Margarite. Preston Place was set within a large estate two kilometers south of the village of Eccleston. The manor was surrounded by formal gardens, parkland, farmland, and woodland. Originally built in the seventeenth century, it was replaced in 1870 by a much larger structure designed by Alfred Waterhouse.

"Try not to be shocked," he told her. "The estate house is encased by every possible permutation of the gothic style, including turrets, pinnacles, arched windows, octagonal towers, and buttresses." He laughed. "As my mother will undoubtedly point out, the buttresses are both regular and flying."

Margarite gasped as they approached the house, surrounded by formal gardens. To the east of the manor, a series of terraces led to a fish pond. Stretching along the middle terrace was a long rectangular pool containing three fountains. On each side of the pool were two compartments framed by yew hedges. Between these compartments were two statues. The one to the south depicted a stag at bay; that to the north was of a rearing horse. From the end of the pool, steps led down to a yellow terracotta cottage. It was in the form of a round, colonnaded Ionic temple with a shallow domed roof.

"The manor is magnificent," Margarite gushed.

"But the gardens are my favorite."

James smirked. "Wait until you see the inside of the house."

Margarite was not disappointed. The interior of the home was as lavish as the exterior, with more Gothic detailing. The library was immense and boasted painted panels of the Canterbury Pilgrims. The octagonal great hall contained an organ. The hangings for the drawing room included yards of purple damask and *sarsenet* silk trimmed with gold lace.

"It is breathtaking." Margarite looked up at James and placed her hands on his cheeks.

James encircled her small waist and kissed her. "I..."

"I do hope I am interrupting something," a cultured female voice interjected.

Margarite turned to see a tall, largish woman with strongly marked features which must once have been quite handsome. She wore a dramatic floor length gown of ruby velvet. The long sleeves and low neck of the gown were complemented by a *parure*, or tiered necklace, made of gold and platinum set with rubies.

Margarite, who wore the understated jade suit, blanched. But she remembered what James had told her as she returned to her apartment to dress that morning: "My mother will think better of you for being simply dressed. She is happiest when the distinction of rank is preserved."

"Hello, Mother." James approached her, somewhat cautiously it appeared to Margarite. "May I present Madame Fusani, soon to be..."

Lady Arthur interrupted, "In my day, a lady was incapable of feeling physical attraction, let alone

286

expressing it, until she had been instructed to do so by her mama."

James blushed.

Margarite curtsied. "I applaud the sentiment, Lady Arthur. When James and I have daughters, I will teach them to seek instruction from both their mother and their grandmother. With your permission, of course." Margarite hid a smile. A strong woman, she thought, I like her already.

Lady Arthur sat on a small brocaded chair.

"As I was beginning to say, Mother..."

Lady Arthur held up her hand for silence. For several minutes, no one breathed. Then, the mature woman held out her hand to Margarite. "I had heard from Johnathan that I should be prepared for this. And I was prepared to be disagreeable. Excessively so. But I think perhaps I may enjoy having another woman in the family." She rang a small crystal bell.

"Yes, My Lady?" an aged butler responded.

"I think we would like some coffee, Archer, coffee and brandy." She sniffed. "And bow to my son's fiancée when you enter the room, Archer. Please, do not be such a snob."

She added in a stage whisper as he left the room, "Archer is as touchy as a beauty losing her looks; we all pander to him."

James snorted, drawing his mother's attention. "And you, young man, I wish to have a word. In private."

****

The sun was setting, reflecting in the pool, when James joined Margarite in the yellow terracotta cottage in the form of an Ionic temple.

"I love it here, James. Thank you." She kissed his cheek.

"And I love you." He pulled a small velvet pouch from his pocket. "And my mother hopes you love this." He got on one knee and took her hand. "Margarite, will you marry me?"

Margarite gasped, as James pulled a sparkling diamond ring from the blue velvet bag.

"It is a royal heirloom," he explained as he slipped it on her finger. "A square-cut central diamond flanked by six diamond baguettes. The setting is platinum."

Margarite began to cry.

"We can replace it with something else, if you like."

"You will have to cut off my finger first, My Grace." Margarite threw her arms around the man she had loved since their first meeting. "What fun we shall have creating issue," she said. "Do you suppose we could start now?"

A word about the author...

C.K. Charlotte is an author, attorney, and former law professor. She has clerked for a federal judge, served as a partner with a large Midwest law firm, and worked as senior counsel of a multi-national corporation. Most recently, she served as a law school professor in the U.S. and China. C.K. published numerous articles and a law school textbook before returning to her first love, fiction writing.

C.K. lives with her husband on a lake outside of Charlotte, where she is hard at work on her next book. She is the proud mother of the perfect daughter and the co-owner of a mischievous black cat. When not writing, she enjoys sailing and traveling.

Please visit C.K. at www.ckcharlotte.com.